D0044759

THE GREATEST SUPERPOWER

a novel by Alex Sanchez

CAPSTONE EDITIONS
a capstone imprint

The Greatest Superpower is published by Capstone Editions, an imprint of Capstone.
1710 Roe Crest Drive
North Mankato, Minnesota 56003
www.capstonepub.com

Library of Congress Cataloging-in-Publication Data is available on the Library of Congress website.

ISBN: 978-1-68446-2780 (hardcover)
ISBN: 978-1-68446-3275 (eBook PDF)

Summary: It's the summer before eighth grade, and thirteen-year-old Jorge Fuerte wants nothing more than to spend his days hanging out with his fellow comic book-obsessed friends. But then everything changes. His parents announce they're divorcing for a reason Jorge and his twin brother, Cesar, never saw coming—their larger-than-life dad comes out as transgender. As Jorge tries to find a way to stay true to the father he loves, a new girl moves into the neighborhood: cool, confident, quirky Zoey. Jorge must face his fears and choose between being loyal to his brother or truthful about his family's secret. Although he's no superhero, Jorge already has the world's greatest superpower—if he decides to use it.

Image Credits: author photo [pg. 352] by Bill Hitz; childhood photo [pg. 351] courtesy of Alex Sanchez; Shutterstock: Betelejze, (brick) design element throughout

Cover illustration by Brann Garvey

Designed by Tracy Davies

Consultant Credits: Sabra L. Katz-Wise, PhD, Assistant Professor at Boston Children's Hospital, Harvard Medical School, and the Harvard T. H. Chan School of Public Health

Printed and bound in China. 3741

THE GREATEST SUPERPOWER

For Pancho,
furry friend,
loyal companion,
beloved pain in the butt.
Thanks for all you shared with me.
I never cease missing you.
— A.S.

CHAPTER 1

"On your marks," Dad announces. His brown eyes twinkle across the kitchen table while Mom, my twin brother Cesar, and I inch forward in our seats, raring to start.

"Get . . . set . . . and . . ." Dad teases the words out, tracking the seconds on his watch. "Go!"

Our nightly game of stopwatch cleanup is off and running. Cesar bolts up, clatters our plates together, and sprints to the sink. Right behind him, I sweep up fistfuls of clinking silverware. Dad scoops up serving dishes containing chimichangas, rice, and refried beans. Mom circles around him, grabbing napkins and placemats. And King—my knee-high, white and nut-brown Jack Russell terrier—dodges our footsteps, licking the tile floor.

Cesar throws me the hot sauce in a final pass. Mom switches on the dishwasher. And Dad hops up, patting the ceiling like a six-foot-one oversized kid.

"Time!" he shouts in his deep, gravelly Mexican American accent. "Nine minutes, forty-three seconds." Not our best time, but decent.

Dad wipes his big, hairy hands on the XXL-sized Superman apron I gave him last Father's Day. Then he slings one arm around Cesar's shoulder and the other across mine. "Good game, great moves."

"Okay, fellas, come sit back down," Mom says, replacing the centerpiece vase on the chunky wooden table that serves as our family's headquarters. She's still wearing her office clothes—gray skirt suit, crisp white shirt, and silver necklace—looking like a company CEO about to deliver the yearly report. "Your dad and I need to discuss something important with you."

I plop down in my chair again. Summer vacation has arrived, and I know what's coming. "We already know what you're going to say."

"How's that?" Mom asks, exchanging an anxious glance with Dad.

"Same spiel every summer," I say. "You want us to use our time wisely and productively, blah, blah, blah . . ." I toss King a rubber ball, but he ignores it, too busy hunting down every microscopic crumb that might've landed on the floor during dinner.

"I'm afraid we need to discuss something different this time," Dad says as he sits next to Mom.

"Can you guys make it quick?" Cesar asks, distracted while texting his life's play-by-play to his girlfriend. "Victoria wants to talk to me."

Cesar and I might be twins, but we don't look alike—we're fraternal, not identical. And we're different in more than just looks. We also have totally different friends and personalities. Cesar is the cool, popular soccer jock—complete with a cool, popular girlfriend. I'm the shy, nerdy comics geek.

"Put your phone down, please, Cesar," Mom says. Her blue eyes are shimmering. Dad reaches to hold her hand, but she slides it away.

Cesar and I glance at each other. Something is off—I've sensed it all evening. Dad, usually pretty jokey, has been weirdly off his game. And Mom, normally the quiet one, kept bringing up goofy stuff about work.

"Dad and I know this will be hard for you boys," Mom says now. Her voice catches like she's trying to hold back tears. "I-I don't know how to say this, so I'll just say it: Dad and I are getting a divorce."

A siren goes off inside my head as if somebody yanked a fire alarm. I turn to Cesar, hoping he'll make sense of this. Even though he's only eight minutes older, I look up to him as my big brother. But he's staring into space as though someone has clubbed him with a phone. Face pale. Mouth dangling open. Eyes glazed over.

Everyone sits silently—except King, whose toenails click across the tile floor.

"We understand this hurts," Dad says in his low rumbly voice. His eyes glisten as much as Mom's. "It's sad for all of us."

"If it's sad for everyone," I ask, "then why are you breaking up?"

"Yeah, what's wrong?" Cesar asks, emerging from his daze. "How can we fix it?"

"Mijo," Dad says—Spanish for *my son*. "This isn't something you can fix. It's because of personal things."

"Things that make it impossible for us to stay together," Mom says, her voice shaking.

"Well, can't you guys go to couples counseling or something?" Cesar insists. "That's what Victoria's parents did. . . ."

"Yeah, you can work it out," I say, backing Cesar up. "Like you always tell us to."

"Dad and I have tried," Mom says, twisting and fidgeting with her necklace. "We've been seeing a therapist on Saturday mornings for more than a year."

When Cesar and I asked where they were going, they would only say it was their "special time." We speculated the mystery outings were some sappy, rekindle-the-flame middle-age couple's thing. Nothing like this.

"So you're just going to leave us in the dark about what's wrong?" Cesar asks.

Mom turns to Dad. "Maybe you'd better go ahead," she says. Now she's the one who reaches for his hand. He grasps hers back, holding it tight.

"I need to tell you boys something. I . . ." He clears his throat. "I'm transgender."

The word takes a moment to register. Then a giggle bubbles out of me. I know what transgender means: Sometimes a person born a boy knows deep inside they're really a girl—or vice versa. My friends and I have seen videos of that Olympic champion, the one with six kids, who was once called the "world's greatest athlete," transforming into a fashion beauty.

It's impossible to imagine Dad like that. To start, he isn't built like a lean, lanky world-famous track star; he's shaped more like a big, bulgy sack of tamale flour. And though he isn't bad looking, his face is as rough and craggy as a Lincoln statue. He's a *guy*. My role model. My hero. I want to be just like him when I grow up. That doesn't include becoming a woman.

"Dad . . . ?" Cesar says. "You're kidding . . . right?"

"Of course he's kidding," I say. This has to be one of Dad's wacky jokes. Like on Christmas morning, when a six-foot-one Easter bunny, complete with a big costume head, woke us up and explained he was helping Santa, who was sick with the flu. After giving us presents, the giant rabbit hopped away down the street while Cesar and I watched in wide-eyed wonder. Dad is *that* kind of dad: the fun one. The one all our friends wish they had.

"I've wanted to talk with you boys about this for a long time, but first I needed to sort it out myself." His forehead is breaking out in a sweat. He grabs a paper napkin and wipes it across his wide brow as the words pour out. "Ever since I was little, whenever I looked at myself in the mirror and saw a boy, it didn't match how I felt in here." He pats the spot over his heart. "Inside, I knew I was a girl, even though outside I looked like a boy."

Cesar squirms in his seat. I squirm in mine.

"One day your grandmother, your abuelita, caught me trying on my sister's dress," Dad goes on. "When she told your abuelito, he beat me so hard the bruises took a month to heal. After that, I buried my secret deep inside." He balls up the paper napkin in his fist. "Times were so different then. There was no internet. Not so much news. I had no words to describe what I felt. I believed I was the only person in the world like me, who felt like this. So I tried to be a good son, a nice Catholic boy." He glances down at his thick hands. "I have lived a lie for too long. I need to be honest. With myself. And with you."

Dad uncrumples the wadded napkin, smooths it out across his apron-covered lap, and glances up with damp eyes.

"But I want you to know that I love you boys and your mom as much as ever. Nothing can change that. I'm still your dad, no matter what. I'll always be here for you. And we'll always be a family."

Tears are trickling down Mom's cheeks. Dad hands her a clean napkin.

"So then . . . ?" I ask. "Can we all stay together?"

"Honey, I'm sorry," Mom says, dabbing her cheeks. "I married a husband, not a wife. I know some women can make that work, but I can't."

"I'm sorry too, boys," Dad says. "Sometimes honesty comes with a price."

"No!" Cesar bursts out. "How can you do this? Don't you realize what people will say? Can't you at least wait till we go to college?"

"I wish I could," Dad says. "But I can't hide anymore."

Cesar quivers like a volcano. Angry tears erupt from his eyes. "Thanks for ruining our lives!"

"Cesar, stop. Calm down," Mom says. "I know you're upset. Try to control yourself."

"*Me?*" He leaps to his feet, bumping the table, and gestures to Dad. "*He's* the one who needs to control himself." The glass vase falls over, splintering into shards.

As Mom rushes to pick up the pieces, Dad rises to block Cesar. "Sit down and talk. Please, mijo."

"Don't call me that." Cesar's face burns red as lava. He's always had a hot temper, but he rarely gets this mad. "I'm not your son anymore."

Dad winces, his face crumbling, his whole body cringing. He keeps back as Cesar brushes past him, storming out of the room. Cesar's footsteps tromp up the stairs. A moment later, his bedroom door slams so hard the walls rattle all the way downstairs. Even King glances up.

It feels like an asteroid has smashed into our home. My average, ordinary, suburban San Antonio family has abruptly gone kablooey. I sit in shock.

Mom massages her temples, frowning sadly at Dad, who's still wearing his Superman apron. He glances at me, waiting for my response.

A sudden rush of anger surges through me—at Dad, at Mom, at Cesar, at everything. I push out of my chair. "Would you take off that stupid apron?"

I stomp upstairs with King racing after me. And when we get inside my room, I slam the door—not as hard as Cesar, but hard enough.

CHAPTER 2

I lie in bed, staring at the ceiling. King presses against me and scratches his ear. I hold up my phone to text my best friends, Darnell and Chang, and tell them what happened. But every time I try to type, a steamroller of emotions knocks me flat: confusion. Fear. Anger.

Downstairs, Mom and Dad are arguing, too far away to make out their words. Over the past year they've gotten into more and more fights, usually about little stuff. Where did Dad put the mini vacuum? Why didn't Mom say she would be late for dinner? Nothing really major. Until now.

The arguing dies down. Then footsteps pad up the stairs, and Dad knocks on my door. "Jorge . . . ? You okay?"

King leaps off the mattress, trots across the carpet, and waits for me to open up. I stay in bed. "Go away!"

Dad jiggles the doorknob, but I locked it. "I know you're

mad," he tells me. "You probably feel a lot of things. If you want to talk, I'm here, mijo."

I stay silent, too upset to talk.

After a moment, Dad's heavy footsteps plod down the hall and stop. "Cesar?"

I climb from bed and press an ear to my door. At my feet, King tilts his head, observing me.

Not a peep comes from Cesar, and after a moment, Dad's footsteps continue toward his and Mom's room. I return to bed, and King hops up beside me, tail wagging, his mouth full of squeaky ball.

I stay awake until the house is quiet and I'm sure Mom and Dad have gone to bed. Then I peek out to the hall. A slice of light glows from beneath Cesar's door a few feet away.

I pad down the carpet with King beside me and knock lightly. "Cesar?" I whisper.

"Yeah?" Cesar opens up. His eyes are red and puffy, like mine when I've been crying.

Usually, people never guess we're twins. Cesar is an inch taller than me and bulked out from wrestling and weight-lifting, giving him the shape of a prized Spanish bull. Like Dad, he's got brown skin, with coal-colored hair and eyes so dark they look black. In contrast, I'm as skinny as an enchilada with sandy blond hair, baby blues like Mom, and skin so white you can see my purplish veins through my wrists and thighs.

"You all right?" I ask, wedging past him into the room.

He wipes his cheek. "Yeah . . . *you* okay?"

"Yeah." I drop into his chair. "What do you think'll happen with Mom and Dad?"

"Who knows?" Cesar stares at the sports trophies, school plaques, and awards lining his shelves. "All I know is he's not going to ruin my life. I won't let him. As far as I'm concerned, he no longer exists."

I nod, even though I know he can't mean that. He and Dad have always been best friends. They used to spend hours in the driveway playing soccer.

"Have you told anybody what Dad said?" I ask, glancing at Cesar's phone.

"Are you *nuts*? The only thing I told Victoria is that Mom and Dad are getting divorced. End of story. And that's all you'd better tell anyone too."

Cesar suddenly swings out, punching my arm—not hard, just enough to make his point. There are days when he socks me so often you'd think my bicep is a bell that needs ringing on the hour. Sometimes I slug him back, but then I risk him pounding me harder. Better to just let him get it out of his system.

"Promise you won't tell anybody about him," Cesar says. "If word gets out, people'll treat us like freaks."

"I won't tell," I say. I wouldn't even know how to *start* to tell.

"Good. Otherwise I'll disown you." He gives my shoulder a gentle squeeze—his signature move: strike, then stroke. "Now," he says with a yawn, "go to sleep."

I glance at his double bed. When we were little I used to sleep over all the time—after a scary movie, if it was thundering, if the power went out. "Can I stay with you tonight?"

"Bro," he says gently. "We're going to be in eighth grade soon."

I glance down, embarrassed that I asked. "I know, it's just . . . I don't want to be alone. Not tonight."

Cesar lets out a sigh. "All right, you can stay." He slings an arm around my shoulder. "But only tonight, okay? We're going to get through this. We don't need him. We'll be fine without him."

I nod.

After I sneak downstairs to let King out to the patio for a minute, the three of us climb into bed. I nestle in the middle with Cesar on one side and King on the other. Then I say a silent prayer that in the morning I'll wake to find this whole evening was just a loopy dream.

CHAPTER 3

The sharp aroma of brewing coffee rouses me in the morning, and the memory of last night hits me like an ice-cold glass of water. I slide down beneath the warm covers, wanting to go back to sleep. But the memories make it impossible. I pop back up.

Beside me on the bed, Cesar breathes softly. Still asleep, he looks so peaceful.

King stands at the door, tail wagging, eager to get out. I slip quietly from between the sheets and head to the bathroom. King dashes downstairs.

When I pass Cesar's door again after my shower, he's on the phone, talking about soccer camp. I dress and tread cautiously down the stairs, unsure what I'll see: Dad squeezed into Mom's gauzy lilac bathrobe? Clunking around in high heels? My imagination runs riot.

I peer into the kitchen from behind the doorway. Mom has already left for her accounting job downtown. Dad stands at the sliding glass door, wearing a crisp red polo shirt—*men's*—and his usual jeans. He sips his coffee and watches King chase a butterfly across the patio. Unaware of me, Dad gives himself a scratch in one of the standard man places. If he truly is a woman inside, he gives no hint of it outside.

Maybe he's just having another midlife crisis, I think, *like when the doc warned him he needed to drop thirty pounds or risk a heart attack.*

That very day Dad bought a jogging suit, tennis rackets for the whole family, and a gleaming set of golf clubs. All the groceries he brought home that week were either low-carb or fat-free. But each time he tasted something, he made an *ick* face and declared it "flavor-free." When he and I went running, he gasped and panted for me to slow down. Our family's attempt at tennis proved too hard on his knees. And the golf clubs never even left their bag. Within a week the fitness kick had blown over.

Maybe the same will happen with this transgender thing, I think. *I should just act normal, like nothing happened.*

"Morning," I say, stepping into the kitchen.

Dad swings around, startled. "Good morning." Reassured by my smile, his face relaxes. "I was just picturing banana pancakes. How about I make us some?"

"Sounds good." I pour myself a glass of orange juice, set the table, and watch him mix the bananas and batter.

Despite his manly looks, Dad has never conformed to the macho Latino stereotype. While Cesar and I were growing up, he was the stay-at-home parent, working as a freelance developer for bilingual apps and websites. He was the one who potty trained us, dabbed our runny noses, helped us with homework, and hauled us around to playdates, the library, or our thousandth visit to the Alamo. He chewed us out when we messed up, wiped our tears when we got hurt, and always found a way to make us laugh.

For his most recent birthday, I gave him a mug with *World's Greatest Dad* written inside a heart. Cheesy as that was, it made his eyes tear up. Never did it occur to me he might've been thinking of himself as World's Greatest *Mom*.

While I scroll through my phone, the sound of Cesar showering comes from upstairs. Several minutes later, footsteps pound down the stairway, loud as hooves, and my brother charges into the room, heading straight to the fridge.

"Good morning," Dad calls out. His voice rings with cheer, but his face is lined with apprehension. "How about some hotcakes?"

Cesar answers with silence. I watch from my seat at the table, my legs jiggling nervously as he jams a couple of yogurts into his backpack and turns to leave without so much as a glance in Dad's direction.

"Hold on," Dad orders. "I get you feel upset, but you're too old to be throwing a temper tantrum."

Cesar stops in his tracks, his face flushed red with anger. Or shame. Maybe a mix. "I've got to go—Eric's mom is taking us to a soccer camp meeting."

"First," Dad says, shutting off the stove burner, "we need to get some things straight. Regardless of what you think of me, when I ask you a question, I expect you to answer."

"No, I don't want pancakes," Cesar says.

"Okay," Dad says. "Second, no more slamming doors. That goes for both of you. If you've got something to say, say it with words. Understood?"

I nod. Cesar clenches his jaw tight.

"*Understood?*" Dad repeats. A horn beeps from the driveway.

"Yeah, fine," Cesar says. "Can I go now?"

"I love you very much," Dad says softly. "Both of you. More than you'll ever know."

Cesar's face remains set and stony. The doorbell rings. "I need to go."

"Play well," Dad says. "And have fun."

Cesar surges out to the living room, and a moment later, the front door slams—louder than ever.

I flinch.

Dad sighs and finishes piling pancakes onto the serving

plate. "I know last night was a lot to handle," he says, joining me at the table. "Do you have any questions?"

Only about a million. But I'm not sure I want to deal with the answers. It would only make the whole thing more real. "Do we have any chocolate syrup?"

Dad's mouth droops. Obviously that wasn't the sort of question he hoped for. He brings me the syrup and asks, "Will you let me know when you're ready to talk?"

I nod so he'll drop it. Then I drown my pancakes with chocolate sauce.

* * *

Hoping to take my mind off Dad, I text Chang and Darnell after breakfast and invite them to come over and work on a new comic book. The three of us have been besties since second grade when we bonded over superheroes, nacho-cheese tortilla chips, and being halfies—Chang is half-Chinese, Darnell is half-Jamaican, and I'm half-Mexican.

Creating comic books unites each of our special powers. Chang sketches phenomenal illustrations—true masterpieces. I have a knack for scripting twisty-turny plots. And Darnell has the most amazing talent of all: a superhuman ability to keep Chang and me from spiraling into chaos. He's our editor-in-chief, referee, and spiritual leader.

Shortly after I text him, Chang skids into the driveway on his bike, looking like a ninja Power Ranger: sleek cycle jersey, flared helmet, wraparound shades.

Darnell hitches a ride from his sister. He resembles a West Indian version of the laughing Buddha: big, dark, and lumpy. His T-shirt pictures Yoda—wielding a fudgsicle in place of a light saber—with the words: *Fear leads to anger. Anger leads to hate. Hate leads to suffering. Suffering leads to ice cream.*

We gather the chips and salsa necessary to fuel our creativity and head to my room with King trailing. For us to all fit, we move aside the hefty white cardboard boxes crammed with my comics collection.

"So I found a contest for us to enter," Darnell says as we sprawl out on the carpet. "But our hero needs to be fresh, original, not a knockoff—with a superpower never seen before."

While our fingers turn nacho-cheese yellow, we struggle to come up with an idea. Darnell and Chang do most of the brainstorming. My thoughts keep circling back to Dad wanting to be a woman and Cesar making me promise not to say anything. I'm concentrating so hard on *not* thinking about it that it's the *only* thing I can think about.

"Come on, guys, think," Darnell says. "Use the Force. Use the Force!"

"Every superpower has already been used," Chang

protests. "Flying? Done. Invisibility? Done. Shape-shifting? Done. Breathing underwater—?"

"Wait, go back," I blurt out, the words flying from my mouth faster than I can stop them. "What if our hero could shape-shift into a woman?"

Chang and Darnell stare at me so hard I'm sure they can see inside my mind—at my thoughts of Dad.

"Sorry," I say. "Brain fart."

"No," Darnell says. "It's brilliant."

"What powers would the hero gain by morphing into a woman?" Chang asks, chuckling. He flutters his fingers over his heart. "Being able to talk about *feeeeelings*?"

"We'll figure it out," Darnell says. "I think the idea is he wouldn't just do drag, he'd actually jump genders. Is that what you were thinking, Jorge?"

Actually I'm thinking that I want to knock myself in the head for suggesting the nutty idea.

"Maybe Chang is right," I say. "It might work better if it were the other way around: a girl transforming into a guy. Like Mulan . . . or Joan of Arc. That would be more convincing. Guys are expected to have more power."

"But see?" Darnell says. "Girls turning into guys has been done to death. A guy morphing into a girl would be totally new and original, wouldn't it?"

Chang taps a finger to his forehead as his mind scans through the dozens of comic-book heroes in his mental catalog. "The Green Lantern turned into a woman once, but not because he wanted to. It's how Dementor punished him. Why would a guy volunteer to become female?"

I try to picture Dad as a female superhero but only get as far as him wearing his Superman apron.

Darnell nudges my knee. "Hey, you okay?"

I blink. "Huh?"

"You seem like you're orbiting in a different solar system today," Chang says.

I glance down, avoiding their eyes, too tongue-tied to explain. My fingers tug at the carpet. "Um . . . my mom and dad are getting divorced."

Slowly, I lift my gaze. Chang and Darnell sit silent, motionless. As if zapped by a ray gun.

"But, dude," Chang says, "you've got the happiest parents I know outside of TV."

"Maybe they're just having a fight," Darnell says. "My folks threaten to divorce all the time, but the next day they're sharing popcorn in front of the tube."

"No," I say. "Mine have never mentioned divorce before."

"You're not going to move away, are you?" Chang asks.

"I'm not sure what's going to happen. They only told us last night."

"Hey, man, I'm really sorry," Darnell says.

"Me too," Chang says. "You doing okay?"

"Yeah. I just feel sort of spacey, you know? Like my

head's floating away from me." I scratch King's chest while he lies on his back, stroking the air with his paws.

"Well," Darnell says, "let me know if you want to talk, or if you need anything, or whatever."

"Same here," Chang says.

"Thanks." For now, telling them about the divorce feels like all I can handle.

When they get up to leave, Chang throws an arm across my shoulders. Darnell wraps his big buttery arms around both of us. And even though I still feel depressed, I think how lucky I am to have them as friends.

CHAPTER 4

"I've rented a house on Cottonwood Street," Dad announces at dinner later that week.

The move will put him only six blocks from our house. Even so, the idea of him leaving takes away my appetite.

"We've agreed you boys will stay here with me," Mom says. "But you can visit Dad as often as you want."

"Every day?" I ask.

A smile pulls at Dad's lips. "If you like, mijo."

"Well, I'm not going over there," Cesar says out of the corner of his mouth.

"Cesar!" Mom scolds. "That's uncalled for."

"It's okay," Dad says and turns to Cesar. "I know you feel hurt. I'm sorry."

Cesar doesn't respond. He trains his gaze on his baked potato, smothering it with sour cream. I keep quiet.

After dinner, we skip playing stopwatch cleanup. We haven't played since Mom and Dad's announcement. As I make my way to my room, I wonder if we'll ever play again.

* * *

"I can't watch," Mom says.

It's Saturday morning, two weeks since the announcement, and I'm helping Dad close up his boxes for the move. Mom presses a fist to her eyes, pushing back tears. And seeing her, my throat clenches too.

Dad tries to put his arm around her, but Mom pulls away and grabs her purse. "I'm going to a friend's house," she says.

He and I watch through the living room window as Mom backs the minivan out of the driveway, nearly scraping Dad's car.

"Can't you just stop all this?" I grumble and shove one of his boxes toward the door.

"I'm sorry, Jorge. I can't."

"Then finish the packing yourself," I mutter and go to my room.

I'm flipping through a comic when Dad's cousin, Raul, shows up with a moving truck. From my window, I see them struggling with Dad's home-office furniture and drag myself downstairs to help.

Raul greets me and tries to make friendly conversation, but I hardly utter a word. I can't stop wondering if Dad has told him why he's getting divorced. *Is he going to tell every-body else, too? What about our friends' parents?*

Cesar stays in his room all morning, supposedly still asleep. When Dad is fully packed, he goes upstairs to say goodbye. I follow him.

"Cesar?" Dad knocks on the closed door. "I'm going now. Can you come out, please? I'd like to give you a hug."

The door stays shut, the room silent. Dad glances at me, wondering what to do.

"Cesar?" I say. "Open up. He just wants to say goodbye."

Still only silence.

Dad jiggles the doorknob—locked. He lets out a sigh. "Okay, mijo. Whenever you want to talk, I'll be only six blocks away. I'm still your dad, and I love you." He wipes his cheeks and turns to me. "Let's go."

Outside, I climb into the car with King. As we pull out of the driveway, I glance up at Cesar's window. He peeks out at us from behind the blinds, then quickly backs away again.

* * *

Dad's new home is typical Tex-Mex style with stucco walls and a red clay tile roof. Inside, King scouts each room, nose pressed vacuum-like to the floor, inspecting every crack and corner. The layout is identical to our existing house but with everything flipped one hundred and eighty degrees in a mirror image. Each time I turn to go right, I have to stop and veer left instead.

"I don't like this place," I tell Dad. "It's too confusing."

He pulls a framed family photo from a box and props it up on his desk. "Well, I hope you and Cesar give it a chance."

I don't want to give it a chance. After all the boxes are unloaded, he invites me to stay and eat with him and Raul. When I tell them I'm not hungry, they exchange a nervous glance.

"Are you sure?" Dad asks.

"See you whenever," I mutter and leave with King.

At home, I wander into Dad's vacant office. The once-crammed room now stands empty and abandoned. The only signs of life are a kid's handprint—Cesar's or mine—smudged on one blank wall. Crayon scrawls mark another corner, next to the gray smear of a wayward ball.

A hollow feeling aches in my chest. I picture Dad working at his desk, peering at his computer screen while an opera plays on the speakers. He hums along: *Tam-dee-dee-um-tam* . . . As the music picks up speed, he raises a hand from his keyboard. Waving an invisible baton, he helps the diva sing her way through the tricky aria. And when she finishes her final note, he applauds. "Bravo!"

Returning to the present, I slump against an empty wall and slide down to the rug. King's wet nose pokes my ear, his warm tongue lapping at the salty tears dripping down my cheeks as the ache in my chest grows stronger.

* * *

"Six blocks isn't so far," I tell King as we head back to Dad's the next day. He forges ahead, sniffing and peeing, thrilled to explore new territory.

While Dad shows the delivery guys where to put his new furniture, I unpack boxes, clean up the patio, and text with Chang and Darnell about our proposed comic. They refuse to give up on my accidentally blurted-out trans hero idea. They think it's awesome.

King and I are still at Dad's as dinnertime approaches, so we help him inaugurate the everything-on-the-opposite-side kitchen. He straps on his Superman apron and whips up a massive spread of arroz con pollo, black beans, tortillas, and guacamole. Over mouthfuls of food, I tell him about the comic book contest.

"We need to invent an original superhero with a power nobody's used before. But the only thing we've come up with is a guy who shape-shifts into a woman."

Dad breaks into a huge smile. "You told them about me?"

"*No*," I snap. "The idea just sort of popped out. But it doesn't make sense. How would becoming a woman be a superpower?"

"Hmm . . . well, men typically have more physical strength, earn more money, have shorter restroom lines. . . ." He cracks

a grin at his own joke. "But they lose a lot of power by getting crammed into the guy box."

"The *what* box?"

With his fingers, Dad draws a square in the air. "The box
that says men should be tough, decisive, in control . . . that
boys aren't supposed to cry. Or feel scared. Or sad. Or hurt.
Or anything else that's considered *weak and girly*. Those
feelings make us human. But guys aren't supposed to have
them. What's left?"

Cesar pops into my mind, his temper erupting like a volcano. "Anger?"

"Bingo," Dad says, scooping some beans onto his rice.
"No wonder your superheroes go around clobbering people.
They're boxed in. Emotionally constipated."

"Dad, do you mind? We're eating."

"At the same time," he goes on, "women get shoved into
their own box. They're told how they should look, act, talk,
and behave. They're allowed all the soft, fuzzy feelings men
aren't allowed, but heaven forbid they get angry or show
authority or ambition."

"So if our superhero shape-shifted into a woman," I ask,
"what power could they gain?"

Dad mulls it over and passes me the guac. "Maybe more
empathy? Being able to step into another person's shoes, see
the world through their eyes. Women—not all, but most—
tend to have that strength. More often than men."

"But how would that be a superpower?"

"Well, more empathy could help your hero understand the bad guys, rather than just clobbering them. Imagine if everybody took time to see things from the other person's perspective. There would be fewer wars, less arguments. It would probably solve half the world's problems."

"Okay, let's say you're right about seeing things from the bad guys' point of view—then what?"

"Maybe the superhero could get the bad guys to have more empathy too. Then they could talk things out. Talking is harder than fighting."

I think of Cesar refusing to talk to Dad. "Harder? How?"

"Because you have to listen and be vulnerable . . . be willing to compromise and make sacrifices . . . give and take. You have to deal with problems rather than trying to clobber them."

"So our hero wouldn't clobber anybody?" I fake a yawn, let my head drop to the table, and pretend to snore.

"You think clobbering is what makes a hero?" Dad asks. "Or is it being strong enough to be vulnerable and show empathy? To feel hurt, and sadness, and fear, and make whatever sacrifices are necessary to do the right thing? Becoming a woman could teach your hero a lot about what a man can be—what a *human being* can be."

I open my eyes and lift my head off the table. "I want to ask you something else."

"I'm listening," he says.

My toes squirm inside my socks. "So . . . how far are you going to go with this woman thing? I mean, like . . . all the way? Like with surgery . . . down *there*?"

Dad blinks, then blinks again. "I haven't decided yet, mijo—one step at a time. For now I've started taking female hormones. They'll help change my body, make my breasts grow."

What for? I wonder. Dad already has major man-boobs. When he goes shirtless at the beach or after a shower, Cesar and I always tease him about them.

"I've joined a transgender support group," he continues. "The gang is having a renaming ceremony for me to leave behind my birth name, Norberto. I will be reborn as *Nor-r-r-ma!*" He sings the word, rolling the *r*.

I recognize the name as the title of one of Dad's favorite operas, the story of a love-torn Druid priestess. He's always loved describing opera's larger-than-life characters and zigzagging plots. Kind of like my life is turning out.

"And," he continues, "I'm asking people to refer to me as *she*."

I stop chewing. Although I knew transgender people changed pronouns, this is *my dad*. I manage to swallow and say, "That's going to feel weird."

"To you, maybe. But to me it feels like what I should've been called all along. Imagine if people called you *she* all the time, even though you know you're a boy. How would you feel?"

"Mad," I say, thinking back to first grade when this one jerk kid told me I threw like a girl. I almost punched him.

"That's how I've felt my whole life," Dad says sadly. "Angry. And hurt."

I try to imagine calling him *she*. "Can't I just keep calling you Dad?"

"Of course you can. I'm still your dad. I'll always be your dad."

I serve myself more chicken. "So what happens if you become a woman but then decide you don't like it?"

"That's a risk I'm willing to take. For once I want to feel like I belong in my own skin. The label *male* has never felt like it fit, no matter how hard I tried. I always felt like I was pretending. Maybe *female* won't fully fit either, but hopefully it'll feel more honest. That's what this is about: Finding the courage to be me."

"Haven't you always been you?" I ask.

"Inside, yes. Outside, no."

Although I've finished eating, I slide my fork back and forth across the empty plate. "You're not scared? Of, like, changing your body? Or what people might say?"

"Sure, I get scared sometimes. Changing your body can be a scary thing. But mostly I'm scared people won't like me—that they'll laugh at me or reject me. It upsets some people to see a trans person. Who knows why? Maybe they feel threatened by people who are different. It makes them question things: What does it mean to be male or female? It unsettles them. They get scared. The only way some people know how to handle fear is with anger . . . even violence." He rubs a napkin across his jowly chin. "This isn't a decision I've made lightly, mijo. I've thought about it long and hard."

I slink down in my seat, not wanting to imagine how people might react to him—or to me.

"Ice cream for dessert?" Dad asks.

"No, thanks." My stomach is full to bursting. So is my head.

CHAPTER 5

Like he promised, Cesar refuses to set foot in Dad's new home. He blocks Dad's calls and texts. He unfriends him on social media. He hides in his room whenever Dad stops by and won't open the door when Dad knocks and tries to talk. Instead he pastes up a big red sign that threatens: *DANGER—KEEP OUT!*

"Does that include me?" I ask.

Cesar answers with a silent smirk that I take to mean *no*. As twins, we've always been close. Cesar used to constantly stop by my room or we'd hang out in his—playing games, sharing homework, confiding secrets, talking about anything and everything.

But since we started middle school, we've grown apart. He's gotten busy with sports, clubs, and activities. I've gotten more involved with comics. And we started to hang out

with different friends. I miss the closeness we had before . . .
now more than ever.

One evening I venture past his *KEEP OUT* sign. In
between texting, he's pumping iron on the bench press set
Dad and Mom gave him last Christmas. I've tried it a few
times, but it's too much work.

"Want me to spot you?" I ask.

"Sure, thanks."

I position myself behind the barbell. And while Cesar
puffs and grunts, I debate how to bring up the subject I came
to talk about—without him transforming into the raging
Hulk.

"Can I talk to you about Dad?" I ask.

"No." Cesar lifts the barbell, and his face twists up like
Bruce Banner when he's about to turn green and mean.
"He's a freak and a liar."

"He's trying to be honest," I say.

"Too late." Cesar breathes hard as he pumps the weights.
"I don't want to hear it."

"Well then," I explode, "who the heck am I supposed to
talk to?"

"Why do you have to talk to *anyone* about him? Just do
what I'm doing: pretend he doesn't exist."

"If he doesn't exist, why are you so mad at him?"

Cesar doesn't answer. The barbell clangs into its cradle,
and I stomp out past the *KEEP OUT* sign to my room.

* * *

Talking with Mom isn't much more help. One morning when she doesn't emerge from her room to go to work, I tap on her door. "Mom? You feeling okay?"

"Come in, honey." Her voice is hoarse and sniffly. She's still in bed, sitting against the headboard. The nightstand is littered with crumpled tissues. She pats the bedspread. "Want to sit with me?"

I scoot beside her. "Are you sick?"

"Just feeling a little blue," she says. "I thought I'd be able to handle Dad moving out better. Sometimes I miss him so much my chest hurts." She blows her nose on a tissue. "Every morning I wake up wondering how he could do this."

"Me too," I say.

Mom pulls me to her. "We'll get through this."

It feels good to rest my head on her shoulder and breathe in her faint, sleepy scent. Then her phone rings. The screen shows Dad's photo.

Mom wraps her hand around the phone as if she's strangling it and punches the SILENCE button so hard her finger turns pink.

I lean away. "Are you all right?"

She plunks the phone onto the nightstand. "I will be. I have an appointment with the therapist later—the one your dad and I went to." Her breath calms, and she gently combs her fingers through my hair. "Would you like to come with me?"

I pull away, surprised. "What for?"

"It might do you good. We could blow off steam. Both of us."

I don't want to blow off steam in front of some stranger. And I don't want to watch Mom blow off steam either. It would feel like I'm taking sides. What I want is for all of us to be back together. One family. One home.

"I'm not going," I say, rising to my feet. "I don't want to."

"Okay, sweetie, you don't have to. It was just a thought. I want to make sure you're all right." She exhales a little puff of air from the corner of her mouth. "If it upsets you to go over to Dad's, you don't have to go—you know that, don't you?"

Why is she bringing that up? "It doesn't upset me. I'm fine."

I leave her room and go down to breakfast, feeling more mixed up than ever. Who can I talk to? Each time I've gotten together with Chang and Darnell in the month since Dad's announcement, I've obsessed about whether to spill the beans about Dad and be done with it. Since he's staying in the neighborhood, they're bound to run into him sometime. San Antonio isn't some vast anonymous metropolis.

But how do I explain everything to them? I'm having a hard enough time trying to understand it myself. And what if they blab about it? Or ditch me? They're too important for me to risk it.

King is the only one I have left. When we're alone, I confide in him about how my life sucks. His ears prick while he listens. His eyes shine bright with understanding— like dark, glistening chocolates in their eyelash wrappers. And if I wake up scared and lonely in the night, all I have to do is wrap my arm around his warm furry body. His heart's steady thump lulls me back to sleep.

CHAPTER 6

As the summer days grow hotter, the cicadas whir and whine like smoke alarms. On the bark of cypress, oak, and pecan trees all around town, the bugs break through their crusty old skins, emerging with shiny new bodies. And Dad begins his own metamorphosis.

He calls it his "social transition." During the past year, he had already let his thick, black hair grow down to his shoulders. I hadn't thought anything of it at the time. His ponytail didn't make him appear womanly—more like a middle-aged hipster. Now he adds jewelry—a necklace, a bangle bracelet, dangling earrings—and he looks like he belongs in an over-the-hill rock band.

He lets his fingernails grow longer too. Soon they glisten with bright pink or ruby red polish. I train my eyes away, pretending not to notice.

His tweezed eyebrows and makeup are harder to ignore. The shaky, unpracticed eyeliner. Clumpy, overexcited mascara. Thick red lipstick that ends up on his teeth. I struggle not to stare.

"Does it bother you?" he asks one evening. We're sitting on his couch playing video games, and while reloading he catches my sideways glance.

"Huh? Um, no." I race my gaze back to the TV screen.

"How would you feel if I wore a dress?" he asks.

Panic seizes me. I don't want to see my dad in a dress. I want to shake him and shout, "Don't you realize how weird this is for me?" But my thoughts and tongue are too tangled. All I can say is, "Dad, NO!"

I leap to my feet, hook King's collar to the leash, and gallop the six blocks home with King at my side and Dad's question ringing in my ears.

* * *

I don't go back the next day or the day after. Dad texts me, asking when I'm coming over again, but I tell him I'm busy with my comic book. When a car pulls into the driveway, I brace myself, figuring he's come to talk more about the dress thing. But it turns out the car isn't Dad's; it belongs to one of Mom's friends.

Although I try to avoid thinking about Dad, memories of him haunt me at every turn. On the back steps, inviting me to help shell peanuts for the squirrels that nest in our patio's live oak. Calling out to me from the sofa to share a gripping scene from a spy novel. In the kitchen, asking me to taste the chili con carne he made and dropping a meat tidbit for King, pretending it was an accident. Dad's ghost won't leave me in peace.

After three days, I know what I need to do. I march through the scorching summer heat toward Dad's house, rehearsing in my mind what I'll say: *If you want to be a woman, go ahead, knock yourself out. But don't count on me to take any part in it. If you're going to walk around in a dress, I don't want to ever see you again.*

Maybe that will bring him to his senses, make him stop this silliness. Bring him back home. As a guy.

Reaching his doorstep, I punch the doorbell. Then I cross my arms tightly against my chest, steeling myself.

The door opens, and Dad stands there in his jeans and a faded T-shirt. His dark, mascara-lined eyes are shimmering. "I missed you, mijo." His voice rasps soft and sad.

My vision grows wet and blurry. I open my mouth, but not a sound comes out. For a long, wordless moment, we just stare at each other across the threshold. Then Dad opens his arms, and I press into him. He clutches me in a hug that seems to last for hours. And the tears flow. From both of us.

There is no way I could ever ditch my dad, even if he does wear a dress.

* * *

In the kitchen we make ice-cold root beer floats. When Dad bends over to let King lick the empty ice cream carton, his hulking shoulders bring back memories of me riding around on them, pretending to be Superboy, flying high in the sky.

"So . . ." I say, slurping the last drop of root beer from the bottom of my glass. "I guess it would be okay if you . . . you know . . ."

Dad studies me from across the table, waiting. "You mean . . . if I wear a—"

"*Yes,*" I say, not wanting to talk about it. I just want to get it over with before I chicken out.

"Are you sure?" he asks.

"*Go,*" I say, waving him to hurry up.

While he goes upstairs to change, I rinse our glasses, throw away the licked-clean ice cream carton, and play ball with King, trying to avoid thinking about what's coming. By the time Dad's footsteps thump down the stairs, my shirt is damp with sweat. Slowly, I turn toward the doorway. Am I really ready for this?

"You're sure you want to see me?" he asks, poking his head around the doorframe.

I nod, and he steps inside. In place of my big, boxy dad stands a big, bosomy woman. She towers atop a pair of chunky heels, smoothing the fabric of an orange sundress over the roll of her belly.

"Now be honest," he says. "Do I look ridiculous?"

It's my dad's deep, rumbling voice coming out of the lip-sticked mouth. It's my dad's hopeful face glowing beneath the powdery makeup. Yet I can't wrap my mind around the idea that the person standing before me is supposed to be a woman *and* my dad.

I squeeze tight the tennis ball in my hand. "Honestly? Yeah, you do look ridiculous."

He wilts like a flower, gaze dropping to the floor in shame, and a stab of guilt pierces me. I know this is important to him, but I don't want a dad that kids are going to stare at the same way I'm staring at him, trying to make sense of who he is.

"Maybe," I say softly, "you could wear something that doesn't make you stand out like an orange juice ad?"

Dad glances up, a smile creeping across his lips, and rushes to go change. When he reappears, I've gotten over my initial shock. This go-around my jaw doesn't drop. The outfit he changed into—a beige skirt and long-sleeve blouse—helps to tone things down by about ten decibels.

"Better?" he asks. His tweezed eyebrows are quivering.

I chew my bottom lip, fighting the impulse to say, *Give it up. You're never going to convince anybody you're a woman. You're a man!*

But the longing in his eyes makes it clear how much he needs me to accept him. I want him to be happy. And the longer I stare at him, the more he kind of does look like a woman—in a big-boned, matronly sort of way. Maybe with a little help, he could actually pull this off.

"Loads better," I say.

Dad's body relaxes, and his face brightens. "You mean that?"

I nod. "But I think you need help with your makeup." Although it's gotten better, it still looks wobbly. "Maybe we can find some lessons online."

"You'll help me?" he asks.

When I shrug *yes*, he hops up to the ceiling, slapping it so excitedly he nearly teeters off his heels.

Over the next few days, we sit together at the kitchen table with a light-up mirror, a mound of makeup, and Dad's laptop, surfing sites and watching tutorials. I never realized all the trouble women go through to paint up their faces.

As Dad struggles to put on fake eyelashes, I ask, "What's the point of all this?"

"To look pretty." He bats his eyes, but the eyelash springs off, flopping onto the table.

I pick it up and think how weird this all feels. I realize too that there's more to looking like a woman than just makeup. There's also a lot of body language—how women sit, their posture, how they walk. . . . King and I watch from the sidelines as Dad practices crossing the kitchen in heels, tipping and tottering and trying to stay balanced.

I strain to keep a serious face. "You're trying to be funny, aren't you?"

"You want to try?" he answers.

"No thanks." I've never had any desire to dress like a woman. Not in the least.

Dad plunks into a chair, pries off the shiny gray pumps, and nudges them over to me. "Go ahead, give them a shot."

"They're too big," I protest.

King trots over, gives the shoes a sniff, and stares up at me.

"Come on, be a *man*," Dad insists. Now he's *definitely* trying to be funny.

Off come my sneakers. My feet slide easily into the shoes—they're nearly the size of battleships. When I try to stand, it feels like I'm rolling on the high seas. My toes keep sliding down, down, down. I have to brace myself on the table to stay afloat.

"You see?" Dad says as I wade across the kitchen, almost twisting my ankle.

"How can anybody walk in these things?" I mutter and kick off the shoes.

To my wonderment, though, with practice and me cheering him on, little by little Dad gets the hang of it. As summer passes and the start of school gets closer, I no longer cringe at him wearing makeup and a skirt. I find myself thinking of him more and more as *her*. As *she*. As my secret dad, Norma.

CHAPTER 7

"Now, listen," Cesar says as we hustle toward our bus stop on the first morning of classes. "I've busted my butt to claim my place in school. Don't screw it up for me, okay?"

He truly has made his mark. He's a soccer, wrestling, and basketball star. He's going out with one of the school's queen bees, with whom he coanchors the school's morning announcements. His grades have gotten him into Junior Honor Society. And this year he's set on getting elected student body president. His catchphrase has become "Winning isn't everything, it's the *only* thing."

"I'm not going to screw it up," I say. But then I wonder aloud, "Screw it up how?"

Even though nobody is around, Cesar leans into me and whispers, "Don't even *think* of telling anyone about Dad."

"Like I don't know that? But you know eventually somebody's bound to see her." It's something I've been thinking about more and more. "What're we going to do then?"

Cesar glares at me. "I can't think about that right now. And stop calling him *her.*" He went through the roof when I told him Dad's new name was Norma. "Just keep your mouth shut. Don't make me have to kill you."

To show he means it, he raises his fist.

"Cut it out," I tell him. As the glossy yellow bus comes roaring up the street, I step back, just to make certain he doesn't accidentally knock me off the curb.

On the bus, Cesar saunters down the aisle toward the other cool kids in the back row. I join Chang, who's sitting in the same row as last year. His thick, black hair is spiked up and shiny, like a cartoon character who stuck his finger in a light socket. On his lap is his sketchbook.

"What'cha got?" I ask, plopping into the seat beside him. All summer long we've worked on our comic for the contest. The deadline is next week, and we're still scrambling to put something together.

"How's this one?" Chang hands me his latest drawing of the guy-to-girl shape-shifter.

The figure looks like a brawny Thor . . . if he squeezed into Wonder Woman's skimpy corset. His arm and leg muscles bulge like sides of grade-A beef, while two steel cones poke out from his breastplate like upside-down ice cream cones, pointy enough to blind an opponent. His flag-like cape flows boldly over his manly shoulders, while at the same time he sports a dainty pleated skirt. His sturdy work boots taper into women's spiked heels, and his winged helmet is crowned by a diamond tiara worthy of a beauty queen.

I clench my jaw, which Chang, of course, notices.

"You hate it," he says, and before I can stop him, he nabs the sketch from my hand.

"No!" I pry the crumpling wad from his fist. "I like it. It's just, um . . . what's he holding?" It looks as if Thor traded in his huge, powerful hammer for a dollar-store eggbeater.

"That's your department," Chang says. "I was hoping you'd come up with a story for it."

"Hmm." I iron out the wrinkled drawing with my hand. "Maybe it's . . . a gender blender?"

Chang's brown eyes widen. "What the heck's a gender blender?"

"Um . . . it's got the power to scramble a person's gender?"

"That would definitely make guys run scared," Chang says. "It looks like he got caught in it himself."

"Hey." A light bulb goes off in my brain. "What if that's his origin story? Say he was this mild-mannered scientist conducting life-saving lab research on, you know, like gender-linked diseases. . . . But then his experiment blew up, and it mutated him, giving him the ability to turn into a super-woman."

"Me likey." Chang raises his fist for a knuckle bump. "How do you come up with this stuff?"

I shrug. "I guess the same way you come up with drawings."

"Okay, I'm hooked," Chang says. "So how does he-she battle the bad guys?"

"Maybe he uses the gender blender to change guys into girls and girls into guys."

"Muah-ha-ha-ha-ha . . ." Chang cackles and rubs his hands like a mad scientist. "Keep going. Then what?"

"Well, then the person whose gender is changed is able to see the other person's point of view and . . . they talk."

Chang looks confused. "They *talk*?"

"Yeah. Talking is harder than fighting."

It sounded good when Dad said it, but Chang scratches his head, unmoved.

"That's lame, huh?" I say.

"No, it just needs . . ."

"Clobbering?"

"That would be good."

Our bus wheezes to a stop at what looks like a sidewalk party. One after the other, every student on the bus turns to stare out the windows at the commotion.

A happy-faced golden retriever barks and wags its tail, fluttering a rainbow streamer tied there. A balding black guy trumpets a New Year's kazoo, and a white lady with platinum blonde hair tosses a shimmering mist of confetti into the air.

Between the couple stands a brown girl, waving good-bye. Her curly hair is held back by a headband with cat ears. Her eyes are as clear and blue as a cloudless sky.

"Good luck," the adults cheer. "Enjoy your new school!"

The girl boards the bus, smiling sheepishly. Everybody, even the driver, sort of gawks at her. She's pretty to begin with, and the confetti sparkles make her even more dazzling.

The driver's hand slips on the gearshift, and the bus gives an unexpected lurch. The girl pitches headlong, nearly tumbling down the aisle.

Faster than a speeding bullet, I reach for her arm. Her skin is soft as velvet. Her cheeks blossom red. A spray of confetti sprinkles off her like pixie dust. Her sweet, flowery scent wafts into my nostrils, sending a tingle through my body.

"Whoops, thanks," the girl says, regaining her balance. She spots Chang's sketch in my hand. "Oh, wow, that's great. Did you draw it?"

"Um . . ." I point a thumb toward Chang.

He plucks the drawing from my grasp and presents it to the girl as though it were a daisy. "You can have it."

"For real? Thanks."

"Take a seat, please," says the driver.

"Uh-oh," the girl tells us. "See you guys later."

As she continues down the aisle, Chang and I follow her with our eyes, our two heads swiveling in sync as if attached to a single mesmerized neck.

The bus shifts into gear, and Chang leans into me. "My heart's pounding like *pa-boomp, pa-boomp, pa-boomp.*"

"Mine too," I say.

When it comes to girls, we're both nerds. Fifth grade was my only attempt at a girlfriend: Oona Swensen. One day in the cafeteria line, she told Chang she liked me and asked him for my phone number.

"Um, okay," I said when he told me. "But what do I say if she calls?"

His face went blank. "You're asking *me?*"

We agreed I should ask Darnell, who already had a real live girlfriend.

"Much to learn you have, young Padawan," was Darnell's response. He liked to say things that way—like Yoda. Sometimes it was funny, and sometimes it got on my nerves. Like when I asked him what to say if Oona called and he replied, "Just let the maiden talk you must." As if it were that easy.

Oona texted and then phoned me that very afternoon. And the next. And the next. In the week that followed, she texted and called me at least twice every day. Her voice was soft and musical, and she loved to talk about riding horses at a local stable.

"We've got to tell each other a secret we've never told anybody," she said one day. "And it's got to be true." Her confession was that she slept with a clump of horse's mane beneath her pillow. "The barn smell gives me dreams of galloping hooves and green fields. What's your secret?"

"Um . . . let me think." I racked my brain for something I'd never told anyone. "Okay, so, if I'm walking my dog and he poops on somebody's lawn? I'll take out the plastic bag in case anybody's watching and do this big show like I'm scooping up his mess, but I really don't. It's too gross."

Oona burst out laughing. I laughed too and wondered if she *like*-liked me.

"How can I find out if she does?" I asked Darnell the next day.

He stroked his chin, thinking before answering. "Told her you like her have you? Hmm?"

"*Tell* her? Just like that? Say, 'I like you'? Guys really do that?"

"Sure they do. Girls love it—especially if they like the guy."

That night I typed Oona a text telling her: I like you. I stared at the words for a very long time. Then I deleted the message.

I retyped: I like you a lot

I deleted that one too.

Finally I climbed into bed and pulled the covers over my head.

Two days later I was in P.E. when Oona sent me a text: I think it's better if we're just friends . . . OK? Sorry . . . nothing personal

Her message hit me like a kickball in the gut. It was just as well I hadn't texted her. Then again, would things have turned out differently if I *had* told her? I would never know.

I now peer over my shoulder at the cat-ears girl. She waves, wiggling her fingers as if tinkling an air piano. I smile back, my mouth trembling a little.

When I turn forward again, Chang is smiling in her direction too—in a dreamy way I've only seen him get when he's drawing. He's never shown much interest in girls, unless you count Black Widow.

"She seems really nice," I say, snapping him out of his daze.

He nods. "She's cute too."

I try to read what's going on behind his dark, brooding-artist eyes. "I saved her from falling," I say.

"She really liked my drawing," he says.

"She talked to me first," I say.

"I *saw* her first," he says.

"You did not. We both saw her at the same time."

"Nuh-uh," he says. "I'm sitting by the window."

"So what?"

"So I get dibs."

"No, you don't."

"Yeah, I do."

The bus takes a curve, shoving us together. I lean away. If this were one of our usual spats, I'd give in. Arguing with Chang is like trying to wrestle a chew toy from King—he can go on for hours. But the tingle from the girl's soft skin lingers with me. I'm not about to give in.

"We'll ask Darnell," I say.

"Fine," Chang agrees.

The wind whips in through the open window as we bounce and bump toward school, and I realize something. For the first time in weeks, I'd stopped thinking about Dad— for at least a few minutes.

CHAPTER 8

When we get to school, Chang and I set aside our rivalry to compare schedules. For first period homeroom, he has art, and I have language arts. We'll meet up at lunch with Darnell. With that settled, we bump fists, separate, and resume our competition, each of us scanning the crowded lobby for the same pair of cat ears.

At the front of my classroom, next to the whiteboard, the TV is on, scrolling the lunch menu and playing marching band music. From one of the desk chairs, Oona gives me a friendly wave. I wave back with a twinge of nostalgia. There's an empty seat in the front row—not my favorite spot, but at least it's by the windows.

"Oh, hi," says a voice behind me. "I was hoping to see you again."

I turn and see *her*—the girl from the bus. "Um . . . hi."

She grins. "I promise not to crash on top of you this time."

"That's okay," I say. "Do you want the seat by the window?"

"No, thanks. I'm good here." She slides into the desk beside me. "Go ahead: Sit."

I obey.

"So where's your friend?" she asks.

"Art class."

"He draws great," she says.

The bell rings, and I think, *If only I could draw like Chang.*

"Quiet down, please," says our teacher, a thirty-something lady with frizzy hair and leopard-print eyeglass frames.

On the TV, the marching band music stops, and my brother appears with Victoria, his trophy girlfriend. She could be a contestant for Miss Middle School America: creamy skin. Corn-silk hair. Bikini body.

"Goooood morning, Mustangs!" Victoria and Cesar cheer in unison from behind a studio desk. They look like real anchors of a network news show.

I whisper to Cat Ears, "That's my brother."

"For real?" she whispers back. "Cool."

"I'm Cesar Fuerte," Cesar announces in his deep, official newscaster voice.

"I'm Victoria Rogers," Victoria says brightly.

"And together we welcome *you*"—their twin fingers

point at the camera—"to an awesome new year at Lone Star Middle."

"To get us off to a great start," Cesar says, sounding as perky as if he downed a dozen caffeine drinks, "let's all rise for the Pledge of Allegiance."

While our class stands and faces the flag, my gaze steals back to the girl beside me. Her hand curves firmly over her chest. Tiny silver stars sparkle on her nails. Her lips glow candy-apple red.

A million questions spin through my mind. What's her name? Where did she move from? Does she like nacho-cheese tortilla chips?

"To kick off the new academic year," Victoria says when we sit back down, "we want to invite everybody to next week's back-to-school talent show. Cesar and I will be your joint emcees."

The event is an annual tradition and loads of fun. Our family always attends.

"It's your chance to wow us with your talent," Victoria continues.

"And," Cesar says, "get a shot at the hundred-dollar grand prize."

"So dust off your dancing shoes. . . ."

"Tune up your voice. . . ."

"And," they finish together, "come shine in the lime-light."

Not me, I think. *Not even for a million bucks.*

Everybody has a fear of something. Superman: kryptonite. Indiana Jones: snakes. Me: getting up in front of groups.

It always ends badly. Like at kindergarten graduation: I was so nervous to get my diploma in front of everybody that when I crossed the stage, I accidentally detonated a fart louder than an atom bomb.

I'm serious—it nearly blew the roof off.

For an instant nobody said anything. All the adults just stared at me, shell-shocked. Then some kid's toddler brother burst into giggles. I ran offstage, choking down tears.

That trauma had barely subsided when I got assigned the role of the angel Gabriel in our second-grade Christmas pageant. The night of the event, my stomach was as tangled as a knot of rubber bands. When the spotlight moved to me, I announced to Mary she'd found favor with God. . . . then hurled my dinner all over her sandals.

The play had to be stopped for cleanup, and for the rest of the year I got called Barf Boy.

My most recent disaster occurred at our fifth-grade spelling bee. I managed to keep myself together until the final round. In front of the whole school, I walked up to the mic. The principal asked me to spell *aftermath.* The next thing I knew, the stage floor was flying up at me, and my teacher was screaming, "Darnell, catch him!"

When I came to, I was lying on my back, blinking up at the glaring rafter lights. A dozen faces clustered around me.

"Is he dead?" someone asked.

A walkie-talkie crackled as the principal radioed the front office. "We've got a man down. Repeat: Man down."

If I could truly have a superpower, it wouldn't be to fly or be invisible. It would simply be the ability to get up in front of a group without feeling like a prisoner facing a firing squad.

"All right, let's get started," our leopard-glasses teacher says when the TV announcements end. "My goal for language arts is to teach you effective communication. Reading. Writing. Speaking. To start off, rather than me calling roll, you'll each stand up and introduce yourselves."

Every muscle in my body snaps to attention as she points to the whiteboard questions.

"Your name and age. Any brothers or sisters? And one special thing about you—a talent or hobby. Easy peasy. I'll start. My name is Ms. Finnegan. I'm thirty-two years old. Four brothers, no sisters. And one special thing? Three years ago I was on *Everybody's Got Talent*."

My classmates sit up. *EGT* is TV's most popular song-and-dance competition.

"Alas," she continues, "I bombed. One of the judges told me he never forgot a voice, but in my case he'd make an exception."

While other students giggle, I gaze down at my desk, trying to summon telepathic superpowers. *Call on somebody else, please. Not me. . . .*

"Let's start in front," Ms. Finnegan says. "You by the window. Hel-looo . . . ?"

Slowly, I look up. Thirty pairs of eyes are fastened on me—watching, waiting—including those of Cat Ears, who's peering at me with worry.

"I can go first," she tells Ms. Finnegan. "I don't mind."

"You can be next," Ms. Finnegan says and returns to me. "Now come on. I know it can be scary to get up in front of people. Just relax. You can do it."

Sweat is dripping into my body's every crevice: the little nook above my top lip. The crooks of my elbows. The hollows between my toes. I feel like I'm drowning.

Cat Ears offers me a life-raft smile. Shakily I push myself up onto my jelly feet. "Um . . . What am I supposed to say?"

Ms. Finnegan points to the whiteboard. "Your name?"

"Jorge?" I say.

"Terrific," she says. "Your last name?"

"Fuerte?"

She checks my name off her roster. "See? You can do this. Your age? Any brothers or sisters?"

"Thirteen—my age, I mean. One brother—you just saw him."

"Oh, you're Cesar's brother? How lucky. Now, what's something special about you?"

What can I say? That I've Photoshopped my face onto the bodies of seventeen different superheroes? That sometimes when I'm home alone, I secretly dance merengue with my dog? Or that my dad . . .

"I can't think of anything."

"Sure you can," Ms. Finnegan says. "We're all special in some way. Any hobbies?"

"My friends and I make comic books."

"That's special," she says. "I'd love to see one sometime. Thank you, Jorge. Everybody, let's give Jorge a round of applause."

I drop into my chair faster than a cartoon anvil. And while I mop my forehead, Cat Ears gives me a thumbs-up.

"You're on," Ms. Finnegan tells her.

The girl stands, faces the class, and—

"Hey, Catwoman," some loudmouth in the back row heckles. "Where's Batman?"

I turn to see Sam Scruggs, an oversize goon with fiery red hair and a grimace like the Swamp Thing. He's one of the oldest kids at school, having been held back a grade—maybe two. I always steer clear of him. I'm not a fighter. I've never been in a real fight in my life. But watching this girl get picked on causes a protective feeling to rise up in me.

I shoot Scruggs my meanest look: steely jaw. Furrowed brow. Squinted gaze. He doesn't seem to notice.

Cat Ears pretends she doesn't hear him. "My name's Zoey Greenfield-Jones. I just moved here from Austin. I'm thirteen. No brothers or sisters. And something special I do is communicate with animals."

She stands tall, her voice radiating confidence. Her whole demeanor seems so at ease. I wish I could be that unafraid to stand in front of people, that comfortable communicating with—

Wait! What did she just say?

"I'm an interspecies communicator," Zoey continues as students around the room exchange looks. Ms. Finnegan blinks behind her glasses.

"Can you talk with horses?" Oona asks. "I'm worried— my favorite mare's been awfully moody lately."

Zoey nods understandingly. "I'd be happy to go talk—"

Scruggs shouts out, interrupting her: "You're bonkers!"

I whirl around. "Hey! Leave her alone."

"You going to make me?" he says.

"Boys!" Ms. Finnegan shouts, cutting us a death stare. "Quiet."

I ease back in my seat, wondering where I got the guts to stand up to Scruggs. Zoey rewards me with a smile.

"Well, that's certainly a special talent," Ms. Finnegan tells her. "Thank you. Let's have a big hand for Zoey. Next?"

I flash Zoey a double barrel thumbs-up, and, while other people introduce themselves, I picture a collection of little forest animals peering in from the hallway, coming to communicate with her.

Eventually the end-of-class bell calls me back to reality. While chairs scrape and people bustle out, Swamp Thing Scruggs lumbers up the aisle. As he steps closer, I try to avoid eye contact, but when he narrows his beady little eyes at me, I refuse to glance away. For what seems like forever, we're locked into a battle of looks. Finally, he shuffles past.

"Thanks, Jorge." Zoey pumps her fist in a solidarity salute. "Hope to see you in another class."

As she disappears down the hall, I imagine her little flock of woodland creatures trailing after her—and me tagging along.

CHAPTER 9

When the lunch bell clangs, I charge down the hall with the rest of the stampede, get a cheeseburger and onion rings, and step into the cavernous cafeteria. Cesar is sitting at the cool kids' table, talking and joking, his dimpled grin blazing as bright as a movie marquee. On the other side of the room, Darnell is already sitting at our table. I join him and flop into a seat, offering Darnell an onion ring.

"I need your help with Chang," I say.

"Uh-oh." Darnell repays me with some barbecue fries. "Are you guys sparring again about why Thor needs a helmet if he's immortal?"

"No, worse. There's this girl—"

"Whoa, *shh*, here he comes. Yo, Picasso!"

Chang plunks down next to Darnell and flashes me a gloating grin. "Guess who's in my history class?"

"Her name's Zoey," I say.

His smile plummets. "You *talked* to her?"

"Yeah. We all had to stand and introduce ourselves in homeroom."

"Oh. So you didn't actually *talk* to her."

"Actually I *did*. She sat next to me."

"Well, I talked to her too." He unwraps his burger. "Finally I met a girl who didn't ask, 'How long have you been in America? Why don't you have an accent? Can you help me with math?'"

Darnell makes a timeout T with his hands. "Slow down. Who is this girl?"

"Sweet Christmas!" Chang gazes over my shoulder. "There she is."

I spin around. At a table two rows back, Zoey is sitting with Oona and a couple of other girls. They're all glancing at something on Oona's phone.

"What're they looking at?" Darnell asks.

"Maybe horses?" I guess. "Zoey says she can communicate with animals."

"I wonder if she could get Shaquille to stop chewing my pencils," Chang says. Shaquille is his dog.

"Maybe I should ask her to help me with King."

Chang pries his eyes off Zoey. "It seems we were mistaken about Jorge," he says to Darnell.

Darnell inspects me with a curious stare. "Maybe so."

"What're you guys talking about?" I ask.

Chang and Darnell exchange a look.

"You've never been into girls," Chang explains.

"We . . . kind of figured you were gay." Darnell shrugs. "It's okay if you are."

I drop my onion ring. "You're kidding me, right? What about Oona?"

Chang shakes his head. "That's why she broke up with you. She said you never made a move on her."

"We were in *fifth grade*. What was I supposed to do? Ride her on my handlebars to go look for a room? I don't think that's what hotels mean when they say *kids stay free*. I can't believe you guys didn't tell me she said that."

"We figured you'd come out when you were ready," Darnell says.

Chang offers me a mozzarella stick. "She said you never even tried to hold her hand."

"I was *shy*. That doesn't mean I'm gay."

"Well, tell it to Oona," Chang says. "Meanwhile I've got dibs on Zoey."

"You can't call dibs on a girl," Darnell says.

"Yeah," I say happily. "Wait, why not?"

"Because she's a human being, not the last Dorito in the bowl."

"I wouldn't mind if she called dibs on me," Chang says.

"Well, she hasn't," I snap.

Darnell tries to change the subject. "Let's see the sketch you texted me about last night," he tells Chang.

"I gave it to Zoey."

"You gave her our sketch?" Darrell asks. "Dude! We're on deadline. The contest ends next Friday—that's only ten days."

"Chill," Chang says, pulling out his phone. "I've got the photo."

While they look at the picture, I chomp on my cheeseburger, debating whether I should go ahead and let Chang have dibs. I don't want to be at odds with him. He's always been there for me: carrying my books when a sprained ankle put me on crutches; lending me comics even after I spilled salsa on his *X-Men: Age of Apocalypse*; consoling me when my ninja box turtle, Donatello, died. There's got to be a way to resolve our Zoey feud.

"Can you find out which of us she likes better?" I ask Darnell.

"Young Padawans," he says in his Yoda voice. "In grade school you no longer are. If you wish to vie for this celestial princess, you must each show her why she should pick you." He sets down his burger, circles his fingers like he's going to meditate, and lets his eyelids close. "The oracle has spoken."

"Are you up for this?" Chang asks me. "Or do you want to concede?"

I crane my head back around to look at Zoey. She isn't

only cute and confident. She's so natural, so at ease with herself, so comfortable in her skin. She's all the things I admire and want to be.

When she catches the sight of me, Zoey's face lights up. I swing back around to Chang. "Game on."

He frowns—actually it's more like a pout. "Fine, but you're not going to win this."

Darnell breaks out of his Buddha pose. "Are you guys sure she doesn't already have a boyfriend?"

Chang looks at me. "I'll ask her."

"I'll ask too," I say, hoping I'll have her in an afternoon class.

Unfortunately, I don't. Fortunately, neither does Chang. When we get on our after-school bus, she's already in her row, busy talking with the girl beside her.

As we ride toward home, Chang pulls out the Darth Vader colored pencil box Darnell gave him last Christmas and starts a new sketch. He can draw anytime, anywhere, even on a bumpy bus. Meanwhile I shoot my dad—*Norma*—a text, asking if I can come over.

CHAPTER 10

In Norma's driveway, parked beside her sporty red car with the *OPERA LVR* license plate, is cousin Raul's car. I glance between the white coupe and the brick townhouse. I'm not usually nervous around Raul—he used to babysit Cesar and me when we were little and always brought food or presents to family events. But this will be the first time I've ever been around anybody with Dad as Norma. It's been our secret—or at least *my* secret.

I grip my backpack and head inside.

"Is that you, Jorge?" Norma calls when I let myself in.

"Nope, just a burglar."

The house smells of cinnamon-oatmeal cookies. In the kitchen, Dad is peering into the oven with a fully made-up face. Beneath the Superman apron is a blue-checkered housedress.

Raul sits at the table, calmly sipping coffee, as if it's no big deal for my dad to be wearing lipstick and women's flats. "Hi, Jorge."

"'Sup?" I head straight to the snack cabinet, only to find it empty. "Hey, where are the tortilla chips?"

"Hey, yourself," Norma answers. "You finished the bag yesterday, remember?"

"Oh, yeah. Well, you should have a backup for emergencies."

"That *was* the backup." She comes over and wraps an arm around me in a fake chokehold hug. "What I should've done was bought stock in Doritos on the day you were born. By now I'd be rich." She lets me go and slides her hand into an oven mitt. "You'll have to settle for cookies."

"How was your first day back in school?" Raul asks.

"Fine." I peel off my backpack, drop into a chair, and try to act relaxed.

He eyes me over the rim of his glasses as if seeing through my act. "Why don't you stop by my house sometime? Or give me a call. We can talk."

"Thanks." I bury my gaze in my placemat. I know that by "talk," he means talk about Norma. And I know I won't call.

She brings us a plate of cookies and asks Raul, "More coffee?"

"No, thanks." He grabs a cookie and stands to go. "I'll

leave you guys to your father-son bonding. Or should I say *mother*-son?"

"No, no, father-son is fine," Norma says. "I may have stopped wearing the pants, but I'm still the papa."

"Why *don't* you wear pants?" I ask. "Mom hardly ever wears a dress at home."

"Because"—Norma twirls her skirt—"I've been waiting forty-three years for this."

I look away, embarrassed, and check for Raul's reaction. He grins, unfazed. "Better late than never."

While Norma walks him to the door, I pour myself some milk and bite into a cookie. The oatmeal crumbles in my mouth: warm, cinnamony, and full of sweet, comforting raisins.

When she returns I ask, "What does Raul think of you becoming a woman?"

"No problem. He's been around trans people before."

"He has? Where?"

"In clubs."

"What kind of clubs?"

"Gay clubs."

I stop chewing my cookie. "You mean . . . Raul is *gay*? Does Mom know?"

"Sure, she knows."

"How come you guys never told Cesar and me?"

"You never asked. And it never came up."

I sip the cold milk. "So . . ." I say, running my finger-tips across the rough edges of the woven placemat. "Are *you* . . . ?"

She stares blankly at me. "Am I *what*?"

I swallow hard and whisper, "Gay?"

She leans back in surprise. "What? No! I'm not attracted to men."

"But . . . if you're becoming a woman doesn't that mean . . . ?"

"Ay, Jorgito . . . Of course you'd assume that, but no." She pours herself a fresh cup of coffee and sits down. "I've always been attracted to women—*only* women—ever since I was your age. The hormones I'm taking may change that, but chances are I'll stay attracted to women . . . in which case, I technically *would* be gay—a lesbian, actually. Interesting, huh?"

I slowly chew another cookie. "So then . . . why can't you stay married to Mom?"

"Because she's attracted to *men*. We talked through this in counseling. I made my decision to transition and live as a woman. Mom made her decision. I need to respect that she doesn't want to be married to a woman."

"But you're not just *any* woman. You're our dad. Mom says she misses you so much her chest hurts."

"She says that?"

I nod. "Do you still love her?"

"Of course I still love her. You don't stop loving someone simply because you break up. That's what hurts so much."

"If you're both hurting," I argue, "why don't you hurt together? Maybe you'll stop hurting."

The whites of her eyes glisten. "Jorge, I need to respect her decision, just like she respects mine. Getting back together just isn't possible."

I think about Dad living in this house by herself. All alone. Without Mom. Without us. Without anybody. Is becoming a woman worth that?

"Your mom's the most amazing woman I've ever met," Norma continues, lifting her *World's Greatest Dad* mug like she's toasting Mom. "She's a better woman than *I'll* ever be."

"Why don't you tell her that?" I ask. "You said the divorce isn't final until next week, right? If she wanted to get back together, would you?"

Norma pulls the mug away from her lips, leaving the white rim stained with a red kiss mark. "Mijo, I need to respect Mom's decision. Don't you understand?"

No, I start to say but stop short. If she isn't going to talk to Mom, then maybe . . . I take another cookie. "I guess so."

"Good," Norma says, and her bulky shoulders relax. "Now I want to hear about you. How was school? And don't just say *fine.* Let's hear details, drama, the full scoop."

"Well . . . there's this new girl, Zoey, who moved to Magnolia Street. Talk about *amazing.* She's got these insanely blue eyes. And she's sweet, and confident, and kind of quirky, but I like that. She says she can communicate with animals."

"Sounds like she's daring to be different. That's brave—especially in middle school."

"Yeah, the problem is Chang likes her too. I don't want us to fight over her."

"Don't worry about Chang," Norma says, pouring me another glass of milk. "Just be *you*. You're funny and smart and good-looking. Plus you have a big, big heart. Let her see how amazing *you* are."

I roll my eyes.

"What's that look for?" Norma asks.

I dunk a cookie into my milk and watch it slowly break into pieces.

"Come on, out with it," she insists. Like Wonder Woman, Dad has a Lasso of Truth, an invisible coil that now loops tight around me. Resistance is futile.

"It's just . . ." I struggle. "I'm not sure how she would react to . . . you know . . . to *you*."

Norma turns quiet, freeing me to ladle a spoon into my oatmeal cookie milk.

"How have your other friends reacted?" she asks.

The lasso tightens around me again. "I haven't told any-body."

"Jorge, *nobody*? Not even Chang or Darnell?"

"I'm scared they'll ditch me. And if other kids find out, they'll pick on me—and Cesar. I promised him I wouldn't tell anyone. He says if I do, he'll have to kill me."

"Jorge," Dad says again, more softly. "You know he's not going to kill you."

"He might as well. You know he's running for student body president. What if he lost because I blabbed? And what if Victoria dumped him? He's crazy about her. He might not kill me, but he'd never talk to me again."

"So you're going to pass up this amazing girl *you're* wild about so he can be with a girl *he's* wild about? That's heroic."

"Thanks."

"For what? I was being sarcastic. This isn't about Cesar. It's about you twisting yourself into a human pretzel to please other people rather than being honest. Believe me, I know all about that."

"Exactly," I say. "Just like you're worried how other people will react to you—I am too."

Her expression softens, and she drums her flamingo-pink fingernails on the placemat. "All right. I suppose if it took me all these years to come out, I can't expect you boys to open up about it overnight. I'm here if you need me."

"Thanks," I say. "Anyway, as far as Zoey goes, she's probably already got a boyfriend."

"I hope not," Norma says. "She'd be the luckiest girl in

the world to be your girlfriend. And I bet anyone who can communicate with animals must be pretty good at understanding humans too—even a boy with a trans dad."

I think about that and down the last of my milk. "I've got to go let King out."

"Take some cookies," she says and stuffs a whole bunch into a big plastic bag. "Share them with Mom and Cesar." She pauses. "Does he . . . ask about me?"

I jam the cookies into my backpack, avoiding her gaze.

"Truth, Jorge."

"I know he thinks about you. He always asks where I've been, even though he knows."

Norma's face brightens. "That's a good sign. He just needs time to work this out."

"He's too mad to work it out," I mutter.

Her glow dims a little. "I'll give you a ride home on my way to the market." She plucks the grocery list from the fridge door. "I hear we need tortilla chips."

"I can walk home," I say. "I need the exercise."

That isn't the real reason, though. Truth is, I'm not ready for the whole neighborhood to see me with her.

Norma's mouth turns down in a knowing look. "Never mind the chips. I'll get you a jumbo bag of pretzels."

CHAPTER 11

"I brought you guys some oatmeal cookies," I tell Mom and Cesar during dinner. "From Norma."

Cesar cringes as if jabbed by a fork. "Could you please stop calling him that?"

"That's her name now," I say, passing the roasted potatoes across the kitchen table.

"You shouldn't even go over there," he says. "What if somebody sees you?"

"You should visit him too," Mom tells Cesar.

"Visit *her*," I correct.

"I don't see *you* going over there," Cesar tells Mom.

"We talk on the phone every day. Now can you boys give it a rest?" She passes me the pork chops. "How was school today?"

"Great," I say. "I met this new girl who communicates with animals."

"You mean that kooky chick with the cat ears?" Cesar says. "Who the heck brings their parents to the bus stop in *eighth grade?*"

"She's not a kook," I say. "She's daring to be different."

"Victoria and I will find you a normal girl," Cesar says.

I start to say I don't want a normal girl, but that sounds wrong.

Cesar slides Mom the carrots. "Victoria offered to be my campaign manager."

While my brother blabbers on about Victoria, a little pair of dog paws lands on my lap. King is standing on his hind legs, leaning into me. His nose twitches, and his bright eyes shine like a pair of headlights—aimed at my plate.

"Jorge, not at the table," Mom says.

I gently shake him off my lap. "Down, boy." But while she and Cesar keep yakking, I sneak a pork tidbit down to King. He snaps at it so fast his jaws clack.

"Jorge, what did I tell you?" Mom says. "King, come here."

He races across the tile at NASCAR speed, skids to Mom's feet, and glances up at her with a look that says, *Ready when you are.*

"No, I didn't call you for food. Sit. Stay still." She returns to Cesar. "Let me know if you need my help with anything for your campaign."

"Thanks. We've got it under control. Victoria is rehearsing the cheer squad to do a flash mob thing."

On the floor next to Mom, King sits waiting. A thread of drool hangs from his mouth like a fishing line. After several minutes of failing to snag a bite, he glances back toward me. I flash my eyes like a secret signal. He decodes the message instantly.

Making sure Lieutenant Mom isn't watching, he drops to his belly. As stealthy as a soldier slinking back from enemy lines, he makes his way across the floor—head low, tail down. Against all odds, he reaches base camp without a hitch. It would be a unfair to let his bravery go without a reward.

"Jorge!" Mom catches me slipping him a pork medallion. "What did I tell you?"

"Sorry, I won't do it again."

"Seriously? We both know you will. So does he. Put him outside."

Grudgingly, I get up. "Come on, boy."

King scrambles past me toward the sliding glass door, eager to be first out. To him, an open door—*any* door—means a world full of possibilities: food. Fetch. Fun.

He flies out to the patio steps. When the glass door clicks shut behind him—and without me—he whirls about face. His head cocks at an angle. You can practically see the wheels turning inside his brain. I couldn't possibly have meant to strand him out there by himself. Why on earth would I do that?

While the rest of us eat, King paws at the window, waving for our attention. His wet nose smears the glass as if scrawling an S.O.S. When the visuals fail, he switches to audio, warming up with a few soft whimpers—the first tentative notes of the concert to come. His tail rises like a conductor's baton. A moment later, he bursts into a symphony of yelps and yowls.

"*Jorge!*" Mom scolds me.

"You told me to put him out."

She turns back to Cesar, speaking louder, "Who else is running for president?"

"A mathlete and some drama chick," he hollers back.

Outside, our neighbors' dogs chime in with King's barking, sounding like an orchestra. Mr. Wilson's Weimaraner woofs like the woodwinds. Mrs. Yamamoto's Chihuahuas yip and yap like the strings. And the Avilas' bloodhound bays like the brass.

Mom gives in with a sigh. "Let him back inside."

I open the door, and King vaults into the room—first to Mom, then to Cesar, then to me. Unable to contain his joy after such a long, lonesome separation, he snaps up his yellow plastic chew toy and canters around the room, swinging his head like a parading colt.

When he offers to share his slobbery prize, Cesar shoos him away. "No, thanks. I don't want it."

"Jorge," Mom says, "you've got to learn to control King."

"Why don't you take him back to obedience school?" Cesar asks me.

I cringe, remembering the last time I tried that. When King was eight months old, the city offered a basic obedience course at a nearby park. From the moment we arrived, he claimed his role as class clown. While the other dogs learned to sit on command, King turned away from me, stood on his hind legs, and surveyed the crowd like a dance partner scouting a better offer. When I tried to teach him to come, instead he bounded away to a slender girl greyhound. And as his classmates learned to follow on leash, King was the one who led me, nearly tugging my arm from its socket.

"Hey, *I'm* the human," I whispered through clenched teeth. "*You're* the *dog*! That means *I* lead. You *follow. Comprendes?*"

King's eyes beamed with understanding. Then he proudly showed the class how he inserted his nose in my crotch.

After the second lesson, the teacher recommended I wait until King was more mature before trying to train him further. He was essentially kicked out of obedience school.

I tried to train him on my own by watching videos online, but my heart wasn't in it. I enjoyed his wacky antics—and still do, now more than ever. They're like a guardrail around the giant hole Dad left by moving out.

"Did you take him for a walk today?" Mom asks. He's

running circles on the floor, chasing his tail, while we clean up after dinner.

When I first got King, I walked him two or three times a day. He was small as an empanada, and I could easily win the leash wars. But as he grew, the tug-of-war yanked in his favor. Each time I tried to slip the leash on him, he chomped down and shook it as if it were a deadly snake. Once we finally got out the door, he rushed ahead of me, sniffing, panting, peeing—sometimes all three at once. And if somebody appeared on our path, he surged to greet them, dragging me behind as if I were a water skier behind a miniature powerboat.

Over time I got tired of fighting him. Instead I let him burn off his energy chasing squirrels in the patio.

"I think he needs more exercise," Mom says.

"He's okay," I say, handing her plates to load the dishwasher. "I already let him out when I got home from Norma's. Oh, by the way, she told me she's a lesbian."

Cesar glances over from wiping the table. "*What?*"

"Um, yeah," I say, realizing I probably shouldn't have blurted that out. "I asked if she's attracted to guys now . . . but she's still only attracted to women."

Cesar tosses his sponge into the sink. "Can you just shut up about him?"

"Cesar, please don't start again," Mom says.

"*Me?* He's the one who started it."

"I was talking to Mom," I say, and turn back to her. "Dad's still attracted to you. She thinks you're the most amazing woman she's ever met."

"Well, he was the most amazing man I'd ever met," Mom says. For a moment, her eyes tear up, but then her tone hardens. "Until he decided to be a woman. He made his decision. I've made mine."

"But inside she's still the same person," I say softly. "She loves you. And I know you love her. Couldn't we at least try living with her as a woman?"

"No," Cesar says. "Everyone would find out. I could never have friends over. And neither could you."

He's right, I realize. It would mean telling Chang and Darnell. Could I go through with that?

Before I can decide, King bursts out barking and zooms to the front hallway.

"Both of you boys are going to need to deal with your friends at some point," Mom says, pouring detergent into the dishwasher. "You can't hide this forever."

"Just promise me he's not moving back in here as a woman," Cesar pleads.

"Why can't we just try?" I insist.

While Mom glances between Cesar and me, King yips and yowls in the living room.

"Jorge, we already filed for divorce. Now will you go quiet King, please?"

"King, quiet!" I shout, but I stay put. "The divorce isn't final till the end of next week. You can still change your mind."

"Mom," Cesar argues, "how could you let him move back after he lied to you?"

"He didn't lie," Mom says. "In every relationship, people grow and change."

"Not into the opposite sex," Cesar says.

"So you'll think about it?" I ask her.

King barks louder, and Mom slams the dishwasher shut. "Guys, drop it. Both of you. Jorge, go quiet King."

I jog out the doorway, steering clear of Cesar. King is perched on the living room couch, ears pricked, nose pressed to the window glass as he whines and whimpers.

"What's going on, boy?" I pat him and look out at the sidewalk.

Beneath the streetlamps' glow, a girl is listening to her headphones while walking her retriever. Not exactly walk-ing—doing some sort of dance. Shimmy, shimmy, step, twirl. Shimmy, shimmy—

King barks, and the girl turns toward the window. My heart gives a leap. It's Zoey.

"Isn't that the kooky chick from school?" Cesar says, sneaking up behind me.

"Her name's *Zoey*."

"Is she stalking you?"

"No. She doesn't know I live here."

"Why's she walking weird?"

I flick my glance back to the street. Zoey shimmies again, continuing up the sidewalk with her dog. At my side, King whimpers.

Cesar grabs my arm. "Hey, come on. Let's text Victoria and ask her which of her friends might be right for you."

I hesitate, thinking about what Norma said about pretzeling myself. Then I slide away from Cesar's grasp, shouting to Mom, "I'm taking King for a walk!"

CHAPTER 12

I hook the leash to King's collar, but it does little good. The instant I open the front door, the strap whizzes out of my hand. I bound across the front lawn, chasing after him. By the time I catch up, King is already letting Zoey's dog sniff his little pink butt. The retriever's tail wags so deliriously you would've thought King was offering her a sweet-smelling rose.

"Hi," Zoey says, pulling out her earphones.

"King, stop that!" I try to tug him away from her dog's rump. "Um, sorry."

"It's okay. They're just saying hi. Their anal scent is like their news feed."

Hearing her say "anal" transforms me into a giggling six-year-old.

"I know, right?" She giggles with me. "But yeah, their

scent reveals what they ate, where they've been, what they've done. Smell is a dog's main sense, apart from energy."

"King is definitely high energy," I say. "Like a dog tornado." As if to prove my point, he whirls around my ankles, circling me with his leash, nearly tripping me.

Zoey reaches out and steadies my arm. "A dog-nado?"

"Exactly."

King scurries between her legs, pulling the leash and me. Suddenly Zoey's softness is pressing into my chest. My cheeks flare warm. Her eyes lock onto mine. And a tingle runs through my body. We've become the ones sniffing and circling each other.

"Sorry," I say, releasing King's leash. Now it's her dog roping us together. I spin around to let her pass. All this circling is making me dizzy.

"Goldie, sit," Zoey says.

Her dog obeys, and I scoop King up in my arms. "Calm down!"

Zoey gives me a doubtful look. "That's like yelling at a foreigner, thinking that then they'll understand English. You'll have better luck using his language."

"Barking?"

"No." She grins. "Energy—like what do you think he's feeling right now?"

King's tongue flicks my face like a windshield wiper set to *high*. "Excited?"

"See?" Zoey says. "You understand him. He's showing you he's excited. The problem is that by cuddling him, you're telling him you approve."

"I am?" I turn my cheek to escape his slobber.

"If you really want to calm him, the best way is to show him through your own calm, assertive energy. Want to try?" She holds out her hand to switch leashes.

I set King on the sidewalk and give Zoey his leash. He excitedly wags his tail.

"To start," she says, kneeling beside him, "let's move his collar higher on his neck to hold his head up, like at a dog show. A head held high projects confidence. Plus, it'll help you direct his gaze and control his attention." She stands and nudges King's head up with the leash. "See?"

He looks proud. Poised. Dignified. For all of two seconds. Then he lurches toward Goldie.

"*Tsst!*" Zoey hisses like a lighted match, snaps her fingers, and flicks his leash all at once.

King ducks his head and gazes up, looking like he's been Tasered.

"To get his attention," she says, "you make a sharp sound."

But as soon as King recovers from the shock, he starts again toward Goldie.

"*Tsst!*" Zoey yanks his leash. "Sit!"

King draws his head in like a turtle and glances toward Goldie. His chocolate-drop eyes drip with yearning.

Zoey bends over and pushes his rump to the ground. He rolls over for a belly rub.

"No." She calmly pulls him back to his feet. "Sit." After two more tries, he finally sits. "Good boy." She turns to me. "How about if we walk him and Goldie? You can be the leader."

The instant the leash shifts from Zoey's hand to mine, King reverts to his clown self, hopping kangaroo-like toward Goldie. I tug and pull to haul him back.

"Hold on, you want to avoid a leash war," Zoey says. "Look at your body language. See how you're hunched over wrestling with him? You're projecting fear. If you want him to behave differently, you need to act differently too." She snaps her fingers. "*Tsst!*"

I snap my head up.

"I meant that for him," she says, grinning, "but that's good. Stand tall. Shoulders back. Project calm, assertive energy. Show him you're the leader."

"Who are you training?" I mumble. "Him or me?"

"Both, actually. You want a well-trained dog, and your dog wants a well-trained human."

I yank King's leash and start ahead. In charge. In control.

He crosses behind me toward Goldie, twirling me in a circle.

"Whoa, whoa," Zoey says. "Forward is *that* way."

"Tell *him* that," I say, tugging him away from Goldie.

"Try again," Zoey says calmly. "Step up to him with confidence, like you were standing before. Shoulders back. Head high. Calm. Assertive."

I stand straight, crowd up to King, and snap my fingers. *"Tzzt!"*

He stops tugging and glances up.

"See?" Zoey says. "Dogs are pack animals. If you view the world through his eyes, you know he's asking, 'Are you my pack leader?' Answer him with your energy. Tell him 'heel,' look ahead, and start walking."

"What if he doesn't follow?"

"Think positive. Picture him in your mind. You can do it."

I stand straight, imagine King trotting at my side, command, "Heel," and start forward. For an instant, his leash resists. Then Zoey steps alongside me with Goldie, and King actually falls in stride.

"You're doing great," Zoey says. "Always walk in front. When he gets ahead or distracted, you calmly snap his attention back. *Tsst!* See? Like that. No need to yell. Just let him follow the leader. That's *you.*"

"What if he wants to sniff or pee?"

"He only gets to stop when *you* decide. How often do you walk him?"

"Usually I just let him out to the patio, except then he goes crazy chasing squirrels and digging holes."

"Hmm . . . It sounds like he's bored. Dogs need to walk. It's in their DNA. It gives them a purpose. Hanging out in a patio isn't the same."

"How did you learn all this stuff?" I ask.

"From the internet and TV. My dream is to be an animal cognition scientist."

"Sounds like you already are one."

She laughs—a warm, good-natured laugh. I like making her laugh.

"By the way," she says, nodding at King, "you might want to change his name."

"Why? What's wrong with *King*?"

"Nothing, except he's a dog. Dogs like to enjoy life. Being a king is too much work."

"You think he understands what *king* means?"

"Not the word, but the energy in it. I know that sounds unlikely, but you might try a different name."

"Like what?"

Zoey watches King jog happily at our sides, his mouth slack with his usual smile. "Maybe something that suits his personality. Like Chipper. Or Zippy. Or . . . Peppy."

He suddenly barks and wags his tail.

I glance at Zoey. "Did you make him do that?"

"Nope."

"Peppy . . . ?" I cautiously ask. Again he barks.

I stare at Zoey, impressed and a little speechless. Maybe

it's just a coincidence. Or she truly is amazing. What I wouldn't do to be her boyfriend—assuming she doesn't already have one.

While we walk toward her house, two streets over, Zoey starts to do the shimmy step she was doing outside my window. I can't help but ask: "So . . . what're you doing?"

"Practicing a dance thing," she explains. "It's for the talent show next week. If I win, I'm donating the hundred dollars to the pet food pantry."

"You're not scared to go onstage in front of all those people?" I ask.

"A little. But you just hold your head high, believe you can do it, and if you start to get scared, yank your mind back. *Tsst!* Don't let your thoughts go there."

"Has anybody ever told you that you're amazingly self-confident?"

Zoey smiles softly. "You wouldn't think so if you heard what goes on inside my head. Truthfully I'd feel a lot more confident if I had a dance partner. But I don't know anybody here." Three paces later she turns to me. "Unless . . . ?"

I stare back at her. "*Me?* No." I don't dance, unless you count secretly boogying in my room with King—I mean *Peppy.*

"I'll teach you," she says. "Pretty please?"

I imagine standing close, holding her in my arms, and

winning her over. Then I picture the thousand people watching us, and my prior disasters flash before my eyes.

"Sorry," I mutter. "You're better off without me. Take my word for it."

Her lips pucker into a pout. "Are you sure?"

"Positive."

"Well," she says, stopping at the driveway of a ranch-style house, "can you at least watch and tell me what you think of what I've got so far?"

"Sure." I tell Peppy to sit. Miraculously, he obeys. Goldie sits on the other side of me.

"It's still a work in progress," Zoey says. "I haven't figured out all the steps yet."

She puts her ear buds back in, takes a breath, and turns her music on. While the dogs and I watch, she begins to shake her shoulders and move her waist, stepping in one direction, then shimmying the other way, and twirling to the side. Beneath the streetlights, she glimmers like an angel.

Beside me, Peppy pulls at his leash, whimpering to dance with her.

"*Tzzt!* Sit." I push his butt down, but it pops right back up. No matter how much calm, assertive energy I try to use, the sight of Zoey dancing is too much for him.

He stands on his hind legs and twirls in sync with her like a Broadway ballet dog. All he needs is a tutu. Wait . . . why not?

"Hey!" I call out to Zoey. "*He* dances."

She stops in mid-pirouette and pulls out her ear buds. "What?"

"He can dance." I point at Peppy. "Mostly merengue."

"Really? Oh my gosh, that's a great idea. Goldie's too old, but Peppy would be perfect. We've only got a few days till the show, though. Could you bring him over after school tomorrow to try it out?"

"Absolutely." My heart thrums with excitement. "I'll be his handler."

"Awesome." She points to the ranch-style house. "This is where I live."

After we say good night, she walks up the driveway with Goldie. I stand planted on the sidewalk, not wanting our time to end. At the front door, she turns and waves. I wave back. Only when she disappears inside do I finally pull myself away.

As I stride home with my newly named dog, my thoughts race ahead of me. I break ranks to pat him on the side. "Way to go, boy."

CHAPTER 13

When I come down to the kitchen the next morning, back straight, shoulders squared, Cesar glances up from his cereal and phone. "Why are you walking weird?"

"I'm not." I hold my head high. "I'm projecting confidence." I snap my fingers at Peppy, who's pawing the patio door. "*Tzzt!*"

Cesar's head jerks up.

"Zoey's teaching me to communicate through calm, assertive energy," I explain, sliding the glass door open. Peppy barges past me so fast he nearly knocks me over. "By the way, King's name is Peppy now. He likes it better."

Cesar stands to rinse his bowl and coffee mug. "Look, before you go overboard with this Zoey, Victoria suggested you give Emily a chance."

Unlike Cesar and me, Victoria and her twin sister, Emily,

are identical—at least in looks. I've had classes with Emily, and she seems nice, but we've never really talked.

"Why do you want to set me up with her?" I ask, sliding a bagel into the toaster.

"I'm just looking out for you. She'll help boost your brand."

"What *brand*? You're the one campaigning, not me."

"Yeah, but you're my brother. How people see *you* affects *me*."

"Cesar, nobody's going to vote for you because of what girl I like. I'm not interested."

"Come on, just talk to her. I think you'll like her— she's into manga. I'll hunt you down at lunch, and you can meet her."

"I told you: I'm. Not. Interested."

"Listen," Cesar says, resting an arm across my shoulders, "Victoria already told her you'd like to talk to her. You want to hurt the girl's feelings?"

My stomach rumbles. "You guys should've asked me first."

"I told you last night we'd look for someone for you. Come on, it's not like I'm asking you to marry her. Just give her a chance. Please?"

"Fine, I'll talk to her, but that's all."

"Thanks, man." He pats my back and heads out. "I knew I could count on you."

From the patio steps, Peppy barks to be let inside. I set my bagel on the table and slide open the patio door. He charges in as fast as he rushed out. I'm at the fridge pouring myself a glass of milk when I glimpse a white furry streak at the table.

"Hey!" He's climbed onto a chair and is nuzzling my breakfast. "No. *Tzzt!* Stop that."

The plate clatters to the floor. Peppy leaps down, snatches up the bagel in his mouth, and sprints toward the dining room as quickly as a running back rushing for a touchdown.

"Honey, why'd you give him that?" Mom says, hurrying to investigate the commotion. "Carbs aren't good for him."

"I didn't give it to him. He stole it. By the way, after school I'm taking him to see Zoey—that girl I told you about. He's going to dance with her in the talent show."

"I wish her luck," Mom says, rinsing her coffee cup. "Now get a move on or you'll miss the bus."

* * *

"'Sup?" I slide into the seat next to Chang while he shuffles the picture he was drawing into his sketchbook.

"Can I see?" I ask.

He clasps his hands over the book. "It's not ready yet."

"Come on," I say, reaching for it. "I'm sure it's great. You always show me stuff you're working on."

"Not always." He grips the book tighter.

I back down, sensing his grouchiness might be about something else. "Listen, we shouldn't be fighting over Zoey. We're friends. That's more important."

Chang relaxes his grip on the sketchbook. "I was thinking the same thing."

"You were?"

"Yeah. Whichever one of us she chooses is up to her."

"Exactly," I say, confident that I have the edge over him thanks to Peppy. "She'll choose whoever she likes best."

"She'll make up her own mind," he agrees.

"So, no hard feelings?" I ask.

"No hard feelings."

"Good morning, guys," Zoey says when she gets on.

Before I can say hi, Chang whips out his drawing. "I did a new sketch for you."

It isn't our gender-ambiguous hero. This sketch is of a hypermasculine guy flying in the sky, his cape flowing behind him. His face looks vaguely familiar. The mask's eyeholes are diamond-shaped, distinctly Asian. His black hair is as spiky as that of the weasel next to me. And in his pumped-up arms he carries a curly haired girl with a cat-ears headband.

"I love it," Zoey says. "Is that supposed to be me?"

The pink rises in Chang's cheeks. "Could be."

"Isn't he talented?" Zoey asks me.

"Yeah, very."

"How's Peppy today?" she asks.

"Not so good. He stole my breakfast."

"Oh. We'll have to work on—"

"Sit down, please," the driver orders.

"Sorry!" Zoey calls back and whispers to us, "See you guys later."

She heads to her seat, and I turn to Chang. "You said your drawing wasn't ready yet."

"I wanted her to see it first," he says.

"Sneak," I say.

He casts his gaze down but then glances back up. "Who the heck is *Peppy*?"

I don't want to gloat. Well, that's not completely true; I *do* want to gloat—I just don't want to make him feel bad. So I say, "Peppy is King's new name. We ran into Zoey last night during his walk."

"His *walk*? Since when do you take him for walks?"

"Dogs need to walk," I answer. "It's built into their DNA. Zoey wants him to dance with her in the talent show. We're rehearsing at her house after school." I smile proudly, now officially in gloating territory.

"You're going to *her house*? When were you going to tell me all this?"

I shrug. "I didn't want you to feel bad."

He cuts me a hard look. "Now who's the sneak? If you don't want me to feel bad, are you willing to give her up?"

I remember what Dad said about twisting myself into a

pretzel. I don't want Chang to feel bad, but I'm not willing to give up Zoey either. "No," I say.

"Didn't think so," Chang says.

As our bus continues toward school, I think, *I shouldn't have gloated.*

CHAPTER 14

"You guys did a terrific job with your speaking skills yesterday," Ms. Finnegan says when class starts. "Today we'll focus on our listening skills. We're going to learn to take notes."

A voice from the back row grumbles: "*We?* Don't you already know how?"

Ms. Finnegan scowls at Scruggs as if trying to melt him with her laser eyes. I hope she might be able to actually do it. I wish *I* could actually do it.

"Mr. Scruggs?" she says icily. "Do you wish to go to the principal?"

"Nah, thanks. You can go without me. I'll stay here and take notes."

"Mr. Scruggs, I'm warning you. One more remark and out you go."

He shuts up. I doubt it will last.

Ms. Finnegan shows us her way to take notes by dividing a blank notebook page into separate rectangles labeled *Keywords, Questions, Main Ideas,* and *Summary.*

A blue-haired boy with purple-painted fingernails raises his hand. "What do you mean by keywords?"

Scruggs answers, "Like if I say you're so gay, the keyword is—"

Ms. Finnegan slaps her hands together. "That's enough. Collect your belongings."

"I was just helping him understand," Scruggs says, faking innocence.

"Out," Ms. Finnegan snaps, handing him a note for the office.

Good riddance, I write in my page's summary section.

* * *

At lunchtime, I'm first to arrive at our table. I immediately nab Chang's usual seat so today *I* can watch Zoey without wrenching my neck.

She waves to me from her table with Oona and Oona's friends. I wave back. Maybe I should go say hi. Maybe she'll invite me to sit with her. Maybe—

"Hey, bro," Cesar calls out to me.

I turn and see him approaching with Victoria and Emily. The girls aren't *exactly* one hundred percent identical. They're equally cute with blond hair and blue eyes, but Victoria is a smidge taller. And the look in their eyes is different. Victoria gazes straight at you with an unflinching stare. Emily has a shy, uncertain glance, like she might be feeling as awkward as I am about being introduced.

"Jorge, this is Emily," Cesar says. "Emily, this is Jorge."

At the same instant both she and I say, "Nice to meet you."

She blushes. I do too.

"Jorge is into comics," Cesar says. "You like manga. So I thought you guys should talk."

"Are you sitting by yourself?" Victoria asks me and casually nudges her sister.

Emily takes the hint. "Would you like to sit with my group?"

"Um . . ." I falter. It's not every day a cute girl asks me to sit with her. Then I catch sight of Zoey watching me. "Thanks, but I'm waiting for my friends."

Cesar looks like he wants to punch my arm. Fortunately his hands are busy holding his tray. Instead he says, "Well, now that you guys have met, I'll text you each other's numbers."

And as the group walks away, Emily glances over her shoulder at me, smiling. I smile back.

"What's going on with you and Emily?" Darnell asks, lumbering over with his tray.

"Cesar's trying to set me up with her."

"You lucky dog," Darnell says, sitting down across from me.

"Hey," Chang tells me, arriving with his tray. "Why'd you take my seat?"

"I didn't see your name on it."

He deposits himself into the chair beside me as though we're at a movie—the star attraction is Zoey.

"Do you have a new sketch?" Darnell asks him.

"I'm working on it. Hey, Zoey's waving to me."

When he waves back I feel compelled to let him know: "She already waved to me before."

Darnell flags his hands in front of our eyes to get our attention. "Hey, what about our comic book?"

"We should go sit with her," Chang says, ignoring him.

"She's with her friends," I reply, tugging off a piece of my pizza-stuffed pretzel meal. "We can't just barge over."

Chang broods for a moment. "If you don't want to go, I'll go solo."

Pizza sauce squirts from my pretzel onto my hand. "You can't do that. We're a group."

"So?" He's already getting up. "That doesn't mean I can't go sit with her." He takes his tray and strides toward her table.

Darnell hands me a napkin. "If you want to go with him, I can go sit with Sav." He nods to where his girlfriend, Savannah, is sitting with her friends.

I wipe the sauce off my fingers and watch Chang. He's sitting down and impressing the group by transforming a napkin into an origami swan.

"Why can't he go after one of the other girls?" I mutter.

"I was wondering the same about you," Darnell says. "Why don't you go after Emily?"

I wad up my gooey napkin. "Because I like Zoey."

"So if you know what you want," Darnell says, "what's the problem?"

I point my chin toward Chang. "He is."

Darnell gives me a disbelieving look. "What's *really* the problem?"

"*He* is," I insist.

Darnell shakes his head and shifts into a squeaky voice: "Look inside, young Skywalker. Named must be your fear, before banish it you can."

I stare down at my pretzel and sigh. "I'm scared she'll like him better. I'm scared fighting for her will ruin our friendship. I'm scared to lose her. And I'm scared to lose him."

"Many fears you have," Darnell says. "Such is the power of the dark side. Clear your mind of them you must. In the Force believe."

"Come on, be serious," I say.

"I am serious. Here, do something with me." He stretches his arm across the table and hovers it in the air, just above the table. "Put your hand on top of mine."

"Why?"

"Question not. Just do."

Reluctantly, I place my hand atop his. This is probably one of those things his mom has taught him—she's an energy healer.

"Now press down on my arm while you imagine Chang winning her."

It isn't hard to imagine. Chang is presenting Zoey with a completed origami rose. Her cheeks color like a real rose. I struggle and strain to press Darnell's arm down, but he easily throws my hand off. It helps that he outweighs me by several dozen pounds.

"That's not fair," I say. "You're bigger than me."

"Size matters not." He stretches out his arm again. "Do it again, but this time feel the Force flowing through you. Around you. Inside you. And imagine *you* have won her."

"I'm not doing it again. I already feel like a wimp."

"Hmm . . ." Darnell says. "Wimps are those who give in to the dark side."

I tug off another pretzel piece and watch Zoey tuck Chang's origami flower behind her ear. A flicker of fury sparks inside me. No way can I wimp out now. I would never be able to live with myself.

I toss down my pretzel. "All right. I'll try it."

"There is no try." Darnell lifts his arm. "Do or do not."

I rest my hand on his and press down on his arm again.

He resists as strongly as before. A grin slowly creeps across his face. He knows I can't beat him.

Then Zoey gazes over, craning her head to see what Darnell and I are doing.

I imagine being at her house after school with Peppy, just the three of us, and a fresh burst of energy flows through me. As I press down harder, Darnell's arm begins to quaver. The rest of Zoey's table, including Chang, turn to watch us.

I press . . . harder . . . *harder.*

Darnell's arm smacks down to the table—*bang!*—rattling our trays. The origami flower falls out of Zoey's hair.

"You let me win," I tell Darnell.

"No, young apprentice. That is the power of the Force. Now use it."

CHAPTER 15

I can barely sit still during afternoon classes, counting the minutes until I'll be reunited with Zoey. When I stop at home to get Peppy after school, he greets me by defying gravity—bouncing up, down, all around the kitchen floor, as high as if he swallowed a pogo stick.

"All right, already!" As he springs into the air, I catch his squiggly body and try to cuddle him while he wiggles, worms, and wipes me with his tongue. Then I remember Zoey's warning not to reward his excitement and set him on the floor.

"*Tzzt!*" I snap my fingers. "Sit."

He rolls over and offers me his tummy, smiling, tongue lolling, tail wagging.

"No, sit up." I pull him back to his feet and push his butt to the floor. It springs right back up. I try again. After three more times, his rump finally sticks.

"Good boy." I give him a treat from his jar. "Ready to go rehearse with Zoey?"

Peppy dashes across the room and races back with a floppy vinyl pork chop.

"That's very thoughtful," I say. "But I don't think she'd want . . ."

Wait, maybe that's not a bad idea. I grab the baggie with Norma's oatmeal cookies. It isn't a colorful sketch or an origami flower, but at least it's something.

* * *

"Now, behave," I tell Peppy as we approach Zoey's driveway. "No goofy stuff."

Music is thumping from inside the ranch-style house. Behind the big front window, Zoey shimmies and twirls across the living room in black leggings and a T-shirt, absorbed in dancing.

I watch, mesmerized, as her body curves and sways. Gliding, spinning, circling toward the window, her arms in an oval and her curly hair streaming behind her like a comet's tail.

Spotting me, Zoey pitches to a stop.

I wave. She waves back, catching her breath and smiling. Then she glances toward my feet, and her eyes pop wide.

On the lawn in front of me, Peppy is waddling in a

tightening spiral. Sniffing. Seeking just the right spot. Arching his rear. And—

"No, nooo! *Tzzt!*" I yank his leash and snap my fingers. "*Tzzt! Tzzt! Tzzt!*"

Too late. His woeful brown eyes gaze up at me. Beneath him, the first Tootsie Roll plunks onto the grass. I drop his leash, cast aside the bag of cookies, scoop him up, and spin around, searching for someplace to deposit him—somewhere other than on Zoey's lawn. Seeing no other options, I'm forced to set him back down to complete his pooping in peace.

A moment later, Zoey strides out with a plastic bag. "It happens," she says.

"I'm really sorry," I say and hand her the baggie of cookies. "These are for you."

"Thanks." She trades me the doodie bag. "I'm definitely getting the better deal."

While I clean up Peppy's mess—*yuck*—he rolls over for Zoey, and she scratches his chest. He's getting the best deal of all.

Zoey leads me behind the house, stopping at the trash bin, and through the backyard gate. At the kitchen's plate glass door, Goldie sits waiting. Peppy immediately begins to twitch, whimper, and wag his tail. Once inside, the two dogs excitedly check each other's news feeds.

The yellow kitchen smells of apples and cloves. From a

birdcage comes the chirping of a pair of parakeets. And posted to the fridge are Chang's sketches. I resist the urge to stuff them into the disposal.

Zoey brings out some milk to go with the cookies. Goldie settles down into a stove-side doggie bed. After I wash my hands, I drag Peppy past the dog food bowl over to the table.

"I think he's got a bottomless stomach," I say, sitting down diagonally from Zoey. "He never stops eating. I told you he nabbed my breakfast this morning. When I feed him, he explodes into his food bowl and inhales it all in seconds."

The instant I take a cookie, Peppy springs to his hind legs and puts his paws in my lap. "*Tzzt!*" I snap my fingers. "Down."

He drops back to the floor.

"Do you feed him at the table?" Zoey asks.

"Sometimes. Otherwise he won't leave me alone."

"Maybe he's learned you'll give in," she says.

"What else can I do? Look at how he makes those big sad eyes." From Peppy's throat comes a pleading whimper. "Hear that? He makes me feel like I'm torturing him."

"You're not torturing him—you're teaching him the table is your space. Picture a line of yellow police tape he's not allowed to cross. If he steps over it, you give him a little nip. Watch, first you cup your hand like a mouth—your fingers are the teeth—and then you nip his back or neck." Without warning, she pokes me in the ribs. "*Tsst!*"

I flinch, giggling. "Hey, that tickles."

"Right—just a quick touch to show who's in charge. That's one way dogs keep each other in check. He'll learn that any food is yours till you decide he can eat. Go ahead, try it."

I poke her ribs, and she wiggles away. "No, I meant with him."

"Ohhh," I say, teasing.

Peppy is watching us like he wants to join in the play. But when I suddenly nip him, he jumps back, startled.

"Excellent," Zoey says. "See? He'll learn. Now let's put him to a real test."

She moves the plate of cookies from the table to a chair—directly at Peppy's jaw-level. He sprints at them, tail wagging, but just as quickly Zoey prods his shoulder. "*Tsst!* Back behind the line."

Peppy scoots backward behind the invisible line and stops, bewildered. His eyes dart between her and the cookies.

"That's cruel," I say.

"No, it's not. He's learning we're the pack leaders—we decide. To a dog that makes perfect sense. If you're consistent, he'll learn to calm his mind. You'll both be happier."

Peppy stares at the cookies, looking hungry, not happy.

"Let's see if he's ready for the next level," Zoey says. She lowers the cookies from the chair to the floor.

I hold my breath, sure he'll dive at them. Instead he looks meekly up at her, his eyes begging for permission.

Zoey gazes back at him, steely-eyed. Peppy returns his gaze to the cookies—so close, yet so far.

"We'll move the plate away when he finally accepts he can't have the food," she says. "It shouldn't take long. He's smart."

Peppy hangs his head like a vulture. His tongue licks his lips. His nostrils flare. He whimpers in agony.

"It's better if we don't watch him," she says. "That way we communicate we trust him."

But the instant we look away, Peppy slinks toward the cookies.

"*Tsst!*" Zoey snaps her fingers at him.

He shrinks back as if she nipped him. His eyes move from her to the cookies, then to the imaginary line on the floor. Slowly, his body relaxes.

"There he goes," Zoey whispers. "He's surrendering."

A moment later, Peppy exhales a gust of air, drops to his stomach, and rests his nose on his paws.

"If I hadn't seen it with my own eyes . . ." I tell her. "You're amazing."

"Thanks, but not really—anybody can do it. You just have to set your mind to it, like you just did. Give yourself credit for staying calm. You're teaching him by example."

When Zoey brings the cookies back to the table, Peppy doesn't even lift his head. Unbelievable.

"These are really yummy," Zoey says, taking another cookie. "Who made them?"

"My dad." I sip my milk and try not to think about Norma.

Zoey asks, "What?"

"What-*what*?" I answer.

"You got a weird look on your face."

"I did?"

"Uh-huh. Is there something I should know?"

I get that pretzel feeling again. "Um . . . no."

"Okay, well, tell your dad they're great," Zoey says. "How about you? Can you cook?"

"A little. I make pretty good French toast. Do you cook?"

"Once I made an apple pie with Felix, my ex."

"Your *ex* . . . ?" A feeling springs up inside my chest—something between fear and hope.

"We were a couple for two months at school last year," she explains. "Until I found out he was sneaking around with someone else."

"Sorry to hear it," I say. But secretly I'm glad he's out of the picture.

"Thanks," she says. "It sucked. I trusted him. If he liked another girl, why didn't he just say so? He kind of broke my heart."

I don't know what to say to that, so I keep quiet.

"You want to know what's the most important lesson I've learned from dogs?" Zoey continues. "Honesty. They never lie to you. Whether they like something or don't, they let you know. They're like these warm furry messengers of truth."

Norma barges into my mind again. I take another cookie and stay silent.

"I'm still licking my wounds," Zoey says. "I don't think I'm ready for another boyfriend."

I wonder if she's trying to tell me something. Actually, I guess she *is* telling me something. I stare down at Peppy, stuck behind the do-not-cross line.

"And you?" Zoey asks. "Are you going out with anybody?"

I sit up. "Who, *me?*"

"No, I'm asking Peppy. Yes, *you.*"

I shake my head. "No."

"Well," she says, smiling, "with all the cute girls at school, I'm sure you'll be crushing on someone soon."

I urge my mouth into a smile and chew my cookie. If Zoey isn't ready for a boyfriend, what's the rush to tell her about Norma? I don't want to ruin the moment. The kitchen feels so warm and cozy. And it feels so good to be alone with her, hanging out. I wonder if she feels it too.

The doorbell shatters the moment. Peppy leaps up, barking. The parakeets chirp and twitter from their cage. Even Goldie wakes out of her stove-side coma.

While Zoey goes to the front door, I hold Peppy by the collar, shushing him from growling at the commotion. "*Tzzt!* Quiet."

Then I recognize the visitor's voice, and I want to growl too.

CHAPTER 16

"Jorge told me about your dance thing," comes Chang's voice from the front door. "I thought my dog could help you too."

Inside Zoey's kitchen, I clench my teeth to keep from yelling, *Go away, you weaselly copycat!*

"Sure," she tells Chang. "We can audition him."

Chang steps into the kitchen with Shaquille, his brown Shar-Pei, whose thick folds of rumpled fur make him look like he mistakenly climbed inside some bigger dog's coat. He's Peppy's favorite playmate.

The two dogs bound toward each other, tails wagging, leashes tangling. Goldie joins the twitching, twisting mix. In seconds the vortex swirls into a frolicking free-for-all of nuzzling, hopping, and . . . humping.

"*Tzzt!*" I grab Peppy by the collar to hold him still. I'm

mortified, but Zoey calmly leads Goldie back to her doggie bed. And Chang hauls Shaq by the leash over to the fridge.

"Wow, you really like my sketches?" he asks Zoey.

"You bet." She pours him a glass of milk. "I wish I could draw like you."

"I can teach you." He sits down to cookies and starts blathering to Zoey about how he's been drawing and painting since he was three, how his mom sent him to special classes, how he won this award and that award, how his dream is to be a cartoon animator. . . .

"Hey, we need to work on Zoey's dance project," I finally interrupt. My voice comes out louder than I mean, and I blush, embarrassed.

"You're right—we should get started," Zoey says, checking the wall clock. "Anybody want another cookie?"

Chang takes one. "These are great. Did you make them?"

"No, Jorge's dad did."

Chang's face takes on an odd look. "How's your dad doing?"

"Fine," I say and turn to Zoey. "Ready?"

"Let's start by choosing a song," Zoey says and leads us to the living room. She's already moved the furniture to the walls, clearing a space for dancing.

I hurry ahead of Chang, hoping to sit next to Zoey, but she takes the armchair, leaving Chang and me with the sofa.

The three of us scroll through our phones, playing each

other bits and pieces of songs. It seems like all the melodies are either too fast, too slow, or don't have a strong enough beat, until I get to Chayanne's Latin fusion, "Madre Tierra." It's one of my favorite songs.

I nod my head to the beat. Chang taps the sofa's armrest. Zoey rocks from side to side. Shaq pricks his ears. And Peppy rises to his feet.

"I think you found a winner," Zoey told me. "What're the lyrics about?"

I think for a moment and translate the Spanish. "About how you have to give love to receive it. And you have to forgive when people hurt you so you can move on."

"I love it," she says and gets up, improvising some steps to the music.

I watch in awe. We all do: Chang, Shaq, Peppy, and me. She moves so beautifully.

"Okay, let's give it a shot," Zoey says. "Whose dog goes first?"

Chang and I both speak up at once: "Shaq!" "Peppy!"

Zoey glances between us, and I reconsider. Although Peppy is bound to win by sheer enthusiasm, he might not have the needed discipline. Maybe watching Shaq first will prep him.

I wave to Chang. "Shaq can go first."

Shaq trots to Zoey, and Peppy strains at his collar, whimpering to join them. I hold him back while Zoey leads Shaq through some easy steps to start. On all fours, he follows her paces pretty well, his rumpled fur scrunching and spreading like an accordion. But when she coaxes him onto his haunches, his thick fur bunches up around his hips like a hoop skirt, weighing him down. He staggers and wavers, and when Zoey twirls him, he loses his balance, tumbling out from under her.

Thump! Shaq bangs into the side of the couch and utters a painful yelp.

"Are you okay, buddy?" Zoey pets him and turns to Chang. "I'm not sure he's got the coordination for this. Let's see how Peppy does."

"Sorry, man," I tell Chang as he sulks. I feel bad for him, but he shouldn't have brought Shaq in the first place.

The instant I release Peppy, he zooms over to Zoey, wagging his tail and rolling over for a belly scratch.

"Maybe you should teach him with the leash first," I suggest.

Luckily, that does the trick. With Zoey leading him, Peppy learns the steps quicker than I thought possible. Only once or twice does he stumble. When I play the song, he dances and twirls to the music as if it's a game, and he loves being at the center of it. By the time Zoey takes off his leash, he follows on cue, synced in cross-step, and spins beneath her hand at exactly the right height for her to cradle his forepaws.

"He's got this," I say proudly. I hold my palm out to Chang, and he sighs, uncrosses his arms, and slaps me a reluctant five.

During the next hour, we play the song over and over while Zoey cobbles together a whole dance sequence. Peppy obediently follows her prompts. Shaq licks and scratches himself. Chang mopes with frustration.

"Whew, that's enough for today," Zoey finally says, collapsing into a chair. Peppy plops down at her feet, panting, his tongue dangling.

"I've got to admit," Chang tells Zoey, "you guys look terrific."

"Fantastic," I agree.

"Thanks." She dabs a towel across her shimmering face. "But we'll need to rehearse till we've got it down pat. We've only got about a week."

"No problem," I say. "I can bring him every afternoon."

"Works for me," Chang says.

I shoot him a look that clearly says, *Why do YOU need to come?*

"Hmm . . ." Zoey says. "I think Peppy might concentrate better without Shaq around."

"Okay, I'll leave him at home," Chang says.

"I'm sorry," Zoey says. "But the fewer distractions, the better Peppy can focus. Okay?"

"All right," Chang says with a sigh.

I try not to smile, but inside my brain I do a happy dance.

Chang and I help move the furniture back into place and hang out for a while. Finally we tell Zoey goodbye and leave together with our dogs.

Neither of us says much while we walk. Chang is sulking. I'm torn between feeling sad for him and happy for me. I imagine a new superhero, Pretzel Man, able to twist and turn his arms, legs, and neck into a human tangle.

As Chang and I approach the street corner where our paths divide, a familiar fire-engine red sports car appears down the tree-lined street, coming in our direction. I probably don't need to mention its license plate: *OPERA LVR*.

Chang is walking somberly alongside me, his gaze cast down at our dogs. Maybe, by some miracle, he won't look up and recognize Dad's car. And maybe, in a double miracle, Norma won't notice us.

I lift my hand, pretending to shield my face from the sun, but I can't resist peeking through my fingers.

When Norma's car nears, the miracles fail to materialize. Chang glances up. Norma slows down and waves to us—in full makeup and a ruffled-collar blouse.

I whirl around, turning my back to her. Yanking Peppy's leash, I start walking back toward Zoey's, telling Chang, "I think I forgot something."

"Jorge!" he calls after me. "It's your dad."

"No, it's not," I call over my shoulder. I watch as Norma

drives past, shaking her head with dismay, obviously realizing I'm avoiding her.

"I saw him at the supermarket!" Chang shouts from behind me.

I stop dead in my tracks. Slowly, I turn and face him again.

Chang's expression is even more somber than before. "Last week, in the checkout line, he was talking on the phone. I recognized his voice and couldn't figure out why he was wearing makeup and a skirt. Like, what the . . . ? I ducked behind a rack before he could see me."

It takes me a moment before I can speak. "Why didn't you tell me?"

"And say what? 'Dude, I saw your old man dressed like a woman'? Why haven't *you* told *me*?"

I open my mouth to answer. Then close it. Then open it again. "I couldn't. Cesar made me swear not to tell anybody."

"You shouldn't let him bully you," Chang says. He's never been a big fan of Cesar, and vice versa.

"He doesn't bully me. Did you say anything to Darnell?"

"No. The whole thing seemed so weird. I wondered if I'd made a mistake . . . until now." His brow scrunches up as he tries to understand. "Why's your dad dressing like that?"

I strain to think of what to say. The only thing I can come up with is the truth. "He's—*she's*—transgender."

"Since when?"

"Since . . . always, but . . . it's confusing. That's why my parents are getting divorced."

"Oh," Chang says. "So that's how you came up with the trans superhero." He searches my face, still putting everything together. "So . . . are you going to tell Zoey?"

Why is he bringing her up? Suddenly something inside me switches. "You *sneak!*"

His expression turns blank. "What?" he asks. As if he doesn't know.

"You want me to tell her about my dad so she'll bail on me."

"What?" Chang shakes his head. "No. I just don't want you to get your feelings hurt—like with Oona. I think Zoey would want to know."

"Oh, thanks for looking out for me," I say angrily. "If you're so concerned about my feelings, why don't you stop moving in on her?"

"You know what? Fine," he says. "Go ahead and get your heart broken. But don't come crying to me when it happens."

"FYI," I say, "Zoey told me she's not ready for a boyfriend. So just back off."

His face falls. "She said that? Honest?"

I nod, and his brow scrunches up again. At our feet, Shaq and Peppy roll around, wrestling and nipping each other.

"Well, I still like her," Chang says. "And I'm going to be her friend, whether you like it or not."

I curl my fist around Peppy's leash. "I'm warning you: You'd better not say anything about my dad."

"Stop bossing me around, Jorge. She's not your girlfriend. If you care so much about her, shouldn't you be honest with her? Like you should've been with me? And Darnell?"

A stab of guilt jabs me. I know he's right. But is he truly looking out for me or just for himself?

"Stay away from her," I say.

"No," he says.

It feels like a grenade is about to explode in my chest. Luckily, before it can go off, Chang sees my curled-up fist, spins around, and tows Shaq away with him.

CHAPTER 17

As Chang fades down the street, I pull out my phone and text the instigator of this mess.

Did you HAVE to slow down and wave? I type as I charge down the sidewalk with Peppy.

Norma must be home already because she texts me back right away: Did you expect me to pretend that I didn't see you?

Me: Duh!

Norma: I don't get it, Jorge. Only yesterday you wanted Mom to accept me as a woman and for us to stay married. Today you want to hide me from Chang. What exactly do you want?

Right now I mostly want to scream. Loud and long. I type back: Chang says he saw you at the supermarket last week

Norma: I don't remember seeing him.

Me: He's been waiting for me to say something . . . He says I've gotta tell Zoey so she'll dump me and he can win her for himself

Norma: He said that?

Me: Just the part about telling Zoey . . . He claims he doesn't want to see me get hurt

Norma: You don't believe him? He's always been a good friend, hasn't he?

Me: I don't know what to believe anymore . . . I JUST WANT A NORMAL LIFE!

Norma: That's hard to manage with a secret life. I should know. Take Chang's advice. Tell Zoey.

Me: So she can dump me like Mom dumped you?

The instant I hit SEND a sick, queasy feeling grips my stomach. I wish I could reach inside the phone and yank the message back.

I'm sorry, I quickly type. I didn't mean that. I hit SEND and shift from one foot to the other, waiting for what feels like eternity.

You're right, Norma replies. Zoey might dump you. Honesty always brings a risk. But so does hiding.

I let out a sigh—half from relief, half from exhaustion. I'm sick of dealing with this.

Me: Talk to you later, ok?

Norma: Whenever you like, mijo. Love you.

Love you, I type in return.

Mom's minivan is parked in our driveway when I walk up, and Cesar's voice comes from inside. My stomach knots tighter, even though it isn't my fault Chang saw Norma. In the entry hall, I take off Peppy's leash, and he darts toward the kitchen. I draw a big gulp of air and wander slowly after him.

Victoria, Cesar's girlfriend, stands at the counter with Mom and Cesar, helping to cut up salad veggies for dinner. "Hi, Jorge," she says. "Hi, King."

"His name's Peppy now," I explain.

"Oh, I like that. Hi, Peppy." Victoria pets him and grins at me. "Emily liked meeting you today."

"Yeah. I liked meeting her too."

"I sent you her number," Cesar says. "Did you text her?"

"Not yet."

"How'd it go with Zoey?" Mom asks.

"Who's Zoey?" Victoria asks.

"A kook," Cesar answers.

"She is not," I say. "She's—"

Before I can argue more, I spot Peppy on his hind legs, sniffing the countertop. Mom picked up a fresh-roasted chicken at the supermarket—one of our standard meals since Chef Dad moved out. Cesar and I love it—so does Peppy.

"*Tzzt!* Down, boy." I nip him, and he drops his paws from the counter. "Zoey is a new girl," I explain to Victoria.

"Peppy is going to do a dance with her in the talent show."
I turn to Mom. "Rehearsal went great."

"I'm trying to get Emily to do something in the show,"
Victoria says. "Maybe she could do something with our cat."

"Are you dancing with Zoey and Peppy?" Mom asks me.

"In front of all those people? No way. But she taught
me something really cool. Look, I'll show you."

Everybody stares as I carry the serving plate with the
chicken to the table, Peppy trailing at my heels. The roasted
bird is nearly as big as he is.

"Now, watch." I set the platter down and snap my fingers at Peppy. "*Tzzt!* Sit."

He sits, tail wagging, eyes trained up at the tabletop—
toward the chicken.

"First time I've ever seen him sit still," says Victoria.

"*Finally,*" says Cesar.

"That's great," says Mom. "Maybe now he'll quit begging."

"He will," I say. "Wait until you see *this.*" I move the bird
on the plate from the tabletop to a chair.

"Honey, what're you doing?" Mom says. "That's not a
good idea."

"It's okay." As Peppy starts toward the chicken I snap my
fingers. "*Tzzt!* Don't cross that line."

He shrinks back and plops his rump down, although his
eyes remain glued to the chicken.

"*Dude*," Cesar says, impressed. Victoria applauds.

Mom wags her head in disbelief. "If I hadn't seen it with my own eyes. . . . Now please put the chicken back on the table."

"Wait, you really won't believe this. Watch." I move the platter from the chair to the floor while telepathically messaging Peppy: *I'm counting on you, boy. Don't let me down.*

"Jorge, no," Mom says. "That's enough."

"But this is the best part," I insist. Peppy's tongue slathers his lips. I snap my fingers. "*Tzzt!* Sit."

He obeys, although his glassy-eyed gaze stays fixed on the chicken mere inches away.

"Ta-dah!" I take a bow toward our audience. . . . and Peppy flies at the bird.

"No!" Mom shrieks.

Too late. His jaws clamp on a drumstick.

I dive for him, but Peppy dashes out from under me, dragging the entire bird off the plate with him.

"Stop him!" Mom shouts. "He's heading for the hall."

"Cut him off from the other side," Cesar tells me.

Peppy bolts between us, the chicken bouncing beside him. Mom blocks the doorway, cutting off his escape. Cesar and I close in from behind.

Peppy's gaze flicks between us. He's surrounded. The gig is up. In a final, frantic burst, he scrambles beneath the table, bird in tow.

"*Tzzt!*" I throw myself in front of him and nip him with my hand. "Drop it."

His jaws pop open. The drumstick plops out of his mouth.

Mom swoops down and scoops up the bird. "Jorge," she says, "what on earth were you thinking?"

I pull myself up from the floor. "It worked with Norma's cookies."

"Who's Norma?" Victoria asks.

I turn to Cesar. Mom turns to Cesar. Cesar swallows the visible knot in his throat. "Nobody," he tells Victoria. "Just somebody we know."

I hate to watch him squirm, but it's also strangely satisfying to see he's not as unbothered as he pretends.

"Jorge, put Peppy outside," Mom says.

"Come here," I order him. He skulks out the patio door, hanging his head. I feel like I should join him. I shouldn't have tested him in front of everybody.

Mom stares pitifully at the chicken. "I guess I can rinse it off. He only bit into the leg."

"I'll eat that," I offer. If his tongue-baths haven't poisoned me, I doubt a bitten drumstick will.

Victoria scrunches her nose. "I should probably go home."

"Oh, don't go," Mom says. "I'll make you something else. How about a nice tuna salad?"

"Thanks, but I'm not really hungry. I'd better take a rain check."

Cesar walks her out of the kitchen, glaring at me. "Thanks for screwing up dinner with my girlfriend," he says when he returns.

"Sorry. I didn't mean to."

Cesar refuses to eat any of the rinsed chicken. Instead he microwaves a couple of frozen burgers. While he and Mom talk about Victoria, the cheerleading squad, and the speech he plans to give tomorrow for his campaign, I keep quiet, wondering if I should say anything about Chang seeing Norma. It might help him realize other people are bound to see her. Plus, if Chang blabs and Cesar finds out I didn't warn him, he'll be doubly furious.

I'll tell him after dinner, I decide and reach for another piece of chicken.

"Wow, you were hungry," Mom says when we finish eating.

I look down. My plate is a pile of bones. I've stress-eaten every last scrap of bird. "Can I have some stomach medicine?"

Upstairs, I lie in bed rubbing my stomach, mad at myself and dreading talking to Cesar. Next to me, Peppy lies on his back, twisting this way and that, scratching his hind fur on the bedspread.

"Hey," Cesar says, stepping into my doorway with a sheet of paper. "I want you to listen to my speech."

"Um, okay." Surprised, I haul myself up to sitting. Cesar used to ask my opinion all the time, but not so much since we started middle school and *definitely* not since Dad's announcement.

"My name is Cesar Fuerte," he begins. "Fuerte means *strong*, and I believe I'm the strongest candidate. You already know me as the coanchor of our morning news show, as captain of our soccer team, and as student of the month last year. But I'm not here to tell you how great I am. Anybody can do that. I want to tell you what I will do for you as president. Our school has many important problems: Our lockers are too small. We start classes too early in the morning. And there's too much bullying."

I'm taken aback to hear those last words come from him. "Did anyone ever bully you?" I interrupt. He's never mentioned it, but our school has always separated us into different classrooms. I realize I don't know everything that's happened to my brother.

"Yeah," Cesar says. "Now can you shut up and let me finish?" He looks back at his paper. "If you elect me, my number-one job will be to solve our problems and make our school the strongest ever. I can only do that with your help. I'm counting on your vote. Thanks for making me your next president." He puts down his paper. "You like it?"

"It's great." But I can't let what he said go. "I never knew you got bullied. When?"

"In second grade. This jerk, Rufus Reznik, kept mouthing off about me being Mexican."

"So what happened?"

"I told him to let up. When he wouldn't, I punched him. You've got to stand up to people who get in your way in life." He turns to leave.

"Wait," I say.

"What?"

I slide my knees up to my chest. "I, um, need to tell you something."

His eyes narrow at me. "What did you do?"

"Nothing." I take a huge breath and spill it all at once: "Chang-told-me-today-he-saw-Norma-at-the-supermarket-last-week-but-it-wasn't-my-fault-so-you-can't-blame-me."

As the words sink in, Cesar's face turns pale. "Did he tell anybody?"

"Just me."

"What did you tell him?"

"That Dad is trans."

Cesar's fist curl around his speech. "You told him that?"

"What else could I say?"

Peppy sits up on the mattress, agitated by our rising voices.

"I knew this would happen," Cesar says, crushing his sheet in his fist. "Why can't Dad just move out of town?"

"That's not going to happen," I say. "Maybe you two should talk."

"*That's* not going to happen," Cesar says, echoing my words. "I'm *never* talking to him. Why can't he just leave us alone?" He turns and storms down the hall. Six steps later, his door slams.

I flinch. If only Cesar would talk with Dad, maybe we could all find some way to work this out.

On the nightstand, my phone chimes with a text.

Darnell: Sup . . . Chang says Peppy was awesome at your rehearsal

Me: Yeah . . . did he say anything else?

Darnell: He was bummed Shaq didn't make the cut

Me: Yeah, I felt bad for him . . . What else did he say?

Darnell: He's working on a new sketch . . . You guys need to get jamming . . . Where are you with the story?

Me: I'll work on it tonight. As if I don't have enough to deal with. Did he say anything else?

Darnell: About what?

Me: About anything.

Darnell: No . . . But Savannah wants to meet the girl who's causing all the fuss between you guys . . . What if we all go sit with Zoey at her lunch table tomorrow?

OK, I type.

It'll help me keep tabs on Chang.

I drag myself from bed, grab my laptop, and try to conjure up our transgender scientist hero's plotline—after his origin story.

I start typing: He falls in love with a girl who doesn't know he can secretly shape-shift into a woman. He lives a double life, dashing away from their dates to fight evildoers and then rushing back to her. She becomes suspicious of his sudden departures, traces of makeup, inexplicable remnants of women's clothing. She accuses him of cheating on her and breaks down in sobs. He wants to tell her the truth but he can't—it would put her life in peril. . . .

It's the tried-and-true dilemma of superhero sagas: Can the guy have the girl *and* be a superhero? Now the story needs a cruel, original supervillain.

I rifle through the cardboard boxes jamming my room and skim through my comic collection for ideas. When I come across my cherished collector's copy of *Daredevil: Pariah,* I get an idea. It isn't about our comic's villain; it's about my own real-life best frenemy.

To Chang's credit, he didn't blab to Darnell about Dad, even though he could've. It feels crappy to be at odds with him, and I know he'd love to have that Daredevil comic, so although I hate to part with the book, I slip it into my back-pack for tomorrow.

CHAPTER 18

"Seat's taken." Chang's arm blocks my place on the bus the next morning, leaving me stranded in the aisle.

"Hey, come on." I open my backpack. "Here, I want to give you something."

He blinks at the Daredevil comic. "You trying to bribe me?"

"Sit down," the driver growls at me in the rearview.

Chang takes the comic and lets me drop into the seat beside him.

"Thanks," I tell him.

As the bus gets moving, he silently flips through the book.

"I'm sorry I went off on you yesterday," I whisper. "You're honestly not freaked out about my dad?"

"Not anymore—now that I know I'm not hallucinating.

He's always been different—like when he took us to Comic-Con dressed up as the Joker. Remember how everybody wanted a selfie with him? Who else's dad would've done that? Not mine. So what if he's trans? He's always been good to me . . . but you should've told me about him."

"I couldn't."

"Yeah, you could've."

"You don't know how hard this is," I protest. "Put yourself in my shoes. What if people find out and treat Cesar and me like freaks?"

"Some probably will." Chang studies the illustrations of Matt Murdock at his lowest: friendless. Homeless. Beaten up. A man without hope. "But not everybody will."

I'm not convinced Chang is right, but I don't want to keep arguing. "Okay," I say. "Maybe I should've told you. I'm sorry. You won't tell anybody?"

"I'm not a snitch, Jorge. But you need to tell Darnell. I don't want to hide this from him."

"Could, um, *you* tell him?"

"I could . . . but I'm not going to. This is on you. Man up."

Even though I've heard that saying a thousand times before, I'm starting to wonder what it really means.

* * *

When lunchtime comes I hurry to the cafeteria, eager to sit with Zoey like Darnell suggested. At the food station, I'm deciding what to get when Victoria's sister, Emily, steps up.

"Hi, Jorge."

"Oh, hi."

"I almost texted you last night," she says. "But I thought you might be busy."

"I meant to text you too," I lie.

"Really?" She smiles and stands a little taller. "What're you getting to eat?"

"I don't know—the popcorn chicken or a turkey burger? I can't decide."

"Me neither. I hate decisions. The pizza-pretzel thing yesterday was good but messy."

"Yeah, that's what I—"

"Hi, Jorge," Zoey interrupts, appearing beside us. "Did you guys order?"

"Hi, um, not yet, go ahead."

"Thanks." She turns to the serving lady. "I'd like the turkey burger with cheese but with the toppings on the side. And no bun. Instead may I have a whole-wheat roll? Also the mixed veggies, but if you could go easy on the cauliflower that would be spectacular. And no carrots, please. Thanks." She turns to Emily. "Hi, my name's Zoey. You're Victoria, right?"

"No, I'm Emily."

"They're twins," I explain.

"Oh," Zoey says. She and Emily exchange a look I can't quite read—like they're sizing each other up. Then Zoey turns to me. "I heard you're sitting with us today. Awesome." She gives Emily a triumphant smile. "You can join us if you'd like."

"Thanks, but I usually sit with my group." Emily turns to me. "You're still invited to join us whenever you'd like."

I feel pulled in two directions: Emily east and Zoey west. Luckily, the serving lady intervenes, handing Zoey her order and asking Emily and me: "You two ever going to decide?"

"See you," Zoey tells us.

I tell the lunch lady: "The same as that girl had."

"Same here," Emily says and returns to me. "Are you coming to Victoria and Cesar's campaign party Saturday night?"

"Um . . ." Cesar had invited me, but I haven't decided. I'm not a huge fan of parties—too many people. Plus it will be Cesar's crowd, not mine.

"You don't have to decide right now," Emily says. "But I hope you can come." She sets her turkey burger onto her tray. "Think about it and let me know."

I watch her walk away. She looks cute from the back, matching how cute she looks from the front. But she's still not the girl I *like* like.

By the time I reach Zoey's table, she's already surrounded: Chang, Oona, Darnell, Sav, a girl I don't know. . . . The only seat left is at the table's far end, facing a boy from my

English class who has blue hair and purple fingernails. Up close, I realize he's also wearing eyeliner.

"Hi, I'm Noah," he introduces himself as I sit across from him. "And no, I don't have an ark. Want some cheesy fries?"

"No, thanks. I'm fine."

"Oh, go ahead. I don't have cooties." A friendly grin curls on his lips.

I take a couple of fries as a man's voice blares out from the ceiling loudspeakers: "Test-test-test." At the front of the room, our principal, Mr. Richter, has stepped onto a plat-form stage. "Hello, boys and girls. During lunch today you get to hear from your three candidates for president in next week's election."

First to the podium is a dark-eyed girl in a crisply pressed dress. She quotes facts and figures about the school's budget and the changes she'll lobby for. Boy, is she organized.

Next up is a girl with wild, curly blond hair dressed in baggy jeans and a baggier shirt. She gives a lively, rambling talk about improving the school's drama, music, and art activities until Mr. Richter has to cut her off.

Last onstage is Cesar. He memorized last night's speech, so it sounds heartfelt. His words ring with passion—the voice of a winner.

As soon as he thanks the audience, Victoria and the cheerleading squad make a surprise entrance through the hallway door wearing their neon-pink cheering outfits.

They cartwheel and somersault in front of the stage, shouting: "C-E-S-A-R! Who's the guy who'll lead us far? It's Cesar." *Clap-clap, clap.* "Cesar." *Clap-clap, clap.*

They march into the aisles, getting people to chime in until the entire room is chanting, stomping, and swaying. Their extravaganza ends with a chain reaction of splits, arm lifts, and shouting, "Get the fever, vote for Cesar!"

Amid the applause, some loudmouth—probably Scruggs but I'm not sure—shouts, "Show us your boobs!"

Cesar ignores him and applauds the cheerleaders. His smile beams as bright as a lighthouse lamp. He raises his arms in a V for victory. From the applause he gets, it seems like he already has the election sewn up—so long as nobody finds out about Dad.

People return to eating their lunches, I turn to Noah, and a question pops into my mind. Should I ask? Would it be prying? Will he be offended?

"Do you mind if I ask you something?" I whisper. "Are you . . . trans?"

"Gender-fluid." He smiles proudly. "I was born with guy body parts, and I'm okay with that, but inside I feel like I belong more in the middle of the boy-girl spectrum—I'm a lot of both. When I'm around other guys, I feel like I don't fit in . . . like I'm faking it and failing. Like I'm secretly an undercover girl. But with a group of girls, I don't feel like I fit in as a total girl either. It's hard to understand."

"No . . . I think I get it. Sometimes when I'm around my Mexican relatives, I don't feel truly Mexican. But when I'm around my mom's relatives, I feel more Mexican than white."

"Yeah, it's like that." Noah nods enthusiastically. "Zoey told me she sometimes feels the same way—you know, having a white mom and a black dad?"

Zoey must sense we're talking about her—she turns and sends me a grin. I send one back.

"She thinks you're cute," Noah whispers.

"Huh? What makes you think that?"

"We're lab partners in bio. We compared which boys we think are cute."

"And she said *me*? Really?" I glance at her again. "She told me she broke up with her boyfriend and isn't ready to go out with anyone."

"I know." Noah dips a French fry into his cheesy goop. "But that can't last forever."

Zoey presses a napkin to her lips. I imagine transforming into Napkin Man, with the power to fold myself into a handy-sized napkin and fly to her lips.

"Who else was on her cute list?" I ask.

Noah flicks his mascara-rimmed eyes toward Chang.

I sigh. "Any idea how I can win her over?"

"Tell her you like her."

I think back to Oona in fifth grade and how I wimped out telling her. "Have you ever told someone you liked them?"

"Well, no." The color rises to Noah's cheeks. "Not yet. Not out loud. But I will. Someday."

"What if I tell her and she doesn't feel the same way?"

Noah shrugs. "Then at least you'll know."

That isn't very motivating. Better to imagine I stand a chance than to confirm I don't.

"You can do it," he says encouragingly.

"What makes you so sure?"

"The way you spoke up for her the first day of class."

That still doesn't convince me—it's easier to speak up for somebody else than to speak up for myself.

CHAPTER 19

"How do you feel about nacho-cheese tortilla chips?" I ask Zoey in her kitchen after school.

"How do I *feel* about them?" She glances at the jumbo-size bag of chips I brought with me, then at me, as if I'm asking a trick question. "I like them. How do *you* feel about them?"

"They're the world's best invention ever. Their crackly crunch. Sunny color. Spicy, cheesy flavor. I get goosebumps tearing open a new bag. Here, you want to do the honor?"

"You go ahead," Zoey says. "I'll watch."

"You sure? I love that opening burst of tortilla smell. Here . . ." I lean across the table, hold the bag beneath her nose, and rip open the cellophane. "Isn't that phenomenal? The first chip always tastes best. You go ahead."

After she takes a chip, I pluck one out for myself. "I try

to eat my first one really slowww. . . ." I crunch the tortilla between my teeth, curl it into my mouth, and roll the powdery pieces across my tongue.

"Mm," she says, chewing her own. "I see what you mean—delicious."

Naturally, Peppy wants to get in on the action. When he props his paws on my leg, it breaks my heart to shake him off.

"*Tzzt!* Back behind the line," I scold him.

"You're doing really well with him," she says. "Have you seen any progress?"

"Well . . ." Blushing, I give Zoey a recap of last night's chicken-snatching episode. "I wanted to show my mom and brother what you taught me, but I guess I got carried away."

"He tried to steal the whole chicken?" Zoey exclaims. "It sounds like you're not the only one who got carried away. Maybe he sensed you were showing off and followed your example."

"Hmm . . ." I ponder that. "I think he just wanted the chicken."

"The important thing is to be consistent," she says. "No feeding at the table."

I give her a salute. "Never again, commander."

"Good." She dips a chip in the salsa I also brought with me. "Wasn't that an awesome show the cheerleaders did at lunch? So, tell me why I should vote for your brother—other than because he's your brother."

"Well . . . he's got some good ideas, like starting school later in the morning. And he's smart . . . and popular. . . . Since he knows so many people he can probably get things done. When he sets his mind to something, he goes all out for it. And he doesn't choke under pressure. He's like a force of nature."

"Sounds like you admire him."

"I do. He can be bossy and pick on me sometimes, but he's also generous and smart. He helps me with home-work, he's loyal to his friends, and he's a real team player at sports. Even if he weren't my brother, I'd vote for him."

"You've sold me." She takes another chip. "So . . . tell me about that girl Emily. Are you interested in her?"

"Huh?" I shake my head quickly. "No. Cesar's trying to set me up with her, but I'm not interested."

"Why not? She's cute, and she seems nice. I can tell she likes you. You sure you're not interested?"

I study Zoey's expression and wonder why she's being so insistent. Can she sense I like *her*? I think about Noah's advice. Is she waiting for me to say that *she's* the one I'm interested in?

My heart begins to race. My head feels warm. My face grows damp. I feel like I'm stepping out onstage as I say, "I like *you*."

Zoey was about to bite into a chip but stops. The tortilla dangles between us. "Jorge, you're really sweet, but . . . you remember I said I'm not ready for a boyfriend, right?"

"Yeah, I know. I just thought . . . never mind." I stuff a chip in my mouth.

"I just don't think I'm ready," she says awkwardly. "Is that okay?"

"Sure." My relief surprises me. Even though I want Zoey to like me back, what would I do if she did? I haven't thought it through. And I realize something else: She didn't say she *doesn't* like me back. She just isn't ready. Not only that, she thinks I'm sweet.

All in all, I feel like I accomplished something. Something big. Something important.

"Ready to rehearse?" she asks. "I've got some new ideas to try out."

We move to the living room and scoot the furniture against the walls. Like yesterday, I take charge of the music. The awkwardness between us fades as Zoey leads Peppy through the routine. First they review the dance steps and twirls. Then she teaches him to front flip and back flip, jump through the hoop of her arms, and roll over.

Some tricks take more coaching and coaxing than others, but Peppy is game to try anything that earns him a treat from her hip pack. Once they've strung together an entire routine, I film them on her phone.

"Let's see," she says, plopping down on the couch beside me. Her skin is glowing from the exercise, and her hair smells so flowery good I wish I could roll around in it the same way Peppy rubs himself in smells he likes.

"My hips don't look right," Zoey says, studying the video.

"They don't?" They look fine to me.

She grabs my hand. "Help me practice. Please?"

"Dance? I can't. . . . You remember Shaq yesterday? I'm like him—*kersplat.*"

Her eyes sparkle. "*Please?*"

I stand up.

"Great," she says. "So, first put this hand here. . . ." While facing me, she places my right hand on her shoulder. My fingers tremble so much she must think I'm giving her a massage.

"Now hold my right hand up with your left, like this. And move in close."

I do as she says and hope I don't have nacho-cheese breath.

"First let's just move in place—like you're marching. Whoa, easy. That's it. . . . good. Next we'll do a basic salsa step. Move forward with your left foot. . . . and rock back with your right. Now step back with your left. Hold the beat. And back with your right. Rock forward on your left—"

"Wait." I stop. "I'm getting confused."

"Sorry. Let's start over. Don't look at your feet. Look up at me."

That only makes me more nervous. After three steps I screw up again. "I can't do it."

"Shh, yes you can." She presses a finger to my lips—it might as well be a lightning bolt. A spark of electricity zaps through my body. "Try again," she says. "Head high. Shoulders back. Project confidence."

We start again. Zoey's hand and arm steer me while her eyes guide me. This time, I manage to keep going.

"You're doing fantastic," she says, leading me across the carpet.

"*You're* the one doing fantastic," I say. "I'm just following you."

"You know you've got really long lashes," she says.

"Um, is that weird?"

"No, it's a good thing. They're nice."

"Oh . . . thanks. I like yours better."

She laughs. I laugh. The whole time, Peppy tags alongside of us, wanting to join our dance.

"Okay," Zoey tells me. "Now it's your turn to lead." With that, she closes her eyes.

"Wait, what're you doing?" I stop.

She keeps her eyes shut. "Use the pressure from your arm and hands. Cue me where you want to go."

"But what if I mess up?"

"We'll start over."

I take a step forward and, with a slight push of my hands, guide her backward. Next I gently pull her toward me as I step back. Then I move her to the side. It's like controlling an avatar in a video game.

"See?" she says. "You're doing it."

I *am* doing it—until Peppy steps between our feet. I accidentally mash his toes, he lets out a pained yelp, and Zoey stumbles. Together we tumble to the carpet.

"Sorry, you okay?" I ask.

"Yeah, I'm okay. You?" Her eyes are open again—blue and beautiful and only inches from mine. Her breath warms my neck. Her face shines bright.

"I'm okay." I'm more than okay. I'm better than ever in my life. If only I could be her boyfriend . . . and kiss her.

As though reading my mind, Peppy licks my mouth.

"Ugh!" I jerk my head back from his tongue.

Laughing, Zoey sits up, cups Peppy's head in her hands, and kisses him on the forehead. I wipe my mouth, wishing I were him.

From the driveway comes the sound of car doors.

"My parents," Zoey says, scrambling to her feet.

I stay on the carpet, still dazed by the sensation of her so close to me. In the front hallway, the doorknob rattles. I rocket up to standing.

Zoey introduces Peppy and me to her parents, and we talk for a while, until her mom reminds Zoey she has a dentist appointment after school tomorrow.

As Zoey walks me to the door, we agree to rehearse again over the weekend. I can hardly wait. She might not be ready for a boyfriend, but I feel more than ready for a girlfriend: her.

CHAPTER 20

It takes all my superpowers to keep from texting Chang to brag about dancing with Zoey. Instead I text Darnell, swear him to secrecy, and confide that I held her in my arms.

You are learning well, Jedi grasshopper, he writes back. Now what about our comic?

Who cares about some silly, made-up superhero? I want to tell the world about the most amazing girl to ever walk the earth.

I'll work on it tonight, I tell Darnell. But by the time I slide into bed, I've hardly been able to do a lick of work.

* * *

After school the next day, I get off the bus a stop early and head toward Norma's, excited to tell her about Zoey.

I'm a block from her house when she drives up and leans out her window.

"Hop in. I want to swing by Raul's garden for fresh herbs. And . . ."—she waggles her eyebrows—". . . he's got ripe blackberries."

I glance over one shoulder, then the other, scanning the neighborhood.

Norma rolls her eyes in disappointment. "Come on, Jorge. Nobody's watching."

I climb into the car and notice the pale gray woman's business suit she's wearing. "Why are you so dressed up?"

"You like it? I had a meeting with a potential new client—fingers crossed. I need to make up for lost business. Not everybody likes my new look."

I've been worried how Dad's website and app clients would react to her transition. "What if you can't get new customers?"

She lets out a weary sigh, but then a grin tugs at her lips. "I guess I'll have to fall back on my career as a diva." She begins singing along with the opera playing on the stereo.

I cover my ears. "If you're going to be a woman, you'd better do something about that baritone."

She bellows even louder as the aria reaches its crescendo and clutches her heart in an anguished gesture so overacted you don't need to know Italian to grasp its meaning.

"I'm serious," I say. "What if your customers dump you?"

"Jorge, did I ever tell you the story about the boy who got a Christmas stocking full of horse caca?"

"Maybe a million times?"

"Well, here's a million and one: As soon as the boy found the caca, he jumped around, excited, shouting, 'There must be a pony nearby!'"

I sigh. Even though I've heard this story a gazillion times, now is the first time I ask: "So did the boy ever find a pony?"

Norma nods. "There's always a pony somewhere. But you've got to believe you'll find one. Never give up hope, mijo. Now stop worrying about me. Tell me about you. Any news about the daring girl who communicates with animals?"

"She's going to dance with Peppy in the talent show."

"*Peppy*? Who's Peppy?"

"King. His new name's Peppy. He told her he likes it better."

"I can't wait to meet this girl."

I frown. "Meanwhile, Cesar's trying to set me up with Victoria's sister, Emily. She's cute and nice, but I like Zoey better. Zoey says she's not ready for a boyfriend, though. So am I supposed to wait till she's ready? Or is she hinting she doesn't like me that way? But then she asked me to dance with her. And what should I tell Emily—that I'm not interested in her? I don't want to hurt her feelings. And it's not that I *don't* like her, it's that I like Zoey better. It's all so confusing. What do you think?"

"Waiting can be hard," Norma says philosophically. "I know."

"Oh, and I told Cesar that Chang saw you at the market. He freaked out. I think you guys really need to talk."

Norma's face lights up. "He wants to talk?"

"No, but maybe if you just come over and . . ."

She looks at me to finish. "And what?" she asks. "Tackle him before he can slam the door on me? I'm open to suggestions. I text your brother every day saying I love him, just like I've always done—same as I do with you. I can't force him to accept me."

I stare out the window at the passing lawns. "So where's the pony?"

"I wish I knew. We've just got to keep the gate open for when it finally shows up."

"In the meantime," I mutter, "enjoy the caca."

* * *

"Jorge, great to see you," says Raul. He's tending his backyard garden of herbs, veggies, and best of all, blackberries—my favorite. He hands me a straw basket. "Gather as many as you like."

"Thanks." I feel embarrassed I haven't phoned or stopped by like he invited me to. But it feels weird that nobody told me he was gay. It makes me wonder: Who else has some secret they're keeping hidden?

Although I could easily pick and eat every last berry, I don't want to be a pig. I stop after a single basket and gather herbs for Norma so she won't mess up her business duds. When we wave goodbye to Raul, my fingertips are purple with berry juice.

"You want some?" I extend the basket across the seat as we drive away.

"No thanks. Better wait till I change."

"So," I say, between mouthfuls of the sweet, addictive berries, "I talked to Mom about you guys getting back together."

Norma turns down the stereo. "You *what?*"

"I talked to Mom—"

"I heard. What did she say?"

"Well . . . she didn't flat out say no."

Norma's mouth droops. "But she didn't say yes, either."

"No . . . but when I told her you still think she's amazing, she teared up."

Norma sits quietly, her eyes growing misty too. "Jorge, I know you want us to get back together, but you need to accept—"

"Do you remember the story about the boy with the Christmas stocking?" I interrupt.

"Hmm . . ." She gives me a nonplussed look.

I press on. "The divorce won't be final until next Friday, right?"

Norma lets out a defeated sigh. "Yes."

"So we still have time, right?"

"Hold on, I need to get gas," she answers and pulls into a station.

I quickly glance around. "Do you have to get it *now*?" I ask, even though there is nobody at the pumps who might see her.

"I'll only be a minute. You can stay in the car and eat your berries."

While Norma gets out to fill the tank, I calm my nerves by eating the juicy morsels. I'm inspecting my purple tongue in the visor mirror when a battered pickup truck rumbles up to the neighboring pump. The driver is a middle-aged guy with a rough complexion and dark, straggly hair. A few whiskers masquerade as a beard. His crooked nose appears to have been broken more than once.

When the motor stops, I can hear the driver chewing out his passenger—a red-haired teenage boy whose back is to me. Suddenly the driver swings out a fist.

The boy crouches down in the seat, shielding himself as the guy—who I'm guessing is his dad—thwacks him on top of his head.

I stop eating my berries. Instinctively, I glance over my

shoulder. Norma is still standing at the pump—looking toward the truck.

The driver slams out of the pickup. He's a big guy, solidly built. He slides his card in the pump register and shoves the nozzle into the fill spout while muttering something about the boy in the truck.

"Excuse me," Norma calls across the aisle. "You shouldn't hit him."

My muscles tense. I've admired Dad before for speaking up to people about not bullying kids, but it has also always turned me into a bundle of nerves. And that was when Dad was dressed as a man.

The guy tilts his head toward Norma. His brow creases and his eyes squint, like he's struggling to make sense of the husky man's voice coming from the stocky woman in a business skirt. "Did you say something?"

No, I reply in my mind. *Dad, just finish pumping and let's get out of here.*

"Yes," Norma answers. "I said you shouldn't hit him."

The boy pokes his head out of the truck window. I blink. It's Scruggs.

Now *I* duck down in *my* seat. I never expected to see him get smacked by somebody, even if it is his dad. I feel sorry for him, though I don't want to. I crack my window open to hear better and glance back to the gas pumps.

Scruggs's dad is missing a couple of his teeth. Scar tissue

covers his knuckles. The veins throb in his thick neck as he strides across the pavement to Norma. "Was I bothering you over there?"

She backs up in her heels. "No, I just don't believe in hitting children. I know they can be challenging—I have two sons myself. But there are better ways to deal with kids than hitting."

Behind her, the pump clicks to full. My heart pounds. *Let's get out of here.*

At the truck, Scruggs is peering out the open window. Watching. Listening. His dad steps right up into Norma's face. "You telling me how to raise my boy?"

"No. I just—"

The guy cuts her off. "Why're you dressed like a woman? You some sort of freak?"

I shove my berries aside. *I should get out and help her.* Except Scruggs would see me. News about my dad would race through school tomorrow. Life would never be the same for Cesar and me.

I stay in my seat.

Norma's chest rises beneath her pale gray jacket as she edges away from the guy. "I don't think how I dress is your business."

"Yeah, it *is* my business." The guy flexes his fists—his fingers stretch like exploding bombs. "See my boy that you're so worried about watching us? What's he going to think when he hears some freak in a dress telling me how to raise him?"

"All I'm suggesting," Norma says, "is that—"

The guy stops her. "When was the last time you got your butt kicked?"

She leans away from him, giving her head a shake. "Excuse me?"

"You heard me. When was the last time someone kicked the crap out of you?"

My stomach clenches like *I'm* the one about to get hit. I grope inside my backpack for my phone to call 911. But what would I say? *A guy's threatening my dad. No, the guy hasn't actually attacked her yet. Yeah, HER—my dad is trans.*

Unable to take my eyes off Norma, I fumble with my phone.

"I'm not afraid of you," she tells the guy. But when she turns to replace the pump nozzle, she nearly drops it. She's shaking, I realize. So am I.

"You're not scared, huh?" the guy says. His voice is cold. Low. Ominous. "What if I just decked you right now?"

The phone slips out of my hands.

"I'm leaving," Norma says. She turns to step around the guy, but he blocks her path.

She shifts to the side.

Again he checks her.

She stops and looks him dead in the eye. "What do you want?"

"I don't know. Maybe I just want to teach you a lesson. You know I could do that. Ask my boy—he'll tell you. You want that? 'Cause I'm kind of leaning that way."

My heart is racing. The guy sounds crazy. I mean *seriously* crazy. No wonder Scruggs is so messed up. Maybe I should blow the horn. Maybe the guy would back down. But what if it set him off instead?

"Look," Norma tells him, "I'm sorry if you think I butted into your business—"

"I don't just *think* it," the guy interrupts, "you *did* butt in. Say you're sorry. Like you mean it." His lip curls to one side. "Ask me not to hurt you."

That's it, I think. There's no way she's going to let him talk to her like that. Even if the jerk is crazy, she won't just let him bully her. She's big enough to take him on.

But she shoots a glance in my direction, then looks back to the guy. "I'm sorry I butted in," she says. "Please don't hurt me."

I can't believe what I'm hearing. Why is she letting him talk to her that way?

"Satisfied?" she asks, her gaze fixed on him.

The guy stares at her steely-eyed. Then his fist jerks up. Norma flinches. I leap back in my seat.

The man smirks and lets his fist drop. "You disgust me,

you know that?" He spits on the pavement. "You're a man. Act like one."

With that, he swaggers to his pump, shoves the nozzle back in, and climbs into the truck. Scruggs sits up in his seat, staring at Norma, imitating his dad's disgusted sneer. The engine starts. The muffler rumbles as they drive off.

"That was a nightmare," Norma says, opening her door and dropping into the seat beside me. She locks the car and lets out a huge, loud sigh. "You all right, mijo?"

I stay slumped in my seat, embarrassed. Relieved. Absorbing the shock of everything that just happened—and nearly happened.

"Hey," she says softly. "You okay?"

I shake my head and lower my gaze to the floor, disappointed in Dad—and in myself. "Why'd you let him talk to you that way, make you say that stuff?"

"He didn't *make* me say anything. I said it because he was crazy. You think I didn't *want* to take a swing at him?"

"So why didn't you?"

"What would it have accomplished? What if he had a gun? Not to mention I was concerned about *you*."

I sit up, trying to sort my thoughts. Sure, it would've been stupid to fight the jerk. But to watch her cave that way makes me feel sick. "So you just let him talk to you like that?"

"Jorge, what exactly did you want me to do?"

The answer comes easy. "Be a man."

Her eyelids hang heavy as she raises a hand and rubs her forehead. "I can only be who I am."

"I like who you *were* better," I say, grabbing my backpack and yanking open the door.

I start to walk home, listening for footsteps, thinking she'll try to stop me. Instead, I hear the engine start. I keep my gaze forward, expecting her to drive up. She doesn't.

Every few steps, I glance over my shoulder, but Norma never appears. Or phones. Or texts. Although I keep checking, there's no word from her all evening.

CHAPTER 21

On Saturday morning, my phone chimes me awake. The message is from Norma: How are you feeling? You coming over today? I saved your blackberries. ☺

I toss the phone aside and pull the covers back over my head. Next time the chime rings I ignore it, figuring it's Norma again. But then I wonder. When I check the screen, I bolt upright.

Good morning, Zoey has written. U awake?

Me: Yeah, sup?

Zoey: I've got some sort of ☹ news . . . Can't rehearse today . . . Mom needs me to go with her to Austin . . . I'm really sorry . . . Can we do it tomorrow?

Me: Sure

Zoey: Great, thanks! Have a good day ☺

Me: Thanks, you too

I slump down on the mattress and wallow—I was psyched to see her. When I finally haul myself downstairs, Mom is grabbing her keys.

"Morning," she says. "I have to go to the office to ready a presentation for a big meeting Monday. Cesar already left to go to a talent show meeting. Remember to do your chores, okay? There are lunch meats in the fridge if you don't go to Dad's."

"I'm not going over there," I mutter as I pour myself a glass of O.J.

"Oh? Is something wrong?"

Yes, I want to yell. *EVERYTHING is wrong. How could you NOT have known Dad was trans when you married him?*

"Everything's fine," I mumble just as my phone rings. Norma's name flashes on the screen. I hit SILENCE.

Mom glances at the screen. "Are you sure?"

"Yeah."

"Okay." She combs my bangs aside with her fingers and kisses my forehead. "See you this evening."

As she leaves, my phone chimes again. I'm ready to slam it on the counter. Then I see the text is from Emily.

Hi, Jorge . . . Look forward to seeing you tonight . . . You coming?

It takes me a moment to remember the party. I sip my juice, debating, before I answer.

Not sure . . . I'm not feeling so hot

Emily: What's wrong? Are you sick?

Me: No, just feeling blah

Emily: Well then come! It'll help cheer you up ☺

Maybe she's right. Besides, I don't want to let her down.

Me: Can I invite my friends?

Emily: I'm sure it would be OK but maybe I should ask Victoria first . . . It's more her and Cesar's party than mine

I remember Cesar freaking out about Chang seeing Norma. Maybe it's not a good idea to bring Chang and Darnell to Cesar's party.

Never mind, I tell Emily. I'll just go with Cesar

* * *

After dinner that evening, I'm riffling through my shirts deciding what to wear when Cesar shouts from down the hall. "You ready?"

"Almost." I settle on a dark blue long-sleeve Mom gave me with shimmery silver stars. Then I head down the hall to Cesar's room. He stands in front of his dresser mirror, his feet squarely planted, and his arms spread above his head in a V.

"What're you doing?" I ask, stepping into the room.

"It's a power pose Coach taught us. You do it for a minute, three times a day, to amp up your power."

I raise my arms and try it. I don't feel powerful, just goofy. "Am I dressed okay?" I ask, letting my arms drop.

"You look all right." Cesar rubs some sort of cream on his face.

"What's that, makeup?" I reach for the jar.

He snatches it away and shoves the mystery cream into a drawer. "It's none of your beeswax. Stay out of my stuff."

Why is he being so mysterious? It makes me even more curious.

He grabs a bottle of musky cologne, splashes some on each wrist and on his throat. Then he grabs my forearms one at a time and rubs his cologne-damp wrists against mine. "Here, this'll make you smell good for Emily. According to Victoria, she's got a crush on you."

"You mean it? What'd she say?"

"She thinks you're really cute and nice. Apparently you're doing something right."

"Any idea what?"

"Nope. Just keep doing it. Things are going to be okay for you and me, despite—"

I wait for him to finish. "Despite what?"

He shakes his head. "I don't want to think about him tonight."

I know exactly who he means by *him*. For once, we're on the same page. I don't want to think about *her* either.

* * *

Mom drives us to the party in the minivan. Although the girls live only five minutes away, their neighborhood is swankier than ours, full of McMansions with huge lawns.

"Did I tell you their dad is on city council?" Cesar asks Mom. "I think he'll be able to help me get into a good college."

"You're only in eighth grade," Mom says. "And you already have good grades."

"So do a lot of other people," he says. "It's not only *what* you know, it's *who* you know."

I haven't even started thinking about college. It seems so far in the future. Why is he already worrying about it now?

"Here it is," Cesar says, pointing out the window. The house looms nearly as big as Batman's stately Wayne Manor.

"You boys have fun," Mom says, stopping the car. "I'll pick you up at nine."

"Mom, don't be ridiculous," Cesar argues. "The party doesn't end till eleven. We'd look like dorks leaving at nine."

Mom glances at the dashboard clock: It's barely seven. "Okay, nine-thirty."

"*Ten*-thirty," he says. "We're thirteen, remember?"

"Okay, okay, ten o'clock. Not a minute later." The way she smiles makes me wonder if that's what she wanted all along. Mom is a lot smarter at arguing with Cesar than I am. "And keep an eye on each other," she adds.

"We always do," he says and climbs out. Halfway up the

three-car-wide driveway, he stops, digs through a bag, and pins my shirt with a button proclaiming *I've got Cesar fever!*

"I'm going to be in campaign mode tonight, so don't be clingy," he tells me. "Just stay cool. I'm counting on you to help me look good." He hands me the bag. "Can you pass these out for me?"

I nod. "You always look good." Even so, Cesar runs a hand across his thick, black hair. Then he adjusts my collar before we start walking again.

As we approach the house, I see that the front steps' railing is strewn with yellow police tape and a homemade sign on the door warns:

CAUTION! QUARANTINE AREA
ENTRY MAY EXPOSE YOU TO CESAR FEVER!!!

When Cesar steps inside, a cheer breaks out. The place is already packed with students. Immediately he begins chatting up potential voters.

From the crowd, a trio of girls, led by Emily, emerges. "Hi, Jorge!" she shouts over the pop music. "You feeling better?"

"Huh?" It takes a second to remember my morning text. "Oh, yeah. All better, thanks."

"Great." She turns to the girls with her. "You know Jorge? Cesar's brother?"

"Wow, cool," the girls say. I give each of them a *Cesar Fever* button.

"I'm such a klutz," Emily says, fumbling with hers. "Can you help me?"

I study her bare-shouldered top. "Um . . . where?"

"Here's good." She points above her heart and grins, her eyes twinkling.

I lean into her, unsure how to pin her without touching a wrong place. My hands are sweating along with the rest of me, and the minute they brush against her, the button slides through my fingers.

"I'm a klutz too," I say, holding the button out to the nearest friend. "Can you do it?"

Mission accomplished, Emily leaves her friends and leads me to the dining room. While pouring me a soda, she introduces me to her mom, who says something to her about the music.

Emily hands me my drink. "Why don't you mingle? I'll come find you."

Mingle? With who? The kids here are mostly Cesar's crowd—some I know, but they aren't really my friends. Across the dining table, the girls Emily introduced me to— *What were their names?*—talk and laugh.

I raise my blue plastic cup in a wave. They wave back, giggle, and scurry from the room. I wonder about Emily asking me to pin her button. *Was she flirting with me?*

"Dude, go talk with people," Cesar tells me as he strides past with Victoria and their campaign entourage.

Clutching the buttons bag, I wander over to a huddle of guys. "'Sup?" I say, squeezing in. "You guys want Cesar buttons?"

They each take one and continue their jock talk about the school's upcoming soccer game—the first of the season. Although I'm not really into the conversation, I nod, mumbling, "Uh-huh . . . yeah . . ."

"Let's check things outside," says the group's alpha, and the herd heads toward the backyard.

I stay behind without them noticing. I might as well be wearing an invisibility cloak.

"I like your button," says a familiar voice. I turn and see Zoey, sporting a red-and-white striped top hat.

"Wow, hi. Am I glad to see you. I thought you'd gone to Austin."

She smiles. "Just for the day. Oona texted me when I got back. Victoria invited her to the party, and she asked Noah and me to come along."

"Would you like a button?" I hand her one. While she pins it on, a nearby clique of girls stare at her hat, covering their giggles. "Cat in the Hat, right?" I ask Zoey. "I like it. You're brave."

"You kidding? I love the attention."

"So how was Austin?" I ask, pouring her a drink.

"Good. I got to check in with some friends."

"Hey, guys," Oona says, wading through the crowd with

Noah. They look like a matching set, both wearing lipstick and eyeliner. Alongside them comes Emily. She and Zoey deliver each other the same guarded smiles as before.

"Great party," Oona says to me. "I hope Cesar wins."

"Can I have a couple of buttons?" Noah asks.

"Sure, as many as you want." I hand him the bag. "Can you guys help pass them out?"

"We need more ice," Emily says, slipping her fingers into mine. "Jorge, can you help me carry some?"

I gaze down at our entwined hands—how the heck did that happen?

Zoey stares too, as if wondering the same thing.

"You guys circulate," Emily tells the group. "Jorge and I will catch up."

She pulls me away and down the hall. I glance over my shoulder at Zoey, trying to signal her with a gaze that this isn't my idea. But she doesn't appear to be reading my signal.

"Emily?" I say as she leads me past the line of students outside the bathroom. "Emily?" I say louder as she pulls me through the kitchen.

I try to slide out of her hand, but she holds me tighter, guiding me into the cavernous garage. After the music and noise of the party, the concrete room is starkly quiet. And deserted. It's only us.

"I hate parties—too many people," she says, leading me

past the silver sedan and blue SUV to the space I assume is reserved for Wayne Manor's Batmobile. At last we arrive at a horizontal food freezer as big as a casket.

"Would you mind me asking you something?" Emily says, still holding my hand. "Are you interested in Zoey?" A flush spreads from her cheeks down to her shoulders.

I blush too. I should just say yes, but Emily is the first girl I've ever known to have a crush on me. I don't want to hurt her feelings. Plus, her hand feels soft and warm. And I do like her.

"Well . . . I like her," I answer, "but she and her boyfriend broke up, and she's not ready for another boyfriend, so . . ."

A sizeable white, longhaired cat suddenly brushes between our legs.

"Why, hello," Emily says, letting go of my hand and picking up the cat. A plastic clip on its head holds the long hair away from its eyes—one blue and one green. "Meet Regina."

"She's as big as my dog."

"The chicken snatcher?" Emily giggles.

"You heard?"

"Victoria says he's going to be in the talent show. She says I should be in the show too, but I freeze up in front of people."

"Ditto," I say. "I couldn't do it either."

Regina leans out from Emily's arms and sniffs me. I rub her downy fur with my fingertips. "I think she smells Peppy."

"*You* smell good," Emily says, blushing again. *I* blush again too.

"It's Cesar's cologne." While she sniffs toward me, I try not to stare at her mouth. Her lips are red and shiny. Her gaze is intense—like Peppy's when he begs to play.

An uneasy feeling seeps through me. I should go back to the party—*now*. And yet I feel powerless to leave.

Regina purrs like a revving motor between Emily and me. My face burns engine hot. I have to clear my throat before I speak. "They're probably waiting for us . . . wondering what we're doing."

Emily doesn't say anything. She just leans forward. Her lips part, her breath warms my cheek—and our noses collide.

Although I've seen a million movie kisses, I've never paid attention to how people keep their noses out of harm's way. I tilt my head, but she tilts hers too. She seems as inexperienced as me.

Regina squirms out of the way, and suddenly my lips make contact with Emily's. Her mouth feels tender. Little sparks tingle from her skin to mine.

A needle of guilt pricks at me, and in my mind I hear Zoey's voice. "Hey, do you guys need . . . ?" Wait, that actually is her voice.

I pull back from Emily and see Zoey standing in the kitchen doorway, her eyes wide with shock, her face clenched with hurt. I stare back, paralyzed.

Without another word, Zoey swings around and whisks out the door. I return to Emily. Her expression is blank, expectant, waiting for me.

"I've got to go," I say, my thoughts whirling, my mind reeling.

"Wait." Emily takes hold of my arm. "Stay. Please?"

My eyes flick between her and the doorway. I bite into my lip and taste her lip gloss.

"Sorry," I say, pulling away. "I'm really sorry."

I shove my way through the kitchen and the hallway crowd, shouting: "Zoey, wait!"

"Whoa, whoa." Cesar grabs my sleeve as I jostle across the living room. "Where you going?"

"I've got to talk to Zoey."

I spot a red-and-white striped hat disappearing toward the front entry hall, but Cesar keeps his grip on me. "Why's she wearing that kooky hat? And where's Emily?"

Across the room, the front door opens. Zoey hurries outside.

"Sorry," I say, shaking Cesar's hand off me. "I've got to go to her."

CHAPTER 22

"Zoey, wait!" I chase after her as she marches down the street. She's moving so fast her red-and-white hat flies off and bounces across the pavement toward me.

"Got it," I say, scooping it up. I brush the grit off the fuzzy felt. "I'm sorry about—"

"No need to apologize," Zoey interrupts, yanking the hat from my hand. "What you do with some girl is none of my business." She jams the hat back onto her head and resumes her march.

I trot after her. "Would you let me explain, please?"

"What for? We're not a couple. I told you I'm not ready for a boyfriend."

While she keeps walking, I sprint ahead, turn to face her, and jog backward. "Then why are you mad at me?"

"I'm not."

"You're not? You could've fooled—"

A bump in the road snags my heel. Before I can eat black-top, Zoey reaches out to catch me. My stumble brings us close, like when we danced.

Zoey quickly lets go of my arm. "You'd better turn around before you break your neck."

When she starts walking away again, I stride beside her. "If you're not angry, then why'd you run out of the party?"

She stops and faces me. Head held high. Feet wide apart. Fists on hips. Standard superhero pose. "Because you lied to me. You said you weren't interested in Emily."

"I'm not."

"Do you always make out with girls you're not interested in?"

"No, I've never even kissed a girl before." As I say the words, I cringe inside. I didn't mean to admit that. "She kissed me."

"Aw, you poor defenseless thing."

"Okay, you're right—I messed up. I'm sorry. But I was only interested in her because you said you're not ready for a boyfriend. I told you I like *you*."

Her gaze bears down on me, as though her X-ray eyes are testing if I'm lying.

"I really like you. . . . and if you *were* ready for a boy-friend . . ." My heart is beating a million beats a minute. "I'd like it to be me."

The light of the setting sun makes Zoey look shimmery and fragile. She pulls at her fingertips, working herself up to say something. At last she says, "I like you too."

I swallow the knot in my throat. "You *do?*"

Her lips curve into a shy smile. "Yeah, I do."

"Oh. So . . . does that mean you'd like me to be your boyfriend?"

"Yeah, I'd like that. But . . . you have to be honest with me. A hundred percent. I don't want my heart broken again. Okay?"

"Okay but, like, wait—so, we're a couple now?"

Her smile grows bigger. "Yeah. We're a couple now."

"Great," I say. "That's great. *Really* great. *More* than great."

Zoey stares at me like she's waiting for something other than me blabbing. Should I kiss her? What if I'm misreading her? What if she doesn't want to kiss me after I just kissed Emily? What if a car drives up the street? What if, what if, what if?

"So, um . . . do you want to go back to the party?" I ask.

She shakes her head. "Not really. Do you?"

"No. I think it's nicer out here." The street is quiet—the only sound is crickets chirping. The oak trees make a kind of cathedral ceiling above us. The last rays of sun are streaking through their branches, and a breeze scents the air with leaves and Spanish moss.

"Would you like to walk me home?" Zoey asks.

I nod with excitement. "Yeah, I would."

While she texts Oona, my thumbs speed across my own phone, texting Mom and Cesar to let them know I'm walking home. I leave out mention of Zoey—it might make Cesar mad. Before putting away my phone, I shut it off. I don't want any distractions.

Zoey and I set off, walking along the edge of the road in the twilight. In the shadows of a big house, a dog barks.

"Sounds like a Doberman pinscher," Zoey says. A garage light turns on, and sure enough, there stands a black and brown Doberman nearly as huge as a horse.

"You can tell the dog breed just by its bark?" I ask.

"Sometimes. If you heard Peppy next to the Doberman, couldn't you say which was which?"

"Sure, he'd be the one fearlessly yapping."

We saunter toward the main road, and she talks about the different ways animals communicate: sounds, songs, actions. When we cross the street, our hands accidentally bump.

"Sorry," I say.

"My fault," she says.

The next time our hands nudge each other, neither of us apologizes. A block later, her pinky finger pokes out like a hook trolling the waters. I take the bait, and our fingers entwine.

For the rest of the walk, I barely pay attention to where we're going or what Zoey is saying—only to her smooth, tender hand. Next thing I know, we've arrived at her home.

"So . . ." I gently swing our hands between us, not wanting to let go.

"So . . ." she replies, tugging me closer. Her eyes glimmer brightly. Her lips shine, pink and inviting.

I shuffle my feet. "Do you want to . . . ?"

Zoey squeezes my hand in answer, and I take a breath, psyching myself up. It feels like when you're standing so close to the curb's edge that suddenly—*whoosh!*—you tip over. I lean toward her, and we're kissing. And kissing. And *kissing!*

Then her hat tumbles off her head. I bend to catch it, just as she does. Our heads clunk.

Ouch.

"Sorry," I say, handing her the hat. "You okay?"

"Fine." Although she rubs her forehead, she's grinning. "See you and Peppy tomorrow after lunch?"

I nod, already eager to see her again.

"Oh, but can we rehearse at your house?" she asks. "My parents are having friends over. I'll bring you a surprise."

"What surprise?" I ask.

"A *surpriiise.*" She stretches the word out. Then she pecks me one last kiss.

My feet scarcely touch the ground as I soar home, riding

on a cloud of excitement. For the first time in my life, I'm not merely imagining being a superhero—it feels as if I've become one, with powers and abilities beyond those of mere mortals. And later, when I climb into bed, it takes me forever to fall asleep.

CHAPTER 23

I'm happily dreaming of kissing Zoey when she steps on my big toe—hard. A spike of pain shoots through my leg.

"Hey, dog breath," she growls, except it doesn't sound like her. It sounds like Cesar.

I blink my eyes open. My Bat-signal clock reads 11:03 p.m. Cesar hovers over me, wrenching my toe through the bedcovers. Behind him, the ceiling lamp glares like a prison searchlight.

I yank my toe away. "What're you doing?"

"Why'd you make out with Emily and then ditch her?" he answers. "She's upset, and Victoria's pissed at you—big-time."

I sit up, fold my legs out of Cesar's reach, and collect my thoughts. "Emily kissed *me*. I didn't know what to do."

Cesar's brow furrows, and his nostrils flare.

I keep talking: "You said she had a crush on me, and I thought, *Well, I do like her some.* So I kissed her. But then Zoey walked in, and I realized I'd messed up. I felt bad walking out on Emily, but . . . it's Zoey I like."

"*Why?*" Cesar asks. "Everybody at the party was whispering, 'Who's the weird chick with the clown hat?'"

"Cat in the Hat," I correct. "It took guts to wear it. That's what I like about her. And she looked cute."

"She looked like the entertainment." He plops down on my bed and holds his head in his hands. "And now Victoria's threatening to break up with me."

"I bet she's just upset," I try to reassure him. "She won't break up with you. You didn't do anything wrong."

"Yeah, I did. I had you for a brother."

I know he doesn't mean that. He's just being hotheaded.

"Cesar, if she's going to break up with you just because of something I did, maybe you should find a different girlfriend."

"I don't *want* a different girlfriend. From now on, just stay out of my life." He rises to his feet, clenching his fist.

I brace myself for his punch. "You're the one who set me up with Emily."

"And that's the last time I do anything for you." He whirls around and storms out—without the punch.

"Good," I shout.

"Guys, what's all the yelling?" Mom asks from down the hall.

"Jorge is being a pain as usual!" Cesar shouts back.

"*You're* the pain!" I argue.

"Both of you go to sleep," Mom says.

On my bedspread, Peppy cocks his head, trying to make sense of everything. I run a hand across his smooth coat. I shouldn't have kissed Emily. Maybe I shouldn't have gone to the party in the first place. But then Zoey and I might not be a couple.

I need to apologize to Emily. I know that much. She didn't deserve to have me run out on her. Maybe I should tell Cesar I'm sorry too.

I launch from bed and pad down the hallway with Peppy trailing after me. The light is shining from beneath Cesar's door. I quietly test the knob—locked. I press my ear to the *DANGER—KEEP OUT* sign. Inside, I can hear my brother moving around.

I tap lightly on the door, whispering, "Cesar?"

"Go away!"

"I just want to say sorry," I whisper, "if I screwed things up for you with Victoria."

The door swings open. Cesar's eyes smolder. Then his fist shoots out, smacking my shoulder.

The punch doesn't really hurt that much. Actually, it feels more like a relief. Maybe I even smile because he gives me a look like, *Are you nuts?*

"Go to sleep," he mumbles and gently closes the door.

Back beneath my bedcovers, I wrap an arm around Peppy. His warm, wet tongue slathers my face. And although his breath isn't sweet like Zoey's—or Emily's—I think how much simpler life would be if we were all dogs.

* * *

The next morning, I wake to the thuds of Cesar's footsteps going down the stairs while he yammers something about soccer into his phone. A car horn toots outside. He yells bye to Mom, and the front door slams.

I haul my carcass out of bed. After showering, I pass Cesar's closed door, and that's when I remember something. I stop and listen, just in case he came back while I was in the bathroom, but no sound comes from inside.

I try the knob—unlocked.

Glancing both ways down the hall, I step inside. Unlike my room, everything in Cesar's room is in perfect order. Clothes are carefully put away. The bedcovers are stretched tight enough to bounce a coin. The dresser shines clean and tidy. His toiletries are lined up as neatly as a store display.

Quiet as a crook, I open the drawer where he keeps the mysterious skin cream, pull out the jar, and read the label:

MIRACLE WHITE
Skin-Whitening Cream
Exclusive Formula with Dead Sea Minerals
and Licorice Extracts

I stare, surprised. Confused. In shock. I've always admired Cesar's bronze skin—same as Dad's. Next to the two of them, Mom and I look like pasty-white ghosts. Why would he want to lighten his skin?

My thoughts travel back to what he said the other day about getting bullied for being Mexican. That was about the same time he stopped speaking Spanish, I realize now. If a stranger spoke Spanish to him, Cesar would answer them, "I'm not Mexican."

For me, growing up was the opposite. Strangers never spoke to me in Spanish. If I told people my background was Mexican, they almost always said, "You don't look Mexican," as if everybody from a country should look the same. Once someone even told me, "You're not Mexican, you're white."

One Saturday morning last year, Cesar and I were riding our bikes to the mall when the police stopped us. I'm still not sure why. They separated us, and one of them—I was so scared I can't even remember what he looked like—asked me who Cesar was. When I said, "He's my brother," the officer looked back and forth between Cesar and me like he didn't believe me. Then he asked me more questions.

Meanwhile, the other cop frisked Cesar as if he were a thug.

When they finally let us go, I asked Cesar, "Why'd they stop us?"

His lip quivered like he wanted to cry. "'Cause of nothing you'll ever have to worry about."

When we got home and told our parents what happened, Mom got really upset. "Did you make sure you were polite?" she asked.

"Remember, mijo," Dad told Cesar, "you always need to be twice as respectful. Twice as smart. Twice as everything."

I felt bad for Cesar and mad at the cops. Not just at them—at something bigger than them. Something I didn't fully understand.

As I'm slipping Cesar's skin cream back into the drawer, Mom calls from the doorway, "Morning, Jorge."

I nearly leap out of my skin.

"What're you up to?" she asks.

"Um, nothing." I slam the drawer shut.

"You'd better not let Cesar catch you," she says. "You know how private he can be."

"Yeah, I know." Now more than ever.

CHAPTER 24

For breakfast Mom fixes me bright yellow scrambled eggs and crispy bacon. Peppy watches me eat with begging eyes. His nostrils quiver. His mouth waters.

"*Tzzt!*" I snap my fingers. "Back behind the line."

He stops staring, drops down, and rests his head on his paws, surrendering.

With my breakfast safe, I text Darnell: Guess what? BIG news!

Darnell: You found my lost Watchmen comic?

Me: BIGGER NEWS THAN THAT!

Darnell: What??? Speaketh!!!

Me: I made out with Zoey . . . We're going out!

Darnell: No joke?

Me: Still trying to believe it myself

Darnell: Well done, Boy Wonder

Me: What should I tell Chang? I don't want him to feel like a loser . . . I want us to be friends like before

Darnell: Hmm . . . What if you both come over? I'll help you break the news

Me: Can't you just tell him without me?

Darnell: Absolutely, positively not. YOU need to tell him . . . and we can work on the comic. We've only got till Friday. Chang has some sketches of prototype villains for our trans hero

With everything going on, I'd set aside the contest and trans hero. My mind now jets back to Norma at the gas station, getting bullied by Scruggs's dad, and my stomach churns—I don't want to be reminded of all that.

Me: Can't we work on a different character?

Darnell: You got a better idea?

Me: No

Darnell: Then that's what we've got

* * *

When I get to Darnell's, Chang is already there. We transport our convoy of tortilla chips, sodas, and salsa to the family room and sink into the plush sofa and chairs.

"So," Chang says, "since most supervillains are guys, I thought: Why not be more original and make our villain a girl?" He flips open his sketchbook. "Her name's Whirlwind Woman."

In the drawing, a muscled, bright-red woman is spinning

like a mighty cyclone. Her long, black hair whips around her head. Her fists swing out furiously.

She reminds me of someone, but I can't put my finger on who.

"It's very good," Darnell says. "But . . ." He turns to me. "Don't you think she looks a lot like—"

It hits me: "Red Tornado!" The superhero who can generate storms and cyclones. Except in Chang's drawing, I note, "It looks like he put on a woman's wig."

"And bra," Darnell adds, nibbling a tortilla chip.

Chang slams his book shut. "You think it's easy to come up with something new? Everything's been done before."

"I agree," I say, spotting my chance. "We should scrap the contest. And the trans hero."

"Giving up, are you?" Darnell asks, switching to his Yoda voice. "Not if anything to say about it have I."

"I've got something else, but you're not going to like it," Chang mutters.

He flips to a drawing of a green woman with pointy ears and evil-looking spiked eyebrows. She's flanked by an army of little mucus-colored minions.

Darnell and I exchange a wordless glance.

"I know," Chang says. "She looks like the Green Goblin. But she's not. She's called Slimeball. She shoots slime from her wrists."

"Like Spider-Man's webs?"

"Screw it!" Chang tosses his sketchbook aside. "I'm done with this."

"Me too," I say. "I don't want to work on this either."

"Come, come, younglings," Darnell says. "Put our heads together we must. What kind of villain would oppose a trans hero?"

Chang shoots a sly fox grin at me. "Maybe the hero's son?"

I fire him a *shut up!* look. He knows I haven't told Darnell about my dad yet.

"Maybe we should go back to the villain being a man," Darnell suggests. "But the opposite of our hero: a hypermasculine dude."

"*That's* supposed to be original?" Chang asks. "'Hypermasculine' describes ninety-nine point nine percent of comic book characters."

"What if beneath the surface the villain is really insecure about his gender?" Darnell argues. "He feels threatened by anybody who isn't a tough hombre or a weak woman."

Since Darnell isn't letting go of the contest idea, I suggest, "Maybe he wants to wipe out all the girly guys and butch women."

"Ooh, clever you are." Darnell rubs his hands together. "He's a gender bigot. He bullies guys to 'man up.' But . . . I'm not sure what he would tell women."

"He catcalls them," Chang says. "Tells them stuff like, 'Be a babe' and 'Go change some diapers.'"

"Excellent, excellent!" Darnell cheers. "Is all that enough for you to get sketching?"

"I'll give it a shot. But I'm warning you guys: If you don't like what I come up with, draw it yourselves."

"Splendid," says Darnell. "We've got our hero and our villain. Now they need a victim to battle over."

"The hero's girlfriend," I say. "But she's got to fit into the whole gender-bending theme. She's gorgeous, but she's also strong and confident. That's what our hero likes about her. She dares to be different."

"How about if she wears work boots and lumberjack shirts?" Chang asks.

That isn't what I'd had in mind but . . . "That would work."

"Now we're cranking," Darnell says. "How soon can you guys pull it together? We've got to move fast."

By Tuesday, we agree—two days from now. Chang will sketch new drawings, and I'll write up the hero-villain-victim plot line.

Darnell raises his soda glass for a toast. Chang cheers: "One for all, and all for salsa!" And we clink glasses.

The happy mood seems perfect to spring my news about Zoey. Apparently Darnell has the same idea: "So, Jorge, how was the party last night?"

"It was good."

"Who was there?" Chang asks.

"Emily, Oona, Noah . . . Zoey."

"Zoey?" Chang's brow wrinkles in thought. "She didn't tell me she was going."

"Why would she?" I say. "She's not your girlfriend."

"She's not yours either," he grouses.

"Actually, she is."

"Right—in your dreams."

"Whoa, back to your corners, boys." Darnell slices the air as if separating us. "Now, tell us, Jorge, what happened?"

"I walked Zoey home from the party and . . ." I feel the heat rise in my cheeks. "We made out."

"You *made out*?" Chang explodes. "How?"

Darnell bites into a chip. "With their mouths, I hope."

"I meant where, when?"

"In front of her house. When we said good night. I kissed her. On the mouth."

Chang turns somber, stirring a chip in the salsa. "I knew she liked you better. I gave her sketches, origami, chocolates—"

"*Chocolates?*" I interrupt. "When?"

His mouth curves into a sheepish grin. "Yesterday morning—before her trip to Austin."

"You sneak," I say.

"Well, it didn't do any good, did it? She didn't even invite me in. She's only ever treated me like a friend—nothing more." He slumps down in the sofa, looking so hangdog that Darnell and I trade a worried glance.

"You'll find another girl," Darnell says. "You're smart, good-looking, a great artist . . ."

Chang glances up at me. "You really made out with her?"

I nod, feeling a little guilty but mostly proud.

"I guess that's it then. She chose you." His expression turns stern. "But you'd better treat her right. Did you tell her about your dad?"

Before I can glare at him to shut up, Darnell chimes in: "He's right, Jorge. If you're going to be a couple, you need to tell her. It's too big a deal to keep secret."

I stop crunching my chip. "You know . . . about my dad?"

Chang echoes my surprise. "Since when? You didn't tell me you knew."

"Back at you," Darnell says, bobbing a chip in the salsa. "I saw him going to his car in the mall parking lot the other night when I was with my mom. He was wearing a dress."

A queasy feeling grips my stomach. "Your mom saw him too?"

"Yeah, she was like"—he imitates his mom's Jamaican accent—"'Lord have mercy, child, what is this world coming to?'"

I pick up a chair cushion and bury my face.

"But then I pointed out to her," Darnell continues, "how she likes to walk around the house in my dad's boxer shorts."

I pull the pillow away from my face. "Why didn't you guys tell me you knew?"

"*You* should've told *us*," Chang says. "And not through a comic-book character."

I frown. I know he's right but . . . "This is all so new to me. It's like somebody dropped a feelings bomb—*pow!*—smack on top of me. I didn't know what to say."

"You could've started by telling us that," Darnell says.

I fold my arms, feeling scolded. And yet I also feel relieved—as if a steam shovel has lifted a ton of debris from my shoulders. "You guys aren't going to bail on me?"

"*Dude*," Chang says as if I should already know the answer.

"Who would write the plot lines for our comics?" Darnell kids.

"So you don't think the whole thing is too weird?" I persist.

"Your dad's always been different," Darnell says. "More like a mom. Cooking for us, listening to us, telling us life lessons, watching movies with us . . . Lots of times I've wished *my* dad was more like him."

"Me too," Chang says. "Is he still the same—I mean apart from the being-a-woman thing?"

"Yeah, but . . . I just wish things would go back to how they were. I miss the dad I grew up with."

"You want us to go talk to him with you?" Chang offers.

"And say *what*?"

"I don't know. Talk him into going back to being a guy."

"I don't think it would work. He—*she*—says she's always been a woman inside. Now she's matching up her outsides with her insides. She's changed her name to Norma. It's all so confusing." I turn to Darnell. "What would Yoda say?"

Darnell lowers his eyelids halfway and scrunches up his mouth. Then he raises a chip as if pointing a cane and speaks: "Man or woman matters not. Luminous beings are we, not this crude flesh. The Force is what binds us. And we must honor that Force inside everyone . . . whether they be male or female."

Even though his voice sounds funny, I know he means what he's saying. I wish I'd confided in him and Chang sooner.

"So are you going to tell Zoey?" Chang asks.

Not that again—I'd hoped he'd buried that bone.

"I promised Cesar I wouldn't tell anybody," I say. "If it gets around at school, it could ruin his shot at student body president."

"If you *don't* tell Zoey and word gets out," Darnell counters, "it could ruin *your* shot with her."

"What's worth more to you?" Chang asks. "Lying for Cesar or being honest with Zoey?"

I chew on a chip, mulling it over. "What if she doesn't understand?" I ask. "I don't want to lose her."

"She seems pretty understanding to me," Chang says.

"I sense in you much fear," Darnell says. "You must learn

to let go of fear by being willing to let go of the things you most fear losing."

My heart sinks at the idea of letting go of Zoey. We only became a couple twelve hours ago. I get that familiar painful pretzel feeling again.

"All right. I'll tell her when she comes over to rehearse after lunch." I stand to leave, unable to sit still any longer. "She says she's bringing me a surprise—wait until she hears mine."

CHAPTER 25

"Fresh and warm from the oven," Zoey says, arriving at my front door. From her backpack she pulls out a bag of cookies with orange-colored flecks.

"You baked them yourself?" I ask. "What kind are they?"

"Try one." Her blue eyes twinkle with mystery and mischief.

With the very first nibble, my mouth bursts into a fiesta of tastes and textures—sweet, salty, chewy, cheesy, tangy, crunchy . . .

"Man, oh man, what did you put in them?"

She grins proudly. "Your fave food."

"You've got to patent this." I chomp another bite. "You're pure genius."

In the kitchen, I introduce Zoey to Mom, who makes

us iced tea to go with the cookies. While we talk, Cesar's footsteps pad across the floor upstairs. He cold-shouldered me when he returned from his morning soccer meeting, didn't talk to me all during lunch, and doesn't join us now.

After filling up on cookies, Zoey and I take Peppy to rehearse in the garage.

"Ready for your surprise?" she asks, sliding her backpack off her shoulder.

"I thought the cookies were my surprise."

"Nope. Turn around. Cover your eyes."

I turn away and press my hands over my face. Behind me, her backpack zipper strums open. Fabric rustles. The garage's cement walls and floor echo every sound.

"Can I peek?"

"No way. Peppy, come here."

His tags jingle, his toenails click across the concrete, and more fabric crackles.

"Okay," she calls out to me. "You can look now."

I spin around and nearly lose my balance. Gone are the casual jeans, sneakers, and T-shirt. Instead she's all girled up in a poofy, off-the-shoulder white blouse, black heels, sequined eye mask, and a ruffled, flame-red skirt that rises high on one side and trails down to the ground on the other. A rose in her hair completes the look.

I stand there stunned.

Next to Zoey, Peppy looks a little dazed himself. A doggie-sized eye mask is tied behind his ears. A gold-embroidered black cape hangs from his shoulders.

"This was my Halloween costume last year with Goldie," Zoey says. "I thought it would go with the Latin music. Do you like it?"

"Um . . . yeah. You look . . . amazing."

We clear a space amid the cardboard boxes, lawn furniture, and garden tools. Zoey tucks her dog-training snack pack into her waistband. Like before, I take charge of the music. And she and Peppy dive into a full dress rehearsal of their act, including all the tricks and twirls.

Although Zoey does a great job maneuvering her costume, Peppy's legs tangle in the cape. We finally agree to scrap it. Only the eye mask survives.

The next run-through goes without a hitch. Even so . . . it feels like it's missing something.

"What's the matter?" Zoey asks, watching my expression.

"You guys look awesome, but . . . I'm always thinking about stories. What if we put together everything you two are doing into a skit?"

"That sounds awesome. Like what?"

"Let me put on my thinking cap." I concentrate for a moment. "How about if you first come onstage solo and pretend you're dancing with an invisible partner? Like this . . ." I stand and circle my arms around an imaginary girl. "Then Peppy trots onstage. That way he can be a surprise."

"I love it," Zoey says. "Keep going."

"He stops and looks at you, and . . . can you teach him to wave hello with his front paw?"

She tries. It takes some doing, but eventually he gets it.

"Great," I say. "But you turn away from his wave and keep dancing with your imaginary partner, so he barks for your attention. When you still ignore him, he comes and tugs at your skirt. He's had practice pulling my covers off in the morning."

Zoey tries to get Peppy to bite the skirt, but he doesn't understand.

"Maybe if I show him?" I suggest.

I don't know where I get the nerve to get down on all fours in front of her. Maybe her playfulness inspires me. Or maybe I want to make her laugh. Either way, I chomp down on the long end of her skirt. The nylon material is so light and airy I have to be careful not to rip it, but Peppy finally understands what to do.

"Good boy." She pats him on the head. "You too." She pats me on the head, laughing.

"So next," I say, still blushing as I get up, "you shake your finger, scolding him to leave you alone. That'll be his signal to let go of your skirt. You pretend to apologize to your invisible partner and keep dancing. Then maybe Peppy comes crawling to you on his stomach. . . ."

I wiggle my elbows to demonstrate what I mean, and Zoey gets Peppy to do it on cue.

"How are you coming up with all this stuff?" she asks me.

"I don't know. It's just how my mind works. The same way you have a talent with animals. So anyway, then he sits up and begs for a dance."

Slowly but surely, Zoey gets Peppy up on his haunches, pressing his paws together like he's pleading with her.

"Finally you give in to him," I explain, "and wave your partner away. Peppy stands on his hind legs, and you dance with him, and twirl him, and he does all his flips and stuff. Then you clutch your chest like you're exhausted. You thank him by leaning down to kiss him. And he curls his paw over his head like he's shy."

"Aww . . ." Zoey says. "He's going to steal the show."

"And for the grand finale," I say, "your rose will be off-stage. He can run and bring it to you."

"This is going to be so amazing," she says. "Except . . ." She pokes me in the ribs, tickling me. "*You* need to be in it too. He's your dog. It's your story. You can be my partner and make jealous faces at him. You should share the credit."

"No, thanks."

"Oh, come on, why not?"

"Because whenever I get up in front of a crowd, I . . ."

I nearly blurt out my history of farting, fainting, and barfing, but that would be more embarrassing than getting on all fours. "When a crowd is watching me, I feel like I'm going to die. Don't *you* get scared?"

"Sure, I do. But you have to face down your fear. Remember when I said to picture the yellow police tape Peppy wasn't allowed to cross? When I start to feel scared, I train my brain the same way. I tell my fear, 'Don't cross that line. I know you're trying to protect me, but don't worry, we're not going to die. So stay back!' Of course if a car is coming at you, you'd better pay attention to your fear and run your butt off." Her eyes sparkle with encouragement.

I smile. *You talked me into it,* I want to say. But despite her pep talk, my fear breaks through the police tape like Peppy lunging at a chicken dinner.

"Sorry." I shake my head. "I just can't."

Zoey's forehead furrows as if she's straining to think up a new way to persuade me. But when her gaze drifts over my shoulder, her expression changes.

"Hey, can we use that for Peppy's entrance?" She steps across the garage to the skateboard hung on a peg.

"Um, it's Cesar's," I say. "And, well, he's sort of ticked off at me for ditching the party last night."

"Ohh . . ." She puckers her lips in disappointment.

My mouth tingles with the memory of her kiss. "I guess I could ask him."

"Would you?" She tests the wood and wheels. "The worst he can say is no, right?"

"He could say worse," I answer and grab my phone.

Can Zoey and I borrow your skateboard? I text.

While we wait for a reply, Zoey peels off her heels, tucks in her ruffled skirt, and steps on the board. Man, can she ride: frontward, backward, flipping, spinning, skating across the floor as gracefully as she dances. She's flying into the air as Cesar bursts in through the door from the kitchen.

"What do you—" He stops short, blinking at the sight of Zoey airborne.

The wheels slam down onto the concrete floor, and she flips the board to a stop. I clench my teeth into a grin.

"Um, Cesar, meet Zoey. Zoey, this is my brother, Cesar."

"Thrilled to meet you," she says, breathing hard. "Jorge convinced me to vote for you. He told me how smart, dynamic, and determined you are. He's your number-one fan."

While she reaches out and pumps his hand, Cesar casts me a suspicious glance.

"He also told me," she continues, barely pausing, "that you're emceeing the talent show. And I was thinking: How would you like the evening's most spectacular stage act to *also* be one of your greatest campaign opportunities? Of course you would want that, right?"

Cesar hardly has a chance to open his mouth before

Zoey goes on. "So here's my idea: You see that cute little dog over there? He's not just any dog. He's the smartest, swiftest, most eager-to-please dog I've ever come across—and I've met plenty. That's where your skateboard comes in. Thanks to your kindhearted generosity, that ordinary-looking little pooch will make the most adorable stage entrance you've ever seen. People will be cheering and laughing and applauding, and it will all be thanks to you."

Cesar folds his arms, looking unconvinced.

"You can see for yourself," Zoey forges on. "Jorge, can you get your brother a chair?"

"Huh? Um, sure." I hastily unfold a lawn chair. Cesar remains standing.

Zoey calls Peppy over. "Now, to start," she explains to us, "we need to get him comfortable with the board."

At first Peppy recoils from the noisy, clunky, unpredictable slab of wood. But he's no match for Zoey's tender, soft-spoken resolve. She places a treat on the board, luring him. Once he takes the treat, she places another. And another.

Cesar leans over the lawn chair, his brow creasing with interest.

I'm fascinated too. By Zoey. By her command of Peppy. By her command of Cesar.

"Now that he's stopped being afraid," she tells us, "let's get him to stand on it." And dang if she doesn't get him to do it.

Cesar sits down in the chair and leans forward, giving her his full attention.

"Okay, boy, push off," Zoey tells Peppy. He glides on the board across the garage. And when she rewards him with lavish praise, his tail wags more proudly than ever.

"And now for his final feat . . ." Zoey announces. She aims the board toward Cesar's chair and signals Peppy. "Ride to Cesar!"

Peppy pushes off and hops on. He whisks across the room and springs off the board into Cesar's lap, his tail waving like a proud flag.

"Now, I ask you," Zoey says as Peppy licks Cesar's neck, "what student wouldn't vote for a candidate who stands onstage holding the city's cutest, most talented dog in his arms? Your election will be practically guaranteed."

Cesar pulls his face from Peppy's tongue, pets him, and nudges him off his lap. Then, as if remembering, he pulls a *Cesar Fever* bumper sticker from his jeans, leans over, and pastes it on the board.

"Bring it back when you're done," he tells Zoey.

"Thanks," she and I both say in unison. After Cesar leaves, she whispers to me, "I see what you mean. He really is a force of nature."

She says it without irony. I guess she doesn't realize she's a force to reckon with too.

Zoey and Peppy rehearse a few more times, until we call

it a day. I pull off Peppy's mask and turn around, closing my eyes, so Zoey can change out of her costume.

"So will your parents come to the show?" she asks. "I can't wait to meet your dad. We can compare cookie recipes."

My pulse rockets. This is my chance to tell her about Dad. In my mind, I try to picture my fear cordoned behind the yellow police tape. "Zoey . . . I need to tell you something."

"Sure, what?"

I squeeze my eyes shut tighter. "Um . . . my dad . . . ? He and my mom are separated?"

"Oh my gosh, Jorge. I'm so sorry. Why didn't you tell me? I mean . . . I know it can be hard. When I was in fourth grade, my parents separated. I cried every night they were apart."

"I'm sorry to hear it," I say.

"Thanks," she says. "But they went to counseling and got back together. Happy ending. Have your parents tried seeing a couples counselor?"

"Um, yeah." My voice wavers as I strain to open up and tell her the truth.

"You can look now," she says.

I slowly turn and face her. She's back in her jeans and T-shirt, yet she still looks amazing. Unspeakably blue eyes. Button nose. Lips as red as the rose behind her ear.

"If you want to talk about your mom and dad," she says, "I'm here to listen."

Inside me, a battle rages. The more I get to know Zoey, the more I like her—really, really like her. The more I think she would understand about Norma. And the more I stand to lose if she doesn't.

Her gaze moves across my face, searching. My cheeks are boiling. My breath comes fast. My knees are shaking. I have to look away.

"I know it sucks," she says, taking hold of my hand. "I'm really sorry." Then she presses her lips to mine, and all my plans to tell her crumble.

"Rehearsal after school tomorrow?" she asks when she pulls away.

"You bet." I clear my throat and think, *I'll tell her tomorrow.*

And I wish tomorrow would never come.

CHAPTER 26

"So, now that you've met Zoey," I ask Cesar at breakfast Monday morning, "do you still think she's weird?"

"Yep." He slurps his cereal while texting. "She sticks out—it's like she doesn't even care what other people think."

I slip my breakfast pastry into the toaster. "I like that she's brave. Why do you care so much what other people think?"

Cesar chugs the last of his coffee. "Didn't *you* just ask *me* what *I* think?"

"Yeah, 'cause you're my brother."

"So, as your brother, I'm telling you I still think she's weird."

"Okay, guys," Mom interrupts, rushing into the kitchen with her empty coffee mug. "I'm off to my big meeting. Wish me luck."

"For what?" I ask.

"For my presentation—I told you, remember? I'll be home late." She stops and looks at me. "And call your dad. He told me what happened at the gas station. Why didn't you mention it? I'd appreciate knowing things like that. He wants to talk with you and says you haven't answered his calls or texts."

Before I can correct Mom on her pronouns, Cesar claps my back. "Good, you're finally taking my advice."

Mom sends him a frosty glare. "Cesar, you're not calling the shots here. You should phone your dad too."

"I'm not talking to him. Why do you keep pushing him on us after what he did to you?"

"I don't have time for this now." She rinses her coffee cup. "If there's any problem while I'm away—"

"There won't be," Cesar cuts in and swings his gaze in my direction.

"What're you looking at me for?" I say.

"Guys, please try to get along," Mom says, then gives us each a goodbye kiss.

* * *

"What was Mom saying about the gas station?" Cesar asks as we walk to the bus stop.

"Why do you care? You said you don't want to hear about Dad."

He walks somberly for several steps. "Just tell me what happened."

"You know Sam Scruggs? His dad saw Norma when we stopped for gas and tried to pick a fight."

"You mean a *real* fight? A fistfight? What happened?"

I remember Dad caving, and my stomach turns. "Nothing happened. She wouldn't fight him."

"Figures," Cesar mutters.

"Shut up." Even though I'm still mad at Dad, I feel the need to defend her. "You weren't there. You don't know. The guy could've had a gun."

Cesar shields his eyes from the morning sun. "I know one thing: He's probably going to get himself killed one day."

I don't want to think about that. I wish I'd kept my mouth shut, and yet it feels good to hear Cesar sound worried. It confirms what I've suspected: He still cares about Dad.

Down the street, our yellow school bus roars toward us. I think about the new thing I haven't told Cesar. "By the way, Darnell and his mom saw Norma at the mall."

Cesar's eyes flash with panic as the bus screeches to our stop. Before he can say anything, I leap on board.

"'Sup?" I ask Chang as I plunge into my seat. Cesar storms past in the aisle.

"Did you tell Zoey?" Chang asks. "Like you promised?"

Of course that's the first thing he asks.

"Um, it didn't come up."

"What the heck does that mean? How's it supposed to come up unless you bring it up?" He inspects my face. "You're never going to tell her, are you?"

I shrug. Shift. Shuffle my feet. "I'll tell her."

"When?"

"When I'm ready. I'm getting there. I told her about the divorce."

"You did? Really?"

"Yeah. Really."

"Well, that's progress. You didn't think that was a good time to tell her about your dad?"

"Look, it's my decision to choose the best time, not yours."

The bus brakes squeal, and we coast to Zoey's stop.

"Hi, guys." She smiles as she walks past.

"You'd better tell her," Chang whispers as the bus takes off again. "'Cause I'm not keeping your secret anymore."

CHAPTER 27

When I get off the bus, Emily is standing at the cactus hedge by the school doors, talking with some girls from the party. I hunch behind Chang, hoping she won't see me.

But luck is not on my side. One of Emily's friends spots me.

"Hi, Jorge," she calls. Did you have fun at the party?" The rest of Emily's friends giggle.

My cheeks ignite like they're on fire, and Emily turns as red as I feel. "Guys, leave him alone," she says and steps toward me. "Hi, Jorge."

"Um, hi." I shove my hands into my pockets and tell Chang, "You go ahead."

"This is awkward, I know," Emily says. "But . . . I want to say I'm sorry."

"Huh?" I thought she would be mad at me, not apologize.

"I shouldn't have—you know . . ." She glances up and pushes the hair away from her face. "Forgive me?"

"No sweat. I'm sorry too. I shouldn't have . . ." I'm not sure how to finish.

"You're really nice," Emily says and gives me a little wave. "See you later." Her blond hair bounces on her shoulders as she rejoins her friends. And I let out a sigh.

* * *

"Open your hand," Zoey says when I bound into homeroom. I do as I'm told, and she drops a little white-and-tan plush doggie into my palm.

I smile so wide my jaw nearly splits apart. "It looks just like Peppy."

"Hey, watch it," Noah protests as Scruggs stomps down the neighboring aisle, nearly knocking him out of his chair.

In my mind, I'm flung back to the gas station with Scruggs's dad.

"Mr. Scruggs?" calls out Ms. Finnegan. "Do you wish to be sent to—"

"It was an accident." He cuts her off and wedges himself into his seat.

I watch to see what she'll do—hopefully kick him out again. She inhales a sharp breath and clicks her nails on her desk. Then she exhales and says, "Be more careful in the future."

Everybody else exhales too.

"Today we're going to work on our writing skills," Ms. Finnegan announces. "Everyone, please open your notebooks and write a page that answers the question . . ." She pauses and points to the whiteboard. "What's a challenge you've faced, and how did you deal with it? You have twenty minutes to write. After that you'll get the chance to read your essays aloud."

The class responds with a collective groan, and little beads of sweat begin to trickle all over my skin. What challenge can I write about that won't be mortifying to read out loud?

I've barely written half a page about getting lost in the mall at six years old when Ms. Finnegan calls: "Time's up. Who wants to go first?"

Oona raises her hand, stands, and reads about how hard she trained for a horseback riding competition over the summer. "When I didn't make the final cut, I was furious with the judges, my horse, myself—everybody and everything. But I learned a good lesson: No matter how much you want something, you don't always get it. Sometimes, even though you try your hardest, you fall on your butt. After a good cry, I pulled myself up, got back in the saddle, and I'm trying again—training for the next competition. And I'm getting some help from an animal communicator." She grins at Zoey. "I'm keeping my hopes up."

"Thank you, Oona, that was lovely," says Ms. Finnegan. Everybody claps. Scruggs neighs like a horse.

Zoey raises her hand next. I wonder if she'll talk about her parents' separation, but instead she reads about how hard it was to leave behind her friends in Austin.

"I cried a lot," she says. "I wish I could've brought them with me. But my mom told me the best way to deal with having to say goodbye to friends is by making new ones. So that's what I'm doing." She smiles at Oona, Noah, and me. Everyone claps again. Scruggs roars a huge yawn.

Noah goes next. I thought he would read about getting picked on for being gender-fluid, but he tells us about playing soccer in grade school: "People made fun of me because my kick was all wrong. Nobody wanted me on their team. I didn't want to play anymore, but then I thought, *If I give up, I'm letting the haters win.* So I asked the best player in my class to show me what I was doing wrong. I was scared he wouldn't help me, but he did. The way he taught me worked really well. At the next game, I played the best ever. I made my teammates, my parents, and, most importantly, myself proud. Lesson? Don't let others bring you down. Ask for help. And believe you can do it."

Everybody claps, except Scruggs, who yells out, "You still kick like a girl."

"Mr. Scruggs," says Ms. Finnegan. "Since you're so eager to speak, you can go next."

He nearly tips back in his chair. "All right," he says, regaining his balance. "The biggest challenge—"

Ms. Finnegan interrupts. "On your feet, please."

Shooting her a dirty look, Scruggs stands up. "The biggest challenge I've faced was when my baby sister, Ashley, died."

The room turns quiet as a grave. Is he serious? Maybe he's making another stupid joke. He pauses and stares defiantly at us before continuing.

"I was seven years old, and Ashley was four. People always said she was cute as a doll. She was funny, and I loved her a lot. We used to play games together all the time."

Everybody in class looks at each other. A whole other non-jerk side to Scruggs seems to be peeking out.

"Sometimes, while Ma and Pa worked, I would babysit her. We were watching TV one afternoon when she went to use the bathroom. After a while, I realized it had been a long time, and she hadn't come back. I went to look for her and saw the door to the driveway was open. It was dark outside, so I yelled for her: 'Ashley . . . ? Ashley?'"

Scruggs stops to swallow, and it's clear he's getting choked up. Ms. Finnegan quietly says, "You don't have to continue."

Wiping his nose, he goes on reading. "They were building a new house next door on the empty lot where we used to play. The basement had just been dug, and somebody left the construction fence gate open. I looked over the edge. Ashley was lying on the cement floor. Her body didn't look right. Her legs were sticking out wrong. I shouted, 'Ashley . . . ? Ashley?' But she didn't move."

His voice trembles. His eyes stay glued to his paper. "I called nine-one-one like you're supposed to, and the EMTs rushed her to the hospital, but she was dead. I didn't want to tell my pa, but I had to. He yelled at me for not looking after her. When I tried to explain, he wouldn't listen. He still won't. And my ma stares at me like I'm some sort of murderer. Nobody wants to hear me." His jaw quivers as he stares down at his page. "Nobody ever wants to listen."

Ms. Finnegan gently clears her throat. "*We're* listening."

Scruggs glances up, eyes wet, ready to break into sobs. The entire class is watching him.

"Stop staring!" he bursts out, crumpling the page in his fists. "I don't need you—I don't need any of you!"

All eyes swing to Ms. Finnegan. She presses her fingertips to her desk. "I'm very sorry—"

"I don't want anybody to feel sorry for me." He drops into his seat. "Stop staring."

We all turn away.

"Very well," Ms. Finnegan says. "Who would like to go next?"

No hands go up. Everybody is too blown away. What

kind of parents leave a seven-year-old in charge of a four-year-old and then blame him for what happened? Even though I don't want to, I feel bad for Scruggs.

I duck down, hoping Ms. Finnegan won't call on me. When somebody finally stands and reads, I'm too lost in my thoughts to pay attention.

CHAPTER 28

I'm still thinking about Scruggs when I stop in the restroom later on my way to lunch. And there he is, knocking the books out of Noah's hand. The stack slams to the floor as Scruggs clutches Noah by the shirt and lifts him up against the wall.

"Let me go," Noah says, his feet paddling the air as he tries to squirm away.

Scruggs has him pinned. "You ain't going nowhere. Give me your money."

All the other boys have cleared out. Maybe I should too and race to find a hall monitor. But meanwhile Scruggs might hurt Noah.

"Let him go!" I shout, straining to keep my voice steady.

Scruggs whirls around. Noah's face floods with relief.

"*You?*" Scruggs sneers, his contorted face reminding me

of a comic-book villain. "What do you think you're going to do?"

I have no idea, except that I can't simply stand by while Noah gets clobbered.

So I do what I've seen heroes do in a thousand different comics: I put up my dukes, knot up my brow, and clench my jaw into my toughest, meanest look.

Scruggs's grimace transforms into a smirk. "Seriously?" He lets Noah drop and squares off to face me, wadding up his fists.

My body hums with adrenaline as I lean back, adjusting my foothold.

He snorts. "Yeah, you'd better run."

"I'm not running." Although I want to, I know that if I run, next time it will be me jammed against the wall.

Scruggs charges at me, swinging. I duck. His knuckles whiz past my ear so close I hear the *whoosh!*

Noah shouts, "Guys, cut it out!"

I dodge to the side. Scruggs stumbles forward. His face hangs in front of me—a clear shot. All I have to do is swing my fist, but I don't. I guess I'm scared it would only make him madder.

When Scruggs lunges toward me again, I do the only other thing I can think of: I open my fist into a little set of doggie jaws. "*Tzzt!*" I nip him in the side.

His body twitches as if zapped. "Hey, what the—"

As he swings at me again, I duck and poke him in the tender spot beneath the ribs. *"Tzzt!"*

He leaps back, still swinging at me. "Cut it out. Are you crazy?"

Maybe I am, because each time Scruggs swings, my pincher hands snap at him. *"Tzzt! Tzzt!"*

"Quit it." He twists, trying to shield his soft undersides, but it's no use. He crumples to his knees, giggling.

"What's going on?" a voice booms behind us.

I whirl around. In the doorway stands Coach Craddock, the science teacher and soccer coach—a big, gruff ex-Army guy.

I drop my doggie-jaw hands. Scruggs scrambles to his feet. It's Noah who finally speaks up. "They were just kidding around."

What? No way, I think. Although Noah's eyes signal me to be quiet, I tell Coach, "Scruggs took a swing at me."

"You jabbed *me,"* Scruggs counters.

The bell rings, and Coach shifts his gaze between Scruggs, Noah, and me. "Next time you *all* get detention. Now get to class or lunch—wherever you're supposed to be."

Scruggs brushes past me, muttering under his breath: "I'll get you, wacko."

I open my mouth to answer, but Noah tugs my arm, pulling me away. Coach follows Scruggs out while I help Noah collect his books.

"Why'd you say we were kidding around?" I ask. "You can't let Scruggs get away with that. He was going to hurt you."

"What's the school going to do?" Noah says. We finish gathering his stuff and head to the cafeteria. "You've seen what happens when Ms. Finnegan kicks him out of class—he's back the next day, same as before. If I rat on him, he'll pick on me even worse. I've been through this before. Snitches get stitches."

"What about your soccer story?" I ask. "What you said about reaching out for help?"

"That's a *game*, Jorge. Everybody plays by the same rules. In real life, everybody's got their own ideas and different rules."

I'd never looked at it that way, but gauging by Scruggs and his dad, I think Noah might be right.

CHAPTER 29

"Hi, Jorge." Zoey saved a seat for me at her lunch table. She pats it and smiles at me. For the first time in my life I have an honest-to-goodness girlfriend to sit and joke and laugh with.

"Scruggs tried to shake me down for money in the restroom," Noah tells the group. He describes my near fistfight with Scruggs. "But Jorge fended him off. He was awesome."

Blushing, I explain to everybody about the doggie jaws. To demonstrate, I poke Zoey.

She wriggles and laughs. "That's not meant for people."

"Did you guys tell Coach what happened?" Darnell asks.

"I didn't want to snitch," Noah says. "What's the school going to do? My last principal always blamed *me* for getting picked on. She said I made myself a target by wearing makeup and that I should act more like a boy."

"That's ridiculous," says Oona. "No one thinks it's weird when a girl wears pants or a baseball cap. Why can't a guy put on makeup or wear a skirt?"

From across the table, Chang and Darnell peer at me, waiting for me to say something. I glance down at my spaghetti and slurp up a mouthful.

"Did you know girls had to fight for the right to dress like boys?" says Savannah. "My granny told me when she was in high school, she and her friends weren't allowed to wear pants or shorts. They had to campaign to change the dress code. Now guys need to fight for their right to dress like girls."

"It's a lonely battle," says Noah. "Sometimes at home I go full girl. My parents have gotten used to it. But if I came to school in a dress, goons like Scruggs would kick the caca out of me."

"It shouldn't be such a big deal," Zoey says. "Who cares how you want to dress?"

"What about bathrooms?" asks one of Oona's friends. "And locker rooms? I'd feel weird sharing that space with a guy. Even if he was dressed like a girl."

"Trust me," Noah says. "If I came in, you'd have nothing to worry about."

"I don't mean you," the girl says. "I mean some creep."

"You seriously think some guy is going to dress and act like a girl in front of the whole school just to get into your restroom?" Darnell asks.

While the group debates, Chang eyes me. I reply with a look: *I only agreed to tell Zoey, not our entire group.* There would be no going back from a public announcement. It would follow me through the rest of school—until the end of time. I return to shoveling my spaghetti.

"My cousin helped start a gender and sexuality alliance at her school in Dallas," says Zoey. "Maybe we could do something like that here."

"What does that mean?" Savannah asks. "What would we do?"

"The group was mostly kids with gay friends or relatives," Zoey says. "They helped stop bullying and make school safer for everyone. They even got the principal to set up a gender-neutral restroom. My cousin said only the girls use it, though. The boys are too scared."

"Count me in," says Oona. "I'll invite a friend who's questioning."

The other girls chime in, mentioning lesbian and gay friends.

"Would you guys come?" Noah asks Chang, Darnell, and me.

"Come on, boys," Zoey says. "The group shouldn't be only girls."

"Sure, I'll come," Chang says. "I've got an aunt who's bi."

"You *do*?" I nearly choke on a spaghetti noodle. "You never mentioned that."

"She lives in Seattle," he says, as if that explains anything. "She used to be married to a guy. Now she's married to a woman."

What a weasel, I think. *All this time he's been pressuring me—*

"Jorge, what about you?" Zoey asks.

Chang, Darnell, and everybody else at the table glance toward me. My cheeks flame. To admit having gay friends or relatives is one thing, but to reveal my dad is a trans woman is like comparing berries and apples. I go for the berries.

"Sure, um . . . my dad's cousin is gay."

"You never mentioned that," Chang mimics me. "Anybody *else* you want to tell us about?"

Why can't he let up? This isn't his secret—it's not about him. Why can't he just let me say it when I'm ready? I imagine dumping my spaghetti bowl on his head, but even that probably wouldn't make him lay off.

If Zoey is going to find out about Norma, it's better she hears it from me. Even if I'm not ready. Even if telling her at a whole table full of people in the middle of the cafeteria is the worst possible time.

Slowly, I turn to her, open my mouth . . . and shut it again. My throat feels dry. My lungs feel as though invisible arms are squeezing them. I force myself to inhale the hardest breath of my life.

"Well . . . my dad . . . is trans."

The entire group stops eating. It seems like the whole lunchroom goes silent. The only sound is the blood pounding in my ears.

"Your *dad?*" Zoey asks in a small, surprised voice.

I make my head nod yes. And Oona's friend who freaked at the thought of a guy using the girls' bathroom exclaims, "Holy cannoli!"

"But . . ." Oona says. She stops, then starts again. "At school events your dad always looks . . . *normal.* I mean . . . he looks like a guy."

"She only came out this past summer," I explain. "My dad, I mean."

"Wow," Noah says. "I've never seen a trans person in real life—only on TV and videos."

"Maybe she could kick-start our group as a guest speaker," says Savannah.

"I bet the entire school would show up," Oona says.

"Whoa-whoa-whoa!" I hold up my hands and edge back. The idea of my dad coming to school as a woman sends me into panic overdrive. "Wait, slow down a minute."

Everybody grows hushed, and I return to Zoey. Her sky-blue eyes have turned cloudy.

"I wanted to tell you," I explain, "but I was waiting for the right moment. Every time I started to tell you, I thought . . . I was worried you wouldn't like me."

"Just because your dad is trans?"

"I was scared you wouldn't want to go out with me if people thought I was . . . a freak."

"Jorge, anybody who would think that is a jerk. I don't care about those people. I care about *you*."

I slump in my seat. "Are you mad at me?"

She looks disappointed. "I told you I needed you to be honest, didn't I?"

"I was going to tell you this afternoon," I insist. "Honest."

She doesn't look like she believes me. I don't know if I believe me either. With my gaze I beg Darnell to rescue me. *Do something.*

"Jorge wanted to tell you," he says, nudging Chang for backup.

"True that," Chang says.

"*Both* you guys knew about his dad?" Zoey asks.

"We accidentally saw him," says Darnell. "I mean *her*. Each of us, separately."

"Blew me out of the water," Chang says. "But I got over it."

"So if your friends understood," Zoey says to me, "why didn't you think I would?"

"Well . . . because you and I barely know each other. And I've never had a girlfriend before. Not really."

"Coming out can be hard," Noah interjects. "Even if you're coming out about someone else. My parents aren't always very gung ho about telling their friends about me."

Zoey raises her fork and pushes her salad around her plate. "Jorge, I'm not saying you should've told me right away. And I'm not saying you should tell everybody. We've all got private stuff. But if I'm your girlfriend, you're supposed to trust me and be honest. I told you about *my* parents."

It's not the same thing, I think. Before I can say that, the end-of-lunch bell cuts the air like a siren. And over the ensuing roar of students getting up, I blurt out, "Can you guys please not tell anyone about my dad? If word gets out, it could sink Cesar's election."

"We won't tell," says Oona, and everybody agrees.

Chairs scrape the floor. Plates clatter. People pick up their trays. I stay in my seat, not wanting to go anywhere except maybe beneath the table to curl up and hide.

Zoey is the only one who stays, like she's waiting for me to say more.

"I'm sorry I didn't tell you," I say. "I promise not to hold back anything like that again. Ever."

Her expression softens a little, giving me hope.

"Besides," I go on, "that was my only real secret. Apart from that, I'm really pretty boring."

For an instant, Zoey looks as if she might smile. But then she looks away, lining up her silverware neatly on her tray. "Maybe you're right, Jorge. We barely know each other. Maybe we've moved too fast. I'm sorry too, but I'm not sure I'm ready for a boyfriend."

My stomach slips. There has to be some way to fix this. Desperate, I joke, "Well, I'm not *that* boring."

Her face stays serious. "I need to think about all this. Okay?"

I grit my teeth. I shouldn't have joked. "Okay."

Zoey picks up her tray and heads to the return window. Seeing I'm alone, Darnell and Chang make their way back over and stand at the end of the table, waiting for me. I rise and join them.

"Good," Chang says. "Now it's all out in the open."

"*Good?*" I slam my tray back down on the table. "That was a disaster. She doesn't want go out with me now."

"I tried to warn you," Chang says. "You needed to tell her."

"Gentlemen?" says Darnell. "Let it rest. It's done."

I glare at Chang. "Why didn't you ever say anything about your aunt?" I jab my finger in his face. "You're a two-faced weasel."

"Hey, don't try to turn this on me."

"Guys, do you hear me?" Darnell says. "Leave it alone. It's over. Finito."

"You wanted this to happen," I say, smacking my hands against Chang's chest. "You kept pushing me."

"Jorge, hold on." Darnell wedges his arms between us.

Chang dodges around him and pushes me back. "Keep your paws to yourself."

Suddenly we're shoving past Darnell, grabbing each other while Darnell tries to pry us apart. "Guys, break it up!" he shouts.

Chang stumbles, knocking the metal chair beside him to the floor. I trip, and he grabs ahold of me. We hit the floor, one on top of the other. Writhing. Wrestling. Kicking and punching. My fist connects with his jaw. Chang's knuckles fly at my face.

"Stop!" Darnell yells. "Cut it out! Stop!"

A cafeteria monitor fights to separate us. More hands grasp our arms. The next thing I know, Chang and I are being whisked down the hall toward the nurse's office.

CHAPTER 30

In the nurse's office mirror, my swollen eye makes it look like I'm winking. My cheek shines bright pink, and my head throbs. Every inch of me aches.

Chang sits on a cot a few feet away, cringing as the nurse swabs his gashed lip with alcohol.

"Principal Richter wants to see you both," the nurse says. She's speaking gently, but inside my skull, it sounds like she's shouting. She hands us each a cold ice pack.

I avoid making eye contact with Chang as the nurse walks us to the principal's office. I'm still too angry at him. Plus my thoughts are stuck on Zoey. How could she dump me so easily? Doesn't she understand how hard it was for me to open up about my dad?

I wish I could talk to Cesar about it—like we used to talk in the old days. But what's he going to say when I tell him I told my entire group about Norma?

"You can keep the ice packs as long as you need them," the nurse says when we arrive at the main office. "Just leave them with the receptionist when you're done."

Mr. Richter greets us in his doorway. "Looks like you fellas did some serious damage to each other." He motions us to the chairs across from his desk.

Chang sinks into one and presses his ice pack to his lip. I slouch into the other and hold mine to my cheek.

"Fighting on campus is a very serious violation of school rules," Mr. Richter says, taking his seat. "I'd like to hear what happened. Who wants to start?"

Chang levels his gaze at me. I sit up, braced to defend myself if he blames me. To my surprise, he stays quiet. Is he feeling sorry? With his silence, my anger starts to lessen— not completely, I'm not *totally* letting him off the hook for hounding me to the breaking point. But his gashed lip, glistening under the overhead lights, sets off a pang of guilt in my chest. Even though what he did was wrong, I shouldn't have gotten physical with him.

"Come now, boys," says Mr. Richter. "I don't have all day. If neither of you speaks up, I'll have to suspend you both. Is that what you want?"

Although Chang stays silent, his dark-brown eyes urge me to talk.

"I shoved him and things took off from there," I finally admit. "Chang was just defending himself."

"Why did you shove him?" Mr. Richter asks me.

"Because—" I stop myself, not wanting to go into the whole thing about Zoey—and especially not about Norma. "I was mad at him. I lost my temper."

Chang relaxes a little, but Mr. Richter isn't done. He leans toward me in his swivel chair. "What made you mad at Chang?"

I stay silent, and Mr. Richter sighs. "How about you, Chang? What's your side of it?"

"Like Jorge said, he pushed me, and I defended myself. But we shouldn't have gotten into a fight."

"But *why* did Jorge push you? What was the fight about?"

Chang shrugs. "That's for Jorge to tell you."

I shift my ice pack over my eye and keep quiet.

"All right," Mr. Richter says. "Chang, you can return to class. Jorge, you stay so we can talk alone."

As Chang leaves, I give him a little nod of thanks for not blabbing the whole story. He shrugs, as if keeping quiet was no big deal.

So why didn't he feel the same way about keeping quiet with Zoey?

"So, what's going on, Jorge?" Mr. Richter asks when we're alone. "Usually when a person lashes out, there's something bigger going on beneath the surface."

I squirm in my chair. With his bald, egg-shaped head and penetrating stare, Mr. Richter reminds me of Professor X, the super-telepath with extraordinary mind-reading powers. I just hope he can't read my mind now.

"Does it have to do with a girl?" he asks. "Or something going on at home?"

Both, I think and shift the ice pack to my skull, blocking his intrusions. "I don't want to talk about it."

"Very well," he says. "But if you decide to talk, my door is always open."

I glance across the room. His door is closed.

"The penalty for fighting is three days' suspension," he says. "Your mom or dad will need to come pick you up."

The pounding in my head instantly escalates. "My mom!" I blurt out.

Mr. Richter gives me a puzzled look. "Isn't your dad the one who usually comes to parent-teacher days?"

I swallow the knot in my throat. "Yeah, but my dad's really busy with work and stuff lately. I know he won't be able to come." Although I say *he* on purpose, it feels weird now that I've gotten used to saying *she*.

Mr. Richter studies me, one eyebrow raised. "Jorge, is there some reason you don't want your dad to come in?"

A sense of doom oozes through me. I shift the ice pack down over my brow and close my eyes.

"Jorge?" Mr. Richter asks. "What's this about?"

The ice feels cool and soothing on my eyelids. I imagine a teletransporter dismantling my body atom by atom, beaming me up into space, and rematerializing me beneath my bed.

"Jorge . . . ?" Mr. Richter repeats.

I peek out from under the icepack. The principal's face looks grim. I need to come up with something. Maybe just part of the truth would be enough. "My mom and dad separated."

"Oh." Mr. Richter's brow softens. "I didn't know that. I'm very sorry, Jorge. When did that happen?"

"Over the summer."

"Is your dad still in the area?"

"Yes, sir."

"Well, then, I'd like to meet with both your parents."

"Can't my mom just come in? *Please?*"

Mr. Richter takes a breath and lets out a long, loud sigh. "What's her number?"

I rattle it off from memory, but it's not until Mr. Richter is dialing that I remember Mom's big meeting today.

What if she doesn't answer? I think. *Please answer*, I pray as Mr. Richter holds the phone to his ear and waits. *Please, please—*

"Hi, Mrs. Fuerte? This is Principal Richter from Lone Star Middle School. How are you today?"

While he talks, the ice pack condensation trickles down my face like tears at a funeral.

"I'm fine, thanks," says Mr. Richter. "But I regret to tell

you that your son, Jorge, got into a fight. . . . yes, a physical fight . . ." He glances at my bruised face. "He seems okay except for a black eye. . . . I agree—we take incidents like this very seriously. I'd like for you to come in to discuss it. . . . That would be wonderful. I look forward to seeing you."

As he hangs up, I wipe my wet, ice-cold face.

"She's on her way," Mr. Richter says. "You can wait in the reception area."

CHAPTER 31

I slump into a chair, my head throbbing. The waiting area outside the principal's office is like a big, human-sized fish tank. A floor-to-ceiling glass wall looks onto the school's main lobby, beyond which you can see out to the parking lot and road.

While I'm waiting, a handful of students wander into the lobby and start setting up election campaign tables, preparing to canvass students after classes let out. I recognize a couple of Cesar's friends unfolding a *Cesar Fever* sign for their table, but there's no sign of my brother.

My head pounds harder as I think about what'll happen if somebody from my group spills the beans about Dad before I have the chance to warn Cesar. I'm busy imagining the worst when Mom's minivan comes racing down the street, kicking up a cloud of fallen leaves. And inside my chest, my heart speeds up.

The car swings into a visitor parking space and lurches to a stop. I perch at the edge of my seat as Mom climbs out and strides toward the building, eyes narrowed. She flings open the lobby door, rockets past the campaign students like a guided missile, spots me through the glass wall, and locks onto her target.

I scan the waiting area for someplace to take cover and, finding none, shield my face with the cold ice pack.

"No use trying to hide," Mom says, bursting through the door. "Let me see."

"It's no big deal."

"No? Then why am I here?" Gripping my chin with her manicured fingers, she pushes aside the ice pack and examines my swollen eye. "For goodness sake. Does it hurt?"

"Some."

She shovels around the junk in her handbag and pulls out the little bottle of chewable pain reliever she always keeps handy for Cesar and me. "Here." She pours a couple into my palm.

I chomp down on the bubblegum-flavored tablets, and Mom tosses one into her own mouth before turning to the young receptionist behind the counter. "I'm Jorge's mother, here to see Mr. Richter."

While the receptionist phones him, Mom turns back to me. "Before we go in, I want to hear what happened. Who was the fight with?"

"Chang."

Mom's eyes spring wide with surprise. "Your *best friend* Chang? Is he okay?"

"His lip's bleeding, that's all."

"That's *all?*"

"Yeah, we're fine now, everything's fine." It's not the full truth—I still need to sort things out with Chang—but I'm trying to calm Mom down.

"Everything's *not* fine, Jorge. Fistfights are *not* fine." She pulls the ice pack away from my face. "Are you hearing me?"

"Yes."

"Good. So what got into you? What was the fight about?"

"He kept badgering me to tell Zoey about Dad."

Mom looks up to the ceiling, shaking her head. "I knew this would be about your dad."

"Can you please not say anything about Norma to Mr. Richter?" I whisper.

Before Mom can answer, the principal opens his door. "Hi, Mrs. Fuerte. Thanks for coming in."

We follow him into the office and take our seats across from his desk. After they finish chit-chatting, Mr. Richter says, "I explained to Jorge the seriousness of fighting on school grounds."

"Or *anywhere,*" Mom says to me. "You know better than to get into a fistfight. Promise me this'll never happen again. *Ever.*"

"Yes, ma'am."

"I fully agree with you," Mr. Richter says. "Jorge wouldn't tell me what brought on the fight. However, he did mention that you and your husband recently separated. I'm sorry to hear that. I wonder if it might be part of what's troubling Jorge."

The throbbing in my head takes a sudden spike. I beg Mom with my eyes to please, please, *please* not say anything about Norma. She refuses to look my way.

"It's been a difficult time for all of us," Mom finally says and turns to me. "But that's no excuse for fistfights."

"Indeed," says Mr. Richter. "In this case, the penalty is a three-day suspension."

I hope Mom will argue against the suspension, but instead she nods and tells me, "I hope you learn your lesson."

"Yes, let's hope so," Mr. Richter says and rolls his chair back from his desk. "Jorge can return to school on Friday. Now, if you'll excuse me—"

Suddenly it hits me. "What about the talent show Thursday night?" I interrupt. "Can I come?" Even though Zoey dumped me, I hope she's still planning to perform with Peppy.

"I'm sorry, Jorge," says Mr. Richter. "You're not allowed on school grounds during the suspension."

"But my dog will be in the show. Please?" Desperate, I turn to Mom.

For a moment, her lips purse like she's thinking. "It would mean a lot to us," she finally tells Mr. Richter. "The show is a family tradition."

Mr. Richter leans away from his desk. His gaze travels between Mom and me as he mulls it over. "I suppose we could make an exception for that one event. You can come to the show, Jorge, but other than that you're to remain off campus. The receptionist will give you instructions to access your class assignments online."

"Thank you, Mr. Richter," Mom says and gives me a stern look.

I guess what she's thinking and say, "Thanks, Mr. Richter."

He nods, and we stand to leave the office. I practically have to run to keep up with Mom as she hurries to the mini-van. "Thank you too, Mom," I say as I race after her.

"Don't think you're getting off that easy," she answers. "I'm very disappointed in you. As of now, you're grounded. No leaving the house. Understand?"

"Yes, ma'am."

Mom digs through her handbag, pulls out her phone, and dictates a text as we climb into the car: "He got a three-day suspension. You need to talk to him. I'm bringing him now."

I can guess where she's taking me—Norma's. "I don't want to talk to her!" I protest. "This is all her fault."

"No, Jorge." Mom jams the key into the ignition. "Your dad didn't punch Chang, you did."

"Yeah, but none of this would've happened if—"

"Stop blaming your dad!" Mom cuts me off. "Take responsibility. You two need to hash this out, and I need to get back to work. I don't want to hear any more about it."

I slink back in the seat and keep my mouth shut the rest of the way.

CHAPTER 32

"I don't want to talk about it," I complain to Norma.

We're in her kitchen. She's setting out chips and salsa while I sit at the table, arms crossed. For once, I don't feel like eating chips.

"Too bad, mijo," she says. "We need to talk about what happened."

"Fine, you want to know what happened? Chang kept nagging me to tell Zoey about you, so I finally did, and she dumped me. I was so mad at Chang that I pushed him. That's what started the fight."

"Zoey dumped you because of *me*?" Norma asks.

"No. Because I hadn't told her about you, even though I've only known her a week, and I *was* going to tell her."

Norma's mouth flattens into a tight, thin line.

"Go ahead," I mutter. "Say 'I told you so.' You happy now?"

"No, Jorge, I'm not happy. I'm very sorry this happened. I know this is all very upsetting to you."

"No, you don't." I sit up. "You have no idea how hard this is. I feel like a freak. Every night I go to sleep wishing that all of this was just a bad nightmare, and everything will be back to normal when I wake up."

"Things can't go back, mijo. I thought you understood that. I can't live that way anymore."

"It's always about you! *You* get to have a new life. *You* get to be who you really are. What about the rest of us? Did you ever stop to think how this might affect *us*?"

"Of course I did. More than you'll ever know. That's a huge part of why I'm doing this. So I can stick around for you and Cesar, so I can keep being your—"

"Stop saying that! Cesar's right—you're not our dad anymore. Our dad's *dead*."

Norma flinches as though I've struck her. I turn away, too angry to take the words back.

For a long time, we sit in silence. I feel Norma's gaze on me. I keep mine aimed down, fighting the guilt that tugs at me.

"Do you wish I'd finished this?" Norma asks.

I look up as she raises her right hand, shaking the blouse sleeve up her forearm. Thin pink scars crisscross her brown skin, slicing across her veins, a reminder of last year's shaving incident.

"You and Mom said that was an accident."

"Mijo, who cuts their wrists shaving? You think the paramedics hustled me to the hospital in the middle of the night for a *shaving* cut?"

My skin goes cold, goosebumps spreading. I still remember that night. Mom worked late, so Dad made dinner and watched TV with Cesar and me. After we got ready for bed, Dad came up and kissed us goodnight. Nothing unusual in that, except he told us like four times how much he loved us. Finally we both yelled, "We know, Dad!"

It was still night when Cesar and I woke to Mom screaming and calling 911. The EMTs came and rushed Dad away.

Cesar and I were terrified—we didn't understand what the heck was going on—but Mom would only say that Dad had accidentally cut himself shaving. Her explanation seemed weird, and Dad didn't return from the hospital until later that week. He and Mom both backed away from discussing what had happened. It had been an accident, they said, nothing more.

Cesar didn't want to talk about it either, so eventually I gave up asking questions. But now I realize my worst fears— the things I'd been afraid to think—were right.

A shiver runs through me. "You tried to kill yourself?"

Norma stares down at the table. Silent. Avoiding my eyes. I wrap my arms around my chest, waiting. Already guessing the answer.

"Are you sure you want to hear this?" she finally asks.

I barely nod, not at all sure.

Norma glances out the window, runs a hand across her skirt, and returns her eyes to me. "I couldn't see any way out, mijo. I loved your mom. I loved you and Cesar. I loved being your dad. At the same time, the woman inside me was fighting to come out. I felt torn in two directions. When I tried to explain it to your mom, she asked me to wait until you and Cesar finished high school. But I couldn't go on living a lie. Every day I hated myself more and more. Finally something in me snapped."

While she speaks, I sit absolutely still. But inside my mind, I'm reeling. Dad has always been my hero. What if she'd actually gone through with it? How could she even have tried?

"You said you'd always be here for us."

"I know." She slides her blouse sleeve back over her wrist. "I didn't really want to kill myself. I wanted to kill the *pain*. I was hurting so bad I had to do *something*. It was a foolish cry for help." Her red lips slowly curl into an impish smile. "Looking back, the whole thing seems like a bad opera scene."

She must think the joke will help me deal with the shock of what she's saying, but it backfires, reigniting my anger.

"You always want to make a joke. This isn't funny! None of it is. You've made me hate my life. Hate myself. Hate *you*."

I shove my chair back and stand up. I have to get away from her, or I'm going to explode.

"Jorge, stop." Norma stands up after me. "I'm sorry I made a joke. I know this is hard for you, but please hear me out."

"Hear what?" I shout and start out of the room. "More lies?"

"No, the truth." Her flats clack behind me on the hardwood floor. "I'm sorry I lied about cutting myself. I'm sorry I lied about all of this. I wanted to protect you. But I've never lied about loving you and Cesar and Mom."

I stop at the front door and whirl around to face her. "You don't love us. If you did, you wouldn't have done this."

"Jorge, don't you understand? I'm not just doing this for me. I'm doing it so I can stay alive for you and Cesar and Mom." She grabs my arm, stopping me from opening the door. "I'm doing this for *all* of us."

"Let go!" I pull my arm and push her away. "Get off of me."

"No." She throws her thick arms around me. "Not until you listen."

I struggle, but Norma is bigger and stronger. She won't let go. Our breath comes fast. Her chest rises and falls against mine. I swing out, punching her.

Instantly I recoil—I've never hit my dad.

But Norma barely budges. "Go ahead," she says. "I can take it."

Furious, I slug her again—harder—then again—even harder.

"That's good." She stands steady. "Get it all out. Go ahead and hate me for what I'm doing. But don't hate yourself."

As I pound my fists against her, tears rise in my throat. I swallow tight to keep them down.

"Do you hear me?" she asks, still taking my blows. "You've done nothing wrong. You're not a freak. You're the best son a dad could have."

"You're lying again." I stop swinging and drop my fists. "Just like before."

"Jorge, how am I lying? You have always been a wonderful son."

"No!" The tears spring onto my cheeks. "I should've seen you were hurting. I should've helped you." The salt stings my bruises as I bury my face in her shoulder. "I didn't know you were hurting. I'm sorry."

"Shh, mijo," she says, gently patting my back. "There's nothing you could've done. I had to come to terms with this on my own. I never wanted to hurt you."

"Well, guess what?" I say, teary-eyed and snot-nosed. "You hurt me anyway."

"I know, and I'm sorry. I'm very, very sorry. I hope you can forgive me."

I gulp, sobbing. "How can I trust you won't try some-thing like that again?"

"Because that time is over. I've accepted who I am: a woman . . . and your dad. The question is, can *you* accept me?"

Her face is wet with tears. Black mascara tiger stripes streak down her cheeks.

"I don't want to hate you," I say.

"Glad to hear it," she says. "But even if you do, I still love you. I always will."

We stand together for a long while, neither of us say-ing anything, holding each other while our breath falls into sync. Dad's arms encircle me, just like they always have.

"I need to tell you something," I say, pulling away. "Do you remember at the gas station—the boy in the truck?" Norma nods, and I continue. "He's in my class. I didn't want him to see me with you. That's why I didn't get out of the car. I'm sorry."

Norma hands me a tissue from the side table. "Well, can I tell you something? If you *had* gotten out of the car, I would've shooed you back inside."

"I could've at least tried to help you," I say.

"I'm glad you didn't," she says. "Don't be so hard on yourself. We're both learning."

She takes a deep breath. "How about those chips and salsa now?"

I blow my nose and nod. I'm starving.

As we sit in the kitchen, the family photos Norma stuck on the fridge door make me think about Mom. "I want to ask you something else," I say.

"Ask me anything," Norma says. "Just be open to hearing the answer."

I hesitate. Then I go ahead. "Shouldn't you have told Mom about . . . you know . . . the woman thing *before* you got married?"

"I did tell her."

"You *did?*" I sit stunned. "So then . . . why'd she marry you? I mean . . ."

"Well . . . you should probably ask *her* that. But I think we both imagined love could fix me . . . cure my 'problem.'" She says it with air quotes. "We hoped love would get us through it. And in some ways it has . . . just not the way we thought. I might not have made it without her." Norma waits for my response. "Any other questions?"

"No. That's all."

CHAPTER 33

"Do you want to come do your schoolwork at my place while you're suspended?" Norma asks when she drives me home.

"Thanks. Can I let you know?"

"Okay, but you need to do your assignments."

"I know. I will."

We pull into the driveway, and I stay in my seat, looking toward Cesar's room. School will let out soon, he'll come home, and I'll need to fess up about blabbing to my group about Norma.

"Can I tell you a secret?" I ask her.

"Absolutely. You can tell me anything."

"Cesar is using skin whitener."

Norma nods. "I know. He left the jar on his dresser one time." She bites her lip for a moment, like she's keeping something back. "Can I tell *you* a secret?"

"Sure." I nod eagerly.

"When I was younger, I tried to whiten my skin too," she says.

I look at her in surprise. "Why?" I ask.

Norma blushes like she's embarrassed. "It was part of not liking who I was inside. I thought if I could change my skin color, I might like myself more and then other people would like me more too. I'd be happy." She shakes her head. "Oh, the lengths we'll go to try to pretzel ourselves into becoming somebody else. Maybe you and Cesar should talk about that."

"You guys should too," I say.

She nods.

I press back into the seat, feeling sad. I'm not sure why exactly. Sad for her, sad for Cesar, sad for me. I yawn, suddenly sleepy.

"Talk to you later," I tell Norma. I hug her and step up the walkway toward Peppy's excited bark welcoming me home. He greets me, tail wagging, body quivering, tongue flapping all over my face. Dashing across the room, he brings a gift—a sock I thought I'd lost.

"Best thing to happen to me all day," I say and let him out to the patio.

I refill his water bowl and am eating the last of Zoey's cookies when my phone chimes. I glance at the clock. School's out.

The text is from Darnell: Hey, how's your eye??? You OK??

My cheek still hurts—my whole body hurts—but I answer, Yeah, I'm OK

Good, Darnell says. What the heck were you thinking getting into a slugfest with Chang?

Me: I know, I know, I shouldn't have . . . but why did he keep pushing me about my dad?

Darnell: True, he was being jerky . . . but you still shouldn't have gotten physical

Me: I said I know.

The hammering inside my head feels like it's getting worse.

TTYL, I type.

After letting Peppy back in, I head upstairs. Even though I'm home alone, I tiptoe down the hallway to Cesar's open door.

On one wall of his room, the shelves are lined with sports trophies: little polished gold-plated figures kicking soccer balls, shooting basketballs, or swinging baseball bats. Another wall is plastered with plaques and awards. Alongside them, a campaign poster reads, *Who's the leader of the pack? Who will keep our school on track? Cesar for President!*

On his desk is a framed photo of him and Victoria at her parents' barbecue last summer. Next to it is a picture of Cesar and me when we were little, taken at the Ol' West photo kiosk beside the Alamo. We got our picture taken wearing cowboy hats, holsters, and boots. A big sheriff's star shines on Cesar's leather vest. A smaller deputy's badge glimmers on mine. He points his six-shooter at the camera while I gaze at him, admiring him like I always have.

Across the room, his bed is neatly made. I kick off my sneakers and climb on top. The pillows smell like Cesar—a mix of musky cologne, soapy shampoo, and a licorice scent I now know comes from his skin-whitening cream.

Lying back, I think about how he and I used to goof off for hours in this room. We would fall asleep watching TV and wake up with our arms and legs so tangled up it was hard to tell whose were whose. I remember the time he asked me to help him secretly build a little opera stage scene out of toothpicks, glue, and cardboard for Dad's birthday. It took a week, and Dad loved it.

What happened to that Cesar—the brother he used to be?

As I lie there thinking, a blanket of weariness spreads over me. My head is still throbbing. My body aches. My eyelids hang heavy. The day's events are catching up with me. And before I know it, I sink into a doze.

The next thing I know, Cesar is shaking my shoulder. "Hey, why are you on my bed?"

I blink my eyelids open. Peppy is standing on the mattress, tail wagging, tags jingling. He rolls over, offering Cesar his tummy.

"Sorry," I say, sitting up.

Cesar stares closely at my face. "What happened to your eye?"

"I got into a fight with Chang."

Cesar yanks his backpack off. "Yeah? What about?"

I might as well get it over with. "Um . . . it sort of came out at lunch that Dad is trans. But everybody promised not to tell."

Cesar flings his backpack down. "'It sort of came out'? *How?* Chang blabbed, didn't he? I knew he would."

I take a breath. "No. It was me."

Cesar's face twists, his eyes bulge. He looks like he's about to morph into the Hulk. All he needs is green makeup. "Why would you tell people?"

"Because I was lying by not saying anything. I needed to let Zoey know about Norma."

"Stop calling Dad that!" Cesar shouts. "He's not a woman. He's a freak and a liar." Before I can duck, he smacks my shoulder.

I pretend it doesn't hurt, but it makes me mad. "No, *you're* the liar. At least she had the guts to *stop* lying. Not like you, trying to make your skin white."

Cesar's eyes pop wide again. "Keep out of my stuff." He raises his fist again, but I grab ahold of his forearm.

Cesar tries to shake me off. "Let go!" He frees his arm and raises his fist again.

"No!" Leaping to my feet, I fling my arms around him. My heart is racing. My mind is racing. Every cell in my body is racing. "I'm not your punching bag."

As Cesar struggles to pull away, Peppy whimpers for us to stop fighting. My heel accidentally tramples his paw, and he yelps. I lose my balance, tipping over, still holding Cesar. Together we topple to the carpet.

Cesar scrambles on top of me, but I shimmy out from under him. He grabs ahold of me, and we wrestle like when we were little. This time I refuse to let him pin me.

We grapple across the room, grunting and groaning. One moment he's on top of me. The next minute, I wrench out from under him. Then his head bangs against the steel bench press—*bam!*

I let go of him. "Are you hurt?"

Cesar sits up, rubbing the back of his head. When he looks at his fingertips, they're wet with blood.

I move toward him. "Let me see."

"Get out of here!" The anger returns to his eyes like two big brown fists.

"Sorry," I say, scooting back with Peppy.

"And stay out!" Cesar shouts. "You're not my brother anymore."

I get to my feet. "Oh, so now you're cutting me out too?

Pretty soon you won't have anybody left except yourself . . . whoever that is."

Cesar takes that in for a moment before yelling, "Go! Get out!"

"Let's go," I tell Peppy.

We're halfway down the hall when Cesar's door slams. When I get to my room, I slam my door just as loudly.

CHAPTER 34

I talked to Cesar, I text Norma from my bed.

And . . . ? she answers. How did it go?

I debate for a moment how to respond. Well . . . we got into a fight. He banged his head on the bench press . . . He's bleeding a little

I'm on my way, Norma says.

I toss my phone down on the bed. At least they're finally going to talk. I just hope *they* don't get physical.

"He's in his room," I tell Norma when she arrives—in a housedress—and heads upstairs with Peppy trailing behind.

"Cesar?" Norma knocks on his door. "Jorge says your head's bleeding."

"I'm fine!" shouts Cesar. "Go away!"

Norma ignores him. "I'm coming in."

"Get out!" Cesar is standing at his mirror, trying to examine his scalp.

"Let me see," Norma says, plowing toward him.

"Leave me alone!" Cesar's eyes burst wide. I realize this is his first time seeing Dad as Norma. He scrambles away from her, climbs onto the bed, and reverses toward the headboard, pressing back almost hard enough to smash through the wall. "Get away from me."

"Cesar, let me look," she says, bearing down on him.

"Get your hands off!"

Cesar tries to pull away, but Norma towers over him, shoving his hands aside. "Stop that, mijo."

"Don't call me that. I'm not your son."

"No? Whose son are you? The pizza delivery guy's?" She grabs Cesar's head between her big fists. "Now, hold still."

Cesar flinches. "Stop it."

"Oh, come on—you're worse than Peppy when he's hurt." She gently separates Cesar's hair between her manicured fingers and examines the wound. "Jorge, go into Mom's bathroom, second drawer on the left. Bring the antibiotic ointment."

I dash down the hall to Mom's bathroom. When I come back, Norma is standing with her hands on her hips, lecturing: "We're still a family. Nothing will ever change that."

Cesar sits covering his ears. "I'm not listening."

I hand Norma the ointment. She squeezes a dab onto her fingers and leans over Cesar. He tries to push her away.

"I can do it," he tells her. "Just back off, okay?"

"No, not okay. I tried backing off the past three months— it hasn't worked. We need to talk this through." While she rubs ointment into his scalp, Cesar crosses his arms.

"I don't want to talk."

"Well, we're going to." Norma plunks down onto the mattress. "I get that you feel hurt, betrayed, angry. I know all about anger. I've been as mad as you—so angry it was destroying me. I know what you're feeling. And I'm very, very sorry."

Cesar brings his knees up to his chest and circles his arms around them. "Saying you're sorry doesn't change anything."

"Maybe not. But I hope it helps you get ahold of your anger and see my point of view. I didn't do this to hurt you, or Jorge, or Mom. I did it because I had to."

"Why couldn't you have waited?" Cesar demands.

"Tell him about the shaving accident," I say, hoping that might help my brother understand.

"What about it?" Cesar asks.

Norma lets out a sigh. "It wasn't an accident." She pushes up her blouse sleeve. "It was a cry for help. I . . . I tried to hurt myself. It was a gesture—only a gesture."

Cesar stares at the zigzag scar, and for a moment, his face

loses some of its anger. Then it goes tight again. "So you were going to ditch us? You're just lie after lie."

Norma tugs her sleeve back down. "Yes, I lied—past tense. Now I've stopped lying. I faced who I am. And you can too. Come on, mijo, you're a better person than this."

Cesar smirks. *"You're* telling me about being a better person?"

"Yes," Norma says. "One thing I've learned through this is it doesn't matter if you wear pants or a skirt. What matters is in here." She pats her heart. "And in here." She taps her head. "What matters is that you take responsibility and face who you are. For you, that means accepting you have a trans dad—whether you want to or not."

Cesar keeps his knees tucked up, looking wounded.

"I know I hurt you," Norma says. "And I'm sorry. Will you forgive me?"

Peppy's ears prick like he's waiting. So am I.

Outside, a car door slams in the driveway. Mom's home. Peppy tears out to the hall, tags tinkling. The rest of us exchange glances.

"Hello?" Mom calls from downstairs.

"We're in Cesar's room!" Norma yells back.

A moment later, Mom appears in the doorway. "Nice to see the three of you in the same room."

Actually, it's the first time since Dad left that we're *all* in the same room.

"What's going on?"

"The boys had a fight," Norma explains, "and Cesar cut his head."

Mom strides straight over to him, flashing me an angry look. "Jorge, what's gotten into you today?"

"*He* started it. I'm sick of him punching me."

"I punched you 'cause you blabbed to your friends at school," Cesar says. "Now everybody's going to find out about . . ." He points his chin at Norma.

Mom bends over Cesar and inspects where the ointment plasters down his hair. "Honey, you know the news about your dad is going to get out whether you want it to or not."

"You could've at least waited till after the election," Cesar mutters at me.

"I tried. I didn't *want* to tell people. But Chang and Darnell already knew—and *they* haven't ditched me. Why can't *you* tell *your* friends?"

"That's Cesar's decision," Mom says. "He's got a right to decide when he wants to tell his friends."

I think about Chang badgering me, and I know Mom is right. But what about *my* right to tell *my* friends if I want to?

"So I have to wait for Cesar before I can tell anybody? That's not fair. I'm sick of all these secrets. Now Dad says you knew about the whole woman thing before you got married."

"*What?*" Cesar cuts in, turning to Mom. "You *knew?*"

Mom sinks into the desk chair, looking annoyed at Norma.

"We need to clear this up," Norma says firmly. "Once and for all."

"All right," Mom says, but she doesn't sound all right— she sounds anxious. "When your dad and I were dating, we shared a lot with each other about ourselves. That's what dating means: getting to know the other person."

Cesar looks like he's about to explode—again. "He *told* you he was trans?"

"Well, not in those exact words. He said that inside he always felt more like a woman than a man." Mom glances at Norma with a mix of sadness and longing. "Am I remembering right?"

Norma nods silently.

Cesar's anger melts into confusion. "So then why . . . why'd you marry him?"

"Because I loved that tender side of him . . . and I admired his honesty. I know that sounds strange now, but it's true. And I thought, *I can deal with this. We can make it work.* And we did." She exhales a breath out the side of her mouth. "Until he couldn't keep the woman inside any longer."

"You know how hard I tried," Norma whispers softly to her.

"I know," Mom says.

"If you knew about him the whole time," Cesar asks, the

anger returning to his voice, "why didn't you tell us? You lied as much as he did."

Mom glowers at him. "I did *not* lie."

"You lied by keeping it a secret," Cesar insists. "You acted like he was the bad guy."

Mom's face turns pink, like she's embarrassed. "Cesar, I never made your dad the bad guy."

"Yeah, you did. You never told us you knew about him before. What were we supposed to think except that he lied to you?"

Suddenly a new puzzle piece of Cesar's anger at Dad clicks into place—he's been feeling hurt for Mom.

Mom folds her arms like we're ganging up on her. "Fine, maybe I should've handled this differently. Maybe Dad and I should've told you the whole truth. We did the best we could. This hasn't been easy."

"You think it's been easy for *me*?" Cesar says.

"No, I don't. I know it's been hard for *all* of us. And I'm sorry. What more do you want me to say? That we shouldn't have gotten married? That it was a mistake? Let me point out something to both of you: If your dad and I hadn't gotten married, neither of you would be here right now." Mom clenches her jaw like she's trying to stop from crying, and Cesar backs down a little, leaning back on the headboard.

Norma gazes between Cesar and me. "Anything else you boys want to ask?"

Cesar shakes his head *no*. So do I.

"No more fistfights," Norma says, rising to her feet. "Agreed?"

Cesar and I both nod.

"Good." Mom stands. "You staying for dinner?" she asks Norma.

Cesar quickly speaks up. "I'm not hungry."

I guess everything we've talked about hasn't changed Cesar's mind about Dad.

Norma sighs. "Maybe next time. Let's let things cool off." As she passes Cesar's dresser, she stops. "By the way," she tells him, "you should stop wasting your money on whitening cream. It doesn't work—I tried it too."

Cesar's face flames. He glares at me, and I hightail it out of the room.

CHAPTER 35

"Get up, Jorge!" Mom wakes me the next morning. "Even though you're staying home, you still have schoolwork to do." She yanks open the blinds to let in the glaring sunlight. "I'll call you later to check on you. Come on now, get moving."

After breakfast, I dutifully complete my classwork assignments online. Both Mom *and* Dad call to check in on me. Since yesterday, I've also gotten a load of messages from friends who heard about the fight, asking how I'm doing—even a text from Emily. But no word from the person I most hoped to hear from.

When it's time for school to let out, Darnell texts: I'm coming over with Chang, k?

Part of me is still angry at him, but I don't want to stop being friends. Our friendship means too much to me.

K, I answer Darnell. C u soon.

When I answer the doorbell, Peppy springs up and down, wagging his tail. And when I see who else came with Darnell and Chang, my heart leaps, just as happy.

"Ouch," Zoey says, cringing at my black eye. "Does it hurt?"

"Not anymore." Not since she appeared. "I'm okay now."

"Fight each other you must never do again," Darnell proclaims to Chang and me.

Chang's lip is less swollen but crusted with a little red scab. "I'm sorry about your eye," he tells me.

"My fault," I say. "I'm sorry about your lip."

Zoey's gaze moves between him and me. I wonder how much she suspects about the cause of our fight—*her*.

"Do you all want to come inside?" I ask.

"Sure," Darnell and Chang say.

I look at Zoey, feeling hopeful. "Thanks, but I need to take Peppy to rehearse," she says.

Although I'm thrilled she still wants to do the skit with him, as she walks down the street with Peppy and Cesar's skateboard, a jumble of feelings ping-pong inside me: disappointment. Frustration. Sadness.

"I wish that was me with her."

"Give up hope, you must not," Darnell says. "As soon as she heard about your fight, she texted me, asking if you were okay."

"Really?" I ask. "She didn't text *me*."

"Have *you* texted *her*?" Chang asks.

"No. What would I say? I already told her that I'm sorry."

"That's a good start," Darnell says. "But you've got to show her that you mean it. Back it up with actions."

"Like what?"

Darnell clasps his fleshy hands on Chang's and my shoulders. "Men, this will require top-level strategizing . . . and food."

I lead them to the kitchen, bring out the chips, salsa, and sodas, and we take our places around the table.

"Come close . . ." Darnell says in a low voice. "The purpose of this summit is to form a plan for Jedi Jorge to win back Princess Zoey. To start, what are some things she likes?"

"Cookies," I say.

Chang crunches a chip. "Tortilla chips."

"Nay, gentlemen," says Darnell. "This mission demands something greater. Something colossal. Stupendous. Something to prove—beyond a shadow of a doubt—Jorge's determination to win her back. What does she like more than anything in the world?"

"Animals," I say. "But she's already got a dog. And fish. And parakeets."

"Jorge, I've got it!" Darnell pounds the table with his

fist. "You said Zoey asked you to do the talent show with her, right?"

"Um, yeah . . ."

"That would be perfect," Chang says.

"Perfectly *insane*. Have you guys forgotten my disastrous history of getting up in front of people?"

"Oh, yeah," Darnell says. "Your kindergarten fart."

"Hey, problem solved," Chang says. "The other night I saw an infomercial for fart-catcher underwear."

"Fart *what*?" I ask.

"Underwear made from the same stuff as army gasmasks," Chang says. "They had a lady demonstrate."

"Demonstrate, how?" Darnell asks.

"By farting. Some audience members came onstage and sniffed around her. Nobody smelled anything."

"Then how do you know she really farted?" I ask.

"You could hear it. Plus, they had a guy from one of those independent auditing agencies."

"Whoa, hold on," I say. "It's not just when I farted. Remember when I barfed onstage? And how I fainted at the spelling bee? Who knows what could happen this time?"

The guys exchange eye contact. Darnell says, "Then I guess you're not willing to do whatever it takes to win her back."

I swallow the lump at the back of my throat. "She's got

a great routine with Peppy. What if I stepped in, screwed up, and made her lose?"

"Or what if you helped her win?" Chang asks.

"Win or lose," Darnell says, "You'll show her you truly love her."

I try to imagine standing on the school stage with a thousand people watching . . . I can't.

I gaze down at the table, disgusted with myself. "I just can't."

The guys go quiet. Finally Chang murmurs, "I don't think I could do it either."

I look up to Darnell for some wisdom. "Sorry," he says. "The Force I cannot give you. You must find it within."

I shake my head, frustrated. "Can we talk about something else?"

"Sure." Darnell turns to Chang. "Show Jorge your sketches."

Chang steadies his gaze at me. "Okay, but I'm warning you, Jorge, if you don't like—"

"He'll like them," Darnell interrupts and gives me a warning look. "Won't you, Jorge?"

I nod and hope I truly will.

Chang digs into his backpack and cautiously opens his sketchbook. "This is the villain. I kept the name Slimeball."

Like we agreed, the guy appears hypermasculine, but he's not like a typical buff, beefy comic-book guy. He looks like a sleazy slob. Uncombed hair. Facial stubble. Stained white undershirt. His gut cascades over his pants. One flabby bicep is tattooed with the words *Man up!* The other arm portrays a curvy female figure along with the words *Be a babe!*

Before Darnell and I even have a chance to respond, Chang shuts the sketchbook cover. "You don't like it."

"Are you kidding?" I block his arm. "He's perfect. Everything a villain should be: scary, menacing, gross."

"Better than Jabba the Hutt," Darnell says.

"Really? You guys like him?" Chang asks. We nod, and he adds, "I was thinking that instead of shooting slime from his wrists, he lifts his underarms and the gunk squirts out of his armpits."

"Never seen that before," Darnell says.

"Fits the character," I say. "What does the slime do to his victims?"

"You tell us—you're the writer."

"Hmm . . ." I say. "How about if it paralyzes his victims? It creeps into their ears, mouths, noses, into their brains . . ."

"Now you're cranking," says Darnell.

"Then Slimeball sends forth his squad of minions," I continue. "The gender police."

"Like storm troopers," Chang adds.

"Right, except they're hairstylists armed with scissors

and combs, and wardrobe handlers carrying racks of pants and skirts to make people stick to gender roles."

"I can picture the troop already," Chang says. "The minion guys wear football helmets and cowboy boots. The minion women wear corsets, frilly blouses, and big hoop skirts."

"They swarm all over a person like bees," Darnell suggests. "And you can hear the person screaming '*Aaaaaiiiiieeee!*' When the gender police pull away, the person has lost all free will. They're transformed into a brain-dead gender zombie. But how do Slimeball and our hero duke it out?"

"Remember the gender blender?" I say. "It transmits a powerful, high-frequency sound wave, inaudible to human ears. Its vibrations break up the gunk in people's brains and lets them have diverse thoughts again."

"I love, love, love it," Darnell says. He nods at Chang. "Show Jorge your sketch of the hero's girlfriend."

Chang's drawing is exactly like I imagined: The woman wears a plaid lumberjack shirt, jeans, work boots, and a baseball cap—just like a guy. But she has a cute girl's face, big foal-like eyes, and long, slender limbs.

"She looks like Oona," I say.

Chang blushes. "I had to model her after somebody."

"So any ideas for our superhero's name?" I ask.

"How about . . ." Darnell brings his fingertips to his forehead. "The Transgender Avenger?"

"The Trans-venger," Chang says.

"Even better," I say, wishing I'd thought of it.

"Gents, I think we have a winner," Darnell says.

I grin. It feels good to be back together again.

"The contest deadline is Friday at midnight," Darnell reminds us. "That gives us three and a half days. Chang, you send me the sketches. Jorge, you send me the story. I'll put it all together. Now I have to pee." He heads to the bathroom, leaving Chang and me alone.

"So . . . did anybody say anything at school today about my dad?" I ask.

"Nope, everybody's keeping it hush-hush."

"That's a relief." I glance at his split lip. "I'm really sorry. I was stupid and upset."

"Forget it," Chang says. "We all do stupid things—including me. I've been thinking about what Noah said—that coming out can be hard, even if you're coming out about someone else. I shouldn't have pushed you to tell Zoey in front of everyone. That should've been up to you. I'm sorry too."

"So we're good?" I ask.

"*I'm* good," he says. "Are you good?"

"Yeah, I'm good."

"We're *all* good," Darnell says, rejoining us, and I wonder if he left us alone on purpose.

We hang out for a while, finishing up the chips. When the guys are leaving, Chang throws an arm around my shoulders, and Darnell's arms swallow up both of us. It feels like we're almost back to normal—or maybe we're in a *new* normal.

* * *

I'm loading our soda glasses into the dishwasher when Zoey returns with Peppy. His pink tongue dangles toward the front stoop as he pants.

"He looks tuckered out," I say, kneeling to unhook his leash. "How'd he do?"

"Great, except he kept watching the door waiting for you."

I scratch his furry chest. "You could rehearse here tomorrow."

Zoey squiggles her mouth from side to side, thinking it over. "Better not. He needs to get used to doing it without you—we've only got one more day to rehearse. I can pick him up again after school tomorrow."

I stay kneeling, scratching Peppy's chest, wishing Zoey would sit with us.

She forces a tight smile. "Jorge, I've been thinking. . . . I understand why you were scared to tell me about your dad. And I still want to be your friend. I just don't think I'm ready for more than that." She holds out her hand. "No hard feelings, okay?"

I stare at her hand and remember walking her home from the party, our palms pressed together. Maybe if I just *offer* to do the skit, that will be enough to show her how much I want to get back together. Maybe I won't actually have to go through with it. She'll argue that there isn't time for the three of us to rehearse, but since I'll have proven how crazy I am for her, she'll want for us to be a couple again.

I pull myself to my feet, open my mouth to speak, and my knees begin to tremble. But what if she *does* want me to do the skit with her? And what if I chicken out and can't go through with it?

I close my mouth, swallow, and shake her hand. "No hard feelings."

When Zoey says goodbye and steps down the driveway, I command Peppy to sit. "*Tzzt!* Don't cross that line. Stay."

He obeys, and I remember what Zoey said about standing up to fear, refusing to let it take charge, training it to stay behind the yellow police tape. I managed to stand up to Peppy, to Scruggs, to Cesar, so maybe . . .

I yank out my phone and group-text Darnell and Chang. What happens if I offer to do the skit with Zoey but she says it's too late to do it with her?

Darnell: Always looking at the dark side you are

Chang: Maybe better to surprise her

Me: What, just show up backstage before she goes on?

Chang: That way she can't say no

Me: That's nuts

Yep, says Darnell. That's love

"Come on, boy," I call Peppy. He instantly obeys. If I could just get my fear to do the same.

CHAPTER 36

"Cesar, dinner's ready!" Mom yells out the kitchen doorway as she shuttles the meatloaf to the table.

I finish setting our places, sit down, and check my phone, wondering if he'll come downstairs. He has been ignoring us ever since Norma came over last night.

After a few minutes, Mom asks, "Jorge, please go tell him to come eat."

"I'll text him," I say and pull out my phone. Mom says come eat

While we wait, Mom rinses some cooking utensils and wipes down countertops. "Cesar!" she shouts again. Still nothing. "Jorge, would you please go get him?"

I sigh and stand up. Peppy tags along with me. Behind Cesar's *DANGER—KEEP OUT* sign, I can hear him saying something about being president. I silently turn the doorknob and peek inside.

Cesar is standing in front of the mirror, reading from his phone. "I'd like to thank all of you for electing me as your president. I want to keep my pledge—" He spots my reflection. "Don't you know what *keep out* means?"

Peppy squeezes past me into the room. "Mom says come eat," I tell Cesar.

He frowns. "I'm not hungry. I'll eat later. Alone."

"Oh, so now you're cutting Mom out of your life too?" I ask. "You're treating us all like we're your enemies. But I'm not against you, Cesar. Neither is Mom. Or Dad."

I figure he'll tell me to shut up, but he actually seems to be listening, so I keep going. "You didn't used to be this way—so obsessed with winning, so worried what people think of you, always mad at somebody. . . . You used to joke and goof off and help me with stuff. What happened to you?"

"You know what happened," he says.

"No," I say. "It began way before Dad came out. Ever since we started middle school, you've gotten angrier and angrier about *everything*. You get ticked off at anything I do or say. It's like I can't do anything right, like you hate me. And I don't know why. What did I do to you?"

My eyes get wet and blurry. I wait for Cesar to say something. His jaw shifts like he wants to answer, but he can't bring himself to do it. His gaze falls to the floor.

I wipe my cheeks with my hand and head back down to

the kitchen. "He says he's not hungry," I tell Mom. "He'll eat later—alone."

Mom stares at me like she can tell I've been crying. "Thanks, sweetheart. Let's go ahead and eat before it gets cold." She's cutting me a slice of meatloaf when Cesar shuffles into the room.

"I just needed to finish something," he says. He sits at his usual place, serves himself some potatoes, and holds his plate out to Mom for a slice of meatloaf.

Did the stuff I said to him actually make an impression? I'm not sure what to think, but I don't make a big deal out of it. Neither does Mom. The three of us just sit quietly and eat our dinner.

* * *

The next morning Peppy's cold, wet muzzle wakes me. Poking my ear. Sniffing. Snuffling. Licking.

Remembering that I'm suspended from school, I pull the bed sheet over my head. Gradually the bed becomes still. But just as I begin to doze again, Peppy's front paws slam on top of me, pumping my chest as if trying to revive me with CPR.

"Let me sleep." I roll over on the mattress and squinch my eyes shut, but it's no use. I'm awake.

When I head to the kitchen for breakfast, Cesar is already there. He doesn't glower at me, or sulk, or avoid eye contact. He actually says hi and asks if I need anything from school.

"Um . . ." I stall, surprised by his offer. "No, but thanks."

"Text me if you do," he says and heads out, leaving me wondering if he's truly having a change of heart.

While I brush my teeth, my mind wanders to the talent show and Zoey in her red, ruffled skirt and Peppy in his mask. And like a bull charging into a ring, an idea springs into my mind.

As soon as Mom and Cesar have left, I race to my closet. I know I'm supposed to focus on schoolwork, but instead I shove aside shirts and jackets and yank out a cardboard box. From inside, beneath a pile of old shoes and jeans, I pull out last year's Halloween outfit. And as quick as Clark Kent in a phone booth, I slip into the all-black costume: a sleek, dark shirt; shimmery pants; a cape, flowing like the wind; an eye mask to shield my true identity; and a plastic sword to slice the air with my signature Z—*swish, swash, swoosh*!

No longer am I meek, mild-mannered Jorge Antonio Fuerte. I am now the original, very first superhero, striking fear into the hearts of men. I am the great, the bold, the fearless . . . Zorro!

The costume fits tighter than last year, but it's still okay. Now all I have to do is learn the part of the skit that Zoey asked me to dance with her. I grab Peppy's treat jar, lead him to the garage, and cue up our song on my phone.

I thought it would be a cinch to incorporate myself as Zoey's dance partner while leading Peppy through his paces, but from the start, he's confused about what the heck we're doing. So am I.

Zoey made dancing look easy peasy. In reality, it's hard to remember all the steps and make my feet go where I want. And keep pace with the music. And play Zoey's part. And add new steps for me. And lead Peppy through flips and twirls. And reward him with treats.

And, and, and . . . each time we start making headway, I mess up. And when I mess up, Peppy messes up.

The part of the song that would include me lasts barely two minutes, but those two minutes seem to go on forever. Once—only once—do we actually get to the one-minute mark before I flub. The next time, we barely make it to the first chorus.

I plop into the lawn chair, sweaty, exhausted, ready to give up. There's no way I can learn all this in just two days. Without me, Zoey and Peppy have a decent shot at winning. With me, they're bound to crash and burn. Not to mention I haven't even asked her to let me do it.

Peppy lies beside me, panting, absorbing the cool of the concrete floor, and shifting his gaze to the jar of treats. As long as the food keeps coming, he seems okay to keep trying. And each time I think of Zoey, I'm determined to keep going.

"All right, let's try again." I haul myself up and chuck off the costume, stripping down to my boxers, sneakers, and an old beach towel I wrap around my waist like Zoey's skirt. I'll need it for the part of the skit where Peppy tugs at it. I keep the cape on for moral support.

I toss Peppy a treat, and for the one thousand and first time, I start the song. Halfway through the routine, the door to the kitchen swings open. I leap back, startled, my arms flying up, my cape spreading like batwings.

"Geez," I tell Norma. "You scared me."

"Sorry—I shouted your name but you didn't answer. What're you up to? Shouldn't you be doing your school-work?"

I blink, trying to conjure an excuse for dancing around the garage in a cape and towel-skirt. Drawing a blank, I resort to the truth about my plan to surprise Zoey and win her back.

Norma listens patiently, shaking her head. "Jorge, Jorge, Jorge . . ."

"I know, it's stupid. *I'm* stupid."

"No, you're not stupid. You just need to get it through your noggin to be honest. Why don't you just tell Zoey how much you like her?"

"I did . . . before all this. But what if she doesn't feel the same way anymore?"

"That's the risk you take when you open your heart to someone."

I grip my cape, not wanting to think about all this.

"Do you remember," Norma says, "when you asked me what powers a female superhero might have? Here's one—being vulnerable. That's something women tend to do better. And letting yourself be vulnerable takes way more courage than clobbering someone. Be brave, Zorro." She slashes the air with her pointer finger as if it were a sword—*swish, swash, swoosh*!

I wrap the cape tighter around my shoulders.

"You hungry?" she asks. "How about taking a break?"

I go upstairs and put on shorts and a T-shirt. When I come back down, Norma is standing at the kitchen stove, making us grilled ham and cheese. Skillet in one hand, spatula in the other, humming some opera tune. Just like the old days. And for a moment, the empty space in my chest fills up.

"Do you remember the first time you told Mom you loved her?" I ask.

Norma flips a sandwich in the skillet as if it were a flapjack. "The *very* first time? Let me think—it was so long ago. She was probably the first to say it. She was braver than me. I felt too unsure."

"Unsure you loved her?"

"No—of that I was certain. That's why I was scared. I wasn't sure she could love me."

"Why?"

"Because of my secret. I didn't think anybody would ever be able to love me."

"How soon after that did you tell her you felt like a woman?"

"I think it was when she first said she loved me. She was the first person I ever came out to."

"What did she say?"

"That if it was part of who I was, it was part of who she loved." As Norma talks, her eyes tear up. "I'd never imagined anybody would ever say that to me. I didn't think anyone could love me." She flips the other sandwich in the skillet. "But she also warned me that if I ever decided I wanted to live as a woman we could no longer be together. It seemed like a fair compromise. I loved her so much. I was willing to do any—"

"Why can't she just accept you?" I blurt out. "It's not fair. Doesn't it make you mad?"

"Mad, no. Sad, yes. I wish it could be otherwise, but your mom and I had an agreement—that I would keep the woman inside me *inside*. I broke our agreement. And I have to accept the consequences."

"Well, it makes *me* mad."

Norma brings our sandwiches to the table. "I understand, but try to put yourself in your mom's shoes. Suppose Zoey told you she feels like a boy inside and wants to dress and express herself as a boy *outside*—maybe even take hormones, grow facial hair, and have surgery. Would you still want to go out with her?"

I imagine Zoey morphing into a guy with facial hair—not to mention everything else—and my stomach starts to knot. As much as I admire her strength and confidence, I also like her softness. Her gentle touch. Her sweet cinnamon smell. Her tinkling voice. Her girlish giggle.

"I don't think I could like her the same way as a guy. I think I like her because she *is* a girl."

"So can you understand how your mom feels about me?" Norma asks.

It pains me to admit it, but . . . "Yeah."

After we clean up from lunch, I walk Norma to the front door.

"Now do your school assignments," she says. "Let me know how it goes with Zoey. Oh, and please ask one of your friends to film you doing your skit onstage. I'd love to see it."

Her voice sounds sad, and my stomach falls a little. I feel bad that I haven't invited her to come see the show, but if she did come, Cesar would freak out more than ever. And I'm not ready to deal with her coming either.

As Peppy and I watch Norma climb into her car, I picture Zoey walking up the driveway after school. I'll look her straight in the eye and say, "I need to tell you something. I can't hold it in any longer."

Just as I'm imagining telling her, "I really, really like you," my pants explode with a fart.

The thing trumpets so loud even Peppy leaps away. A wave of panic seizes me. What if that happens when I'm with Zoey? The thought makes my stomach wobble. My head feels dizzy. And I lean a hand against the doorframe, more unsure of myself than ever.

CHAPTER 37

I race through half my classwork and reward myself with another rehearsal with Peppy, but I keep stumbling and missing steps. Each time, I feel more and more like giving up. Only the thought of Zoey keeps me going.

The next time I check the clock, it's almost time for school to let out. Zoey will be coming over soon.

I'm finishing changing clothes when the doorbell rings. Peppy races to the door and presses his nose to the bottom, sniffing to suss out who's there.

"Hi," Zoey greets us. "What've you been up to all day?"

I think about Norma encouraging me to share my feelings. Then I remember my shocker fart. "Just hanging out. How was school?"

"Great. Savannah and I talked to Mr. Richter about starting a Gender and Sexuality Alliance."

"For real?"

"Yep. He says okay—only if we change the name to the Diversity Club. Oona thinks that's wimping out. What do you think? You're going to be part of it, aren't you?"

"Sure." If Zoey is part of it, so am I. "Maybe the name isn't as important as what we do."

"Good point." She smiles, her cheeks dimple, and I think about Norma's hypothetical: If Zoey were a boy, would I still want to go out with her—I mean, *him*?

I picture her dressed in work boots and a lumberjack shirt and think, *She would still look as cute.* But then I imagine kissing *boy*-Zoey, and it feels like there are wet worms squirming inside my socks.

When she walks away with Peppy, her curly hair flaps in the breeze. I'm glad she's a girl, not a guy—even though at this point it doesn't make much difference. I promise myself that when she brings Peppy back, I'll definitely tell her about my feelings. But when she returns, I once again chicken out.

* * *

I'm catching up on my classwork at the kitchen table when the front door rattles, and Peppy dashes out to welcome Cesar.

I tap my pen against my history book, listening to his footsteps approach. Since he didn't send me any panicky texts from school saying news leaked about Dad, I'm hoping my group kept our secret.

"'Sup?" I offer a smile as he steps through the doorway.

"'Sup," he answers with a smile. That's a relief.

I refocus on my book and watch from the corner of my eye as my brother peels off his backpack, pours a tall glass of water, sinks into a chair, checks his phone, and puts it down.

I slide my bag of nacho-cheese chips toward him. "You want some?"

He takes a handful. "I talked to Coach Craddock after practice today. I told him about Dad."

I nearly choke on a chip. "You mean—what'd he say?"

"At first, nothing. He just stared at me and scratched his head. Then he asked if Dad had ever hit us or abused us. I said no. He asked if Dad did drugs or got drunk. I said no. He asked if Dad ever left us without food, or clothes, or a roof to sleep under. I said no. Finally he asked, 'So then what's the problem?'"

I lean forward in my chair. "What did you answer?"

Cesar crunches a chip. "That if people find out, they'll treat us like freaks. And I can kiss being president goodbye. So Coach said,"—Cesar mimics Coach Craddock bellowing at soccer games.—"'You think you're the only kid who's ever been embarrassed by a parent? At least you've got a dad. You know how many students at this school hardly ever even *see* their dads?'"

Peppy stands and whimpers as Cesar continues in the booming voice: "'You think I'm only here to coach soccer and teach you science? I'm here to help you learn how to succeed in life. Right now that means you need to stop thinking your dad is doing this to hurt you. If you picture yourself as a victim, you'll always be one.'"

Cesar takes another chip. "It hit me that's what I've been doing. Coach always says, 'When you get tackled in life, you've got two choices. Either stay down feeling sorry for yourself, or pick yourself up and decide that the thing that knocked you flat is going to make you better.'"

It's hard to believe what Cesar is saying. "How could Dad being a woman make you better?"

"That's what I asked," Cesar says. "Coach said, 'Come on, you're smart. Get off your pity-pot and think it through.'" He imitates the coach leaning back, arms crossed, staring across the table. "He wouldn't let me leave until I came up with something. So I thought about how every family's got stuff they don't want other people to know. I thought about how your friends found out Dad is trans, and they haven't ditched you. Are you sure they don't think it's weird?"

"They think it's different, but they say he's always been different from other dads. That's why they like him."

Cesar nods. "And I thought about how you haven't freaked out about all this. You've handled it a lot better than me."

I glance down at the table. Compliments always make me self-conscious.

"You were right when you said I've changed," he continues. "I don't know what happened. I felt like I had to prove I was as good as anybody else. Somehow that turned into showing I was better than everybody else. And it seemed to be working. Everything was going great—soccer, my grades, the morning news show, Victoria. . . . Then the divorce and Dad . . . it felt like my world flipped upside down. Like someone changed the rules midgame. Like suddenly everybody was against me."

"Cesar, the only one against you is you."

Cesar turns quiet, like he's working himself up to say something. "I'm sorry I made you feel like I hate you. I don't hate you. Lots of times I wish I could be more like you."

I tug at my shirt, feeling awkward. "Promise you won't punch me anymore?"

"Promise." A sly grin creeps across his lips. "Unless you punch me first."

I grin. "Deal."

While we talk some more, Peppy wanders out of the room and returns with a tissue in his mouth—probably one he dug out of a bathroom wastebasket. He crouches down, sphinxlike, on the kitchen floor, holding the soft paper between his front paws and shredding it with his jaws into wispy white strands he then swallows.

"He looks like a kid eating cotton candy," Cesar says.

"Booger-flavored cotton candy," I say.

Cesar laughs a little with me for the first time in days—maybe even weeks—and says, "Somebody ought to make booger-flavored dog food."

"A whole line of pooches' favorite flavors," I say, laughing with him. "Boogers. Bugs. Barf."

"Vomit flavor," Cesar says. "Rotten egg."

"Toilet-bowl flavor," I chime in.

"Get this," he says, now completely cracking up. "Our bestseller—"

"Dead mouse?" I interrupt.

"No, better: cat poop." He laughs so hard he has to swig some water to keep from choking, but the water squirts out his nose.

"I think I'm going to hurl," I say.

"Use Peppy's bowl," Cesar says. "He still looks hungry."

Peppy peers up from his tissue and runs his tongue across his lips—amping up our giggles to a whole new level. Each time Cesar or I pause to wheeze in a breath, the other pipes up with a new suggestion—"Stinky cheese!" or "Poopy diapers!"—and a new wave of rib-splitting laughs roll between us.

Our last giggles finally die out as Peppy hoovers his nose across the floor, checking for any wayward shreds of tissue.

"You think he and Zoey'll win the talent show?" Cesar asks.

I blow my nose with a napkin and debate whether to reveal my secret plan. "I don't know. But . . . I'm thinking I might dance with them."

"But you hate getting up in front of groups," Cesar says.

"I know. How do you do it?"

"I just picture everybody cheering and applauding. I visualize it, like in soccer. Coach always says 'believing is seeing.' I act as if I believe it."

"But what if I mess up, and everybody laughs, and Zoey loses because of me?"

Cesar shrugs. "Coach has a Michael Jordan quote up on his wall: 'I've failed over and over and over again in my life. And that is why I succeed.'" He grows quiet and then asks, "Dad hasn't said anything about coming to the show, has he?"

"No." The bad feeling from earlier in the day, the one I had for not inviting Dad to the show, comes back. "She asked me to have somebody film my skit for her."

I expect Cesar to jump on my case for referring to Dad as *she* and *her*. But he doesn't. Instead he turns thoughtful, then pulls out his books and does his homework across the table.

I try not to smile too hard, hopeful I might truly be getting my brother back.

CHAPTER 38

Only eleven hours till showtime, I calculate when I wake up and look at my clock Thursday morning. I leap out of bed, chomp down some breakfast, and as soon as I've raced through my schoolwork, I grab Peppy's treats and lead him to the garage.

In our first run-through, I flub up at the end. Each time after that, we barely make it halfway before I screw up. I'll never pull this off.

The cracked mirror across the garage catches my reflection. I walk over, raise my arms in a power-pose V, and try to imagine an auditorium full of people applauding. Behind me, Peppy does a backflip.

I whirl around. He wags his tail and points his nose toward the bag of treats. I toss him one. He gobbles it down, does a roll, and angles once more toward the treats. Inside my head an idea sparks: *Let's try this differently.*

I cue the music, and this time I let Peppy lead. I follow, feeding him treats. He never seems to worry about what comes next. He just puts one foot in front of the other. Trick, then treat. Trick, then treat. And for the first time . . .

"I made it through my part, boy!"

The next time, I screw up again. My brain keeps telling me to lead. But I don't need to train Peppy—I need to train *me*.

It isn't easy, but we manage to make it through my part of the skit again—once, twice, three times in a row. When we stop to rest, a shiver runs down my back. We might actually pull this off.

* * *

After lunch, I give Peppy the afternoon off. I've got homework, and he needs his energy for the show. I do too.

When school lets out, Zoey comes to get him.

"Whoa," I say, opening the front door. "I like your hair."

Her curls are pulled up and back in a twist, held together by a tortoiseshell comb. Her face looks brighter, more open, more inviting. More than ever I want her back as my girl-friend—hopefully for more than a day.

"Thanks," she says. "My mom found the comb at a vintage store. Are you as excited as I am for tonight?"

I bite into my lip, thinking about my harebrained scheme and feeling all tangled up inside.

"Uh-oh," Zoey says. "What's that look for?"

In my mind I hear Norma's voice: *Tell her how much you like her!* At the same time, another voice screams, *Don't say it! You're going to get hurt again!*

"Um . . . Zoey?"

"Yeah?"

My brow starts to sweat. My legs begin to wobble. "Well . . . I just wanted to tell you . . . "

"Tell me what?"

I can't breathe. I feel like I'm about to pass out. The best I can manage is, "Good luck."

"Thanks," she answers with a giggle.

I feel instant relief . . . and disgust with myself.

As Zoey disappears down the sidewalk with Peppy, I head inside, punching my leg with my fist. I'm sitting on my bed, trying to decide what to do about the show when Cesar comes up the stairs, singing—actually *singing*—and stops in my doorway.

"I saw Zoey leaving with Peppy," he says. "Did you decide if you're going to do the show?"

"I'm still not sure. I haven't talked to her about it. I thought I'd surprise her."

My brother's eyes nearly pop out of his head. "That will definitely be a surprise. But what do you have to lose, I guess. She already dumped you, right?"

"Yeah, but I don't want her to dump me as a friend too."

Cesar nods like he understands. "Well, if you're going to do it, you'd better decide. It starts in two hours."

He leaves to shower and change. I stay sitting in bed and close my eyes, trying to picture people cheering me on. But I can only imagine them laughing at me.

Maybe changing into my outfit will help.

By the time Mom gets home, I'm in full Zorro mode, flourishing my cape and brandishing my sword at my bedroom mirror, trying to psych myself up. From the doorway, she raises a quizzical eyebrow. "What's up with the costume?"

I pull off the eye mask and clear my throat. "Um . . . the talent show?"

"You said you weren't going to be in it."

"I know," I admit. "But now I want to try. I just haven't told Zoey yet because I'm not sure I can go through with it."

"Wow," Mom says. "Complicated."

I nod. "What should I do?"

"Hmm . . . which will you regret more—if you try or if you don't?"

I think about that and suddenly wonder if that's how she decided to marry Dad. Before I can ask, Cesar returns to the doorway dressed in his emcee getup: navy blazer, red necktie, khaki pants, leather loafers.

"You look handsome," Mom says, and a car horn beeps in the driveway.

"Gotta go," Cesar says. "Victoria's mom is taking us."

"Good luck!" Mom calls after him as his footsteps pound down the stairs. She turns back to me. "Let me get changed, and we can go."

As she heads to her room, my phone chimes. The text is from Norma: Ready for your stage debut? I'm cheering for you!

My stomach sinks—I wish I could invite her to come. I always feel stronger, more confident with Dad around. At least I would've before, but now . . . I'm too stressed to deal with Norma.

Thanks, just trying to psych myself up, I reply. Then I plop into my desk chair, feeling like a wimp.

You'll do great, Dad replies. Just believe in yourself as much as I do! I love you.

Love you too, I answer.

I toss my phone aside and flop down on my bed. Why am I so scared of her coming? My friends know I have a trans dad. They don't care. Darnell and Chang have already seen her as Norma, and the others want to meet her.

But then I think about Scruggs and his dad and other jerks at school. What if something were to happen like at the gas station? And what about Cesar? We're just getting back to being brothers. What if inviting Norma makes me lose him again?

I'm still going back and forth when my phone chimes. It's Darnell on our group text: Ready to go win Zoey back?

Or lose her forever, I answer. Hey, do you guys think I should invite my dad?

Chang: Sure, why not?

Me: What if somebody hassles her?

Chang: We can be her bodyguards

Darnell: Have courage, young Skywalker

I read his text and wonder, *Should I go through with it? CAN I go through with it?*

My fingers bloom with sweat as I text Norma: Will you come to the show with Mom and me?

Before I can change my mind, I hit SEND. Then I hold my breath.

Almost immediately Norma replies, I would love to come.

I start to breathe again until she adds: But I don't want to cause any problems. Have you asked your mom?

I didn't think of that. In an instant, I'm racing to Mom's bedroom. "Can Norma come with us?"

Mom studies me for what seems like a century before she asks, "Is that what you want?"

I try to keep my voice steady. "Yes."

"You're *sure*?" she asks, curling her fingers around her blue stone necklace. "And you discussed it with Cesar?"

"Not exactly." I think back to our conversation after our dog-food brainstorm.

Mom lets go of her necklace. "Well, let him know she's coming. And brace yourself."

I wonder which part I should most brace myself for. Cesar? Scruggs? Other students? Parents? Mr. Richter? Zoey? A thousand people watching me onstage?

My thumbs shake as I text Norma: Mom said you can come with us

Almost instantly, she answers, I'm on my way over.

I text Cesar: Norma is coming with us . . . See you soon!

I hit SEND, hoping I haven't just lost my brother again. Then I follow Mom downstairs, my shiny black cape billowing behind me, just like a real superhero's.

CHAPTER 39

"Honey, can you please stop squirming?" Mom asks, gripping my chin and drawing a moustache on my face with eyebrow pencil while we wait for Norma.

I try to stand still. "How do you think people will react to her?"

Mom's hand shakes a little as she fills in my moustache. "I'm trying *not* to think about it. Sara Kozinski thinks I'm crazy to still be friends with your dad. Sally Jenkins gave me an earful about what kind of example this is giving you boys."

"Really?" I say softly. "You never told Cesar and me that."

"It's not your problem, sweetie. You've got enough to deal with." She caps her pencil. "There. You look like a movie star."

Norma's headlight beams sweep the wall as she pulls into the driveway. I figured she would dress up, and boy, has she. She steps out of the car wearing a fancy camel-colored skirt, a gauzy blouse, amber jewelry, makeup, and heels.

Mom glances in the mirror and frowns—she changed from her nice work clothes into a casual shirt and jeans.

"You should've warned me you were going to look better than me," she tells Norma when we step outside.

"I could never look better than you," Norma says, opening the passenger door for her. Dad has always acted like a gentleman—even now. "No matter what you wear, you're still beautiful."

Mom smirks. "Never mind the sweet talk. You should've warned me—that's what girlfriends do."

"Oh," Norma says, letting that sink in. "Right. Sorry." She closes Mom's door and turns to me. "I guess we learn something new every day."

"That's for sure," I say, maneuvering into the backseat with my cape and sword. As we pull out, I check my phone, wondering why Caesar hasn't replied to my text about Norma coming with us. I thought for sure he would protest.

"So, how was your day?" Norma asks Mom as we start toward school.

Mom brings us up to speed on her office's goings-on and asks Norma about her work. They chitchat like nothing has changed between them, even though everything has changed.

The honk of a car horn snaps me out of my thoughts. Inside the blue sedan next to us at the traffic light are Mr. and Mrs. Kozinski and their sixth-grade daughter, Ava.

I dip down in the seat and pull my mask tight.

Through our closed windows, Mom clenches a smile, waves at Mrs. Kozinski, and tells Norma, "I was just telling Jorge about Sara."

Mrs. Kozinski smiles at Mom but gives Norma the stink eye. Mr. Kozinski stares in confusion as Norma waves to them. Ava waves back, then the stoplight turns green, and the Kozinskis speed away.

"Well, we got through that one," Mom says. "But you know everybody's going to be at the school for the show. The Garcias . . . the Gosnolds . . ."

"It'll be our grand debut!" Norma raises her hand in a theatrical flourish.

Mom folds her arms. "Everyone we haven't told."

"I wanted to tell people," Norma says. "But you said, 'No, let's wait.'"

"So this is my fault?" Mom snaps. "I'm to blame?"

"I'm not blaming you," Norma says, reaching out her hand. "I know this is stressful."

Mom keeps her arms folded. "You're not afraid of how people will react?"

"Of course I am," Norma says. "I've lived my entire life afraid. But you know what I'm finding? Most people are just as afraid to say anything."

I chime in: "Darnell's mom saw her, and she's okay with her."

Mom glances over her shoulder, staring at my mask like she wishes she could borrow it.

I look down at my phone. On my way, I text Chang and Darnell. Where r you guys?

Chang: Nearly there

Darnell: Same . . . Meet outside the front doors?

When we arrive, the school parking lot is swarming with cars and families. Norma pulls into an empty space and shuts off the engine. "Showtime."

Mom stays strapped in place, making no move to get out.

"If you're that uneasy," Norma says, "would you rather go in separately?"

"No," Mom says. "I need to face this." She reaches across the seat and tenderly strokes her fingertips through Norma's hair. "I feel so sad."

Norma extends her hand again. This time Mom accepts it.

"Jorge, you go ahead if you want," Mom says. "I just need a minute."

I reach for the door handle but then stop. The thought

of letting them walk in by themselves makes me more nervous than the thought of walking in with them. "I'll wait."

Mom leans back on the headrest, closes her eyelids, and sits quietly. While she psyches herself up or prays or whatever, a parade of people march past us toward the school.

I fidget with my sword, antsy to go. Norma glances at me in the rearview mirror and presses a finger to her lips, signaling me to be patient.

"All right," Mom finally says, opening her eyes. "Everybody ready?"

Norma gives an encouraging nod. "If you are."

I grab the door handle and step out into the stream of people, just as Oona is striding by with her parents. She smiles and waves. "Hi, Zorro."

I freeze, but she doesn't seem to recognize me. I could get used to this mask-wearing thing.

Mom waits until there's a gap in the crowd before stepping out. "Now, let's just walk calmly," she says in a low voice, "and have a normal, ordinary conversation."

"Okay, everyday conversation," Norma replies. "Let's see . . . how do you feel about harem pants?"

"They'd suit your build," Mom says. "But no bright colors."

As we walk up the row of parked cars, I notice Norma has gotten way better at walking in heels. Even so, several people glance over at us. First at me, then at Norma. She trudges onward, head held high, undaunted.

I stop outside the front doors. "Chang and Darnell are supposed to meet us here."

A bunch of kids next to the cactus hedge are talking and joking. If we can just make it past the group unnoticed, we can disappear into the crowd inside. Home free.

"Hey, look," a girl tells the group. "It's Zorro."

"Who's that with him?" another girl asks. "Is it a he or a she?"

"Maybe it's part of the show," jokes a boy.

"If not, it should be," bellows another.

I recognize the voice instantly—it's Scruggs. While his crowd erupts in laughter, I cringe beneath my cape. Mom hears the jokes too, and her face goes tight.

Norma tries to soothe her. "It's okay, dear. They're just kids."

I'm not about to stand by and let Scruggs disrespect Norma like his dad did. I have to stop him, but how? I doubt nipping him with little doggie-jaw hands will work a second time.

At that moment, a voice speaks behind me. "Hi, Mr. Fuerte—uh, I mean . . ."

I turn and see Chang, together with Darnell and both of their parents.

"Just call me Norma." She smiles and shakes hands with

the adults. None of them seem fazed by Dad. I guess Darnell
and Chang prepped them.

"Good to see you, Norberto," says Darnell's dad,
and his mom corrects him: "Didn't you hear her? She's
Norma now."

Apparently more adults haven't discouraged Scruggs
and his group. "I know that freak from the gas station,"
I hear him say. He swaggers in our direction with his crowd.

Not knowing what else to do, I yank out my plastic
sword, flare my cape, and block his path. "Halt in the name
of Zorro!"

Scruggs stops, half-scowling, half-sneering. "You've got
to be kidding."

"Easy, Jorge," Darnell murmurs to me. "We've got this."
He signals Chang to one side of Norma while he flanks her
other side. "Everybody circle up," he says to our group.
"We're moving inside."

I sheathe my sword, and we all surround Norma and
Mom like a human wall. As we shuffle past Scruggs's group,
he levels his gaze at me. I get a creepy, foreboding sense—he
and I aren't finished yet.

Inside the lobby, a throng of students and their families
are funneling toward the auditorium. Some people stare at
us. Some point. Some exchange looks. But it doesn't matter.
In our little circle, we're safe. Protected. Out of harm's way.

Through the crowd, I spot a familiar face. With his blue

hair and sparkling, glittery fingernails, Noah stands out in the sea of people. "Noah!"

His mascara-lined eyes survey my Zorro costume. "Jorge?"

I nod. "Yeah, meet my dad. This is Norma."

Noah stares at Norma like he's starstruck. "Wow, you're doing it," he tells her. "Living my dream."

"There's Mr. Richter," Mom tells Norma, nodding toward the auditorium doors.

As we approach, Mr. Richter's gaze travels between Norma, Mom, and me, then back to Norma. He blinks. Once. Twice. Three times.

Norma extends her hand. "It's good to see you, Roger. Thanks for letting Jorge come tonight."

"Pardon?" says Mr. Richter, shaking her hand. Then suddenly a curtain of recognition rises across his face. "Oh, yes, of course." His gaze tracks us as we move away, until he's greeted by other parents.

Inside the auditorium, seats are filling up—row upon row of people. Even at a distance, the curtained stage appears huge, formidable, ominous. My costume suddenly feels cramped and warm.

"Shouldn't you be going to join Zoey?" Norma asks me.

"Maybe I should just stay with you."

Norma eyes me skeptically. "You haven't told her you want to dance with her, have you?"

"Um . . ."

"There's room in the front row," Chang tells our gang.

"Go ahead," Norma calls back to him. "I need to talk with Jorge."

While the others trek down the aisle, Norma squares her gaze at me. "Have you figured out the greatest superpower?"

I shake my head no.

"What have I been telling you all along?" she asks. "Come on, think."

"Can't you just tell me?"

"You know," she insists. "Listen to the wise voice deep inside you."

My mind flashes back over stuff that's happened over the past few months: her coming out and struggling to be recognized as a woman; her determination to trudge on, even after the incident with Scruggs's dad; her telling me the truth about her suicide attempt; her encouraging me from the very start to be honest with Zoey. . . .

"You mean about being honest and telling your truth?" I feel a little let down. "How's *that* a superpower?"

"Because nothing is as powerful as truth. That's why people are willing to die for it."

I tug at my collar. "I'm not ready to die."

"Jorge, you're not going to die."

"It feels like I might. What if I screw up?"

"If you're honest, you'll come out stronger, mijo.

No matter what happens. Now, go use your superpower. Tell Zoey your truth."

Norma sets her big manicured hand on my shoulder, and I feel something flow through me, deep into my bones. Her belief in me. Her boldness. *Her* superpower. If she can stand up for her truth, I can stand up for mine . . . I hope.

CHAPTER 40

Backstage is bustling like a circus. Gymnast girls tumble and somersault. A boy wearing a jester's hat juggles tennis balls. Coach Craddock, Ms. Finnegan, and other teachers shuttle through the chaos, barking instructions, helping with makeup, shouting orders into their crackling walkie-talkies.

Across the wings, Zoey, wearing her red, ruffled skirt, sequined mask, and poofy white blouse, is helping a ballerina adjust her tutu. Peppy is at her side. Catching my scent, he spins around on his leash and wags his tail. I press a finger to my lips—*keep quiet!*

From the auditorium loudspeakers booms Mr. Richter's voice. "Could everybody please find a seat? The show is about to start."

"Cesar? Victoria?" Ms. Finnegan asks. "You two ready?"

"Almost," says Victoria. She looks like a beauty queen

in a shimmering white evening gown. After clipping a lapel mic to my brother's blazer, she pulls him by the hand to the curtain. "I want to see how many people came."

"Why don't we just wait?" he answers, trying to stand back.

"Look," she says, peeking out at the audience. "It's completely full."

Cesar peers out, blinks, and spins away from the curtain. The color drains from his face, leaving him whiter than any skin cream could. The auditorium lights are still on, and I can guess who he saw sitting in the front row.

Didn't he get my text warning him about Norma? I wonder.

"Everyone please join me in welcoming our hosts," Mr. Richter commands from the loudspeaker. "The stars of our school's morning show, Victoria Rogers and Cesar Fuerte!"

"Curtain up," Ms. Finnegan radios the tech booth. "Lights, lights!"

The curtains part. The audience bursts into applause. The stage lamps' glow spills across the front row, revealing my friends, their parents, my mom, and at the very center, Norma.

While Victoria steps out toward center stage, Cesar stays planted in the wings, as stiff and glassy-eyed as a deer in headlights.

"Cesar, something wrong?" Coach Craddock asks, peering at the audience as if studying a soccer field. When his gaze lands on Norma, he claps Cesar's shoulder. "Remember what we discussed?"

Emerging from his trance, Cesar nods. As he strides out to join Victoria in the spotlight, it's like a switch flips inside him. He's no longer my brother, panicked about our trans dad. He's Cesar Fuerte, the school's star of soccer, stage, and screen.

"Goooood evening, Mustangs!" he and Victoria call out to the crowd. "Together we welcome *you*"—their fingers point at the audience, just like on their TV show—"to the twenty-third annual Lone Star Middle School's Got Talent Show."

"Boy, do we have an amazing lineup tonight," Victoria says over cheers and whistles.

"And an awesome audience," Cesar adds in his deep newscaster's voice. Then he shouts, "Are you excited?"

The crowd cheers louder, except for a single boo from the back row—probably Scruggs. Cesar and Victoria carry on with their note-card script, explaining the phone-polling app set up for the audience. At the end of each performance, people will vote, awarding contestants one to five stars. Prizes include three-ring binders, cookie shop coupons, and the grand prize of a hundred dollars.

While Victoria babbles on, I spin around, newly determined to march toward Zoey, and *wham*! I slam into Emily.

"Sorry, I'm sorry," I say, grabbing her elbow to keep her from toppling over.

She's costumed like a black kitten: furry ears, tail, collar with a tinkling bell. In one arm she holds a soccer ball. In her other arm she cradles Regina, her big white cat. A plastic clip on its head holds the long hair out of its eyes.

"Jorge?" Emily whispers, recognizing my voice.

I nod and ask, "You're in the show too?"

Emily nods. "Victoria talked me into doing something with Regina. I'm so nervous. You want to see? I taught Regina to roll on a ball."

"Um . . ." I glance toward Peppy. He's tugging at his leash, his eyes locked on Regina—his tail wags frantically while Zoey tries to calm him.

"Maybe now's not the best time," I tell Emily. "I need to talk to Zoey."

"Oh, okay," Emily says. "Good luck."

"Thanks, you too."

While two girls with Hula-Hoops whisk past us to the applause welcoming them onstage, I meander through the performers toward Zoey. Peppy tugs his leash in my direction.

"Hi, boy," I greet him.

"Jorge?" At the sound of my voice, Zoey lifts her sequin mask to peer at me. "Why're you dressed like that?"

"I, um . . ." I pet Peppy to calm him—and myself—down,

and think, *Here goes nothing.* "I came to . . . you know . . . help you. As your dance partner?"

Zoey tilts her head, puzzled. "But we haven't rehearsed. You said you could never do it."

"I know but . . ." My forehead is raining sweat. "You wanted me to do it, and so I've been rehearsing with Peppy, and you've rehearsed with him, and he knows his steps, so we should all be good."

Zoey's jaw drops a little. "Except we haven't practiced as a group! We can't just go out there together unrehearsed. That would be insane."

I drop my gaze, feeling like I *am* insane.

"Jorge, why didn't you tell me?"

"Because I was scared you'd say no?"

"Jorge, look at me." I gaze up. Zoey's usually bright, cheery face is a mix of concern and confusion. "What's going on?"

The Hula-Hoop-ers skip back from stage after Cesar and Victoria finish interviewing them. Ms. Finnegan ushers out the string quartet. And I take what must be one of the deepest breaths of my life.

"I wanted to show you I'm willing to do anything—absolutely anything in the world—to go out with you."

Her face relaxes a little. "Oh, Jorge . . . I appreciate that. Honestly, I do. You're very sweet. I like you a lot. But—"

"Do you remember when you told me to face down

my fear?" I interrupt. "That's what I'm doing. And I'm asking you to face down yours. I'm asking you to trust me, to believe that I really, really like you—so much I would never do anything to hurt you. I'm asking you to give me a second chance."

Zoey glances toward the stage and then back at me. "You would really go out in front of all those people for me?"

Adrenaline pumps through my body while doubts swirl through my mind. I wipe the sweat from beneath my mask. "Yeah. I would."

The auditorium thunders with applause as the string quartet plays their last note. Cesar and Victoria start to interview them.

"Zoey?" Ms. Finnegan says, hurrying over with her clipboard. "You're up next. Tell the props assistant what you need help with, then stand by. Good luck."

I nervously clutch at my cape, waiting for Zoey's verdict. As she comes to a decision, her eyes brighten.

"All right, you made your point," she says. "You don't need to go out there to prove it. I get that you care about me." She hesitates, and in that moment, her cheeks bloom with color. "I care about you too. We'll talk later, okay?"

I can barely contain my excitement—and relief. "Absolutely!"

Zoey picks up her skirt's hem and starts toward the stage. I carry the skateboard for her, thrilled beyond belief about what I told her and her response. And that I dodged a bullet—or a whole barrage of bullets from the thousand people in the auditorium whose sights would've been set on me.

Zoey explains the skateboard and the plastic rose to the props guy. Then she adjusts her mask and turns to me, her blue eyes sparkling like sequins. "How do I look?"

"Spectacular."

From the stage, Cesar announces: "Up next is an act unlike any you've ever seen . . ."

"She's a new student at our school this year," Victoria adds. "Let's give a big welcome to Zoey Greenfield-Jones!"

"Here I go," Zoey tells me. "Wish me luck."

"Good luck," I say.

From beneath her mask, she smiles—big and bright and beautiful. Then she takes a step, and *rrrip!*

As her skirt tugs beneath my shoe, my left foot nearly flies out from under me. Zoey freezes in mid-step. Her hand flaps toward her backside, checking her skirt. She glances down, and her face pales.

The torn skirt is dangling to the floor.

My cheeks flame as pink as her underwear. I hop off the skirt hem, yank up the ripped cloth, and cover her rear end. "Oh my god. I'm sorry, Zoey. I'm really, really sorry."

"*Jorge?*" Her voice quavers, and her eyes fill with tears. "What do I do?"

"Zoey?" Ms. Finnegan runs over. "What's the—?" She sees the torn skirt. "Oh no."

"Can you switch me with the next act?" Zoey asks. *"Please?"*

Ms. Finnegan glances at her clipboard. "How?" Her pitch rises with every word she utters. "The next act needs a scene setup, and the act after that just ran to the restroom, and your music is cued, and everything is scripted, and it would throw the whole program out of whack."

Emily rushes over, her face half-painted with whiskers and a kitten nose, carrying her leashed cat. "Do you want Regina's hair clip?"

Zoey shoots the cat a quick glance. "It's too small. Peppy, sit!"

He's whimpering at Regina, whose tail flicks over Emily's arm as if she's casting a fishing line.

"Can you take our place while I fix this?" Zoey asks Emily.

"I haven't finished my makeup," Emily says. "But let me look in my backpack for a bigger clamp."

"Earth to Zoey," Cesar calls out from onstage, trying to sound jokey.

Victoria joins in. "Zoey, are you there? Come in, please."

Zoey tugs my arm. "Get behind me."

"I *am* behind you," I say, still holding the skirt to cover her rear.

"Closer," she says, lining me up like kids playing choo-choo train. "Come on, right foot first."

"Wait, what're we doing?"

"What you came here for," Zoey says.

I balk for an instant, but what choice do I have? I follow her out to my firing squad.

CHAPTER 41

"Get closer," Zoey instructs, pulling me even tighter behind her.

"I can't get any closer." My voice squeaks as we shuffle out from the wings in lockstep. Ahead of us, the stage looms vast and lonely. Above, the lights glare brightly. And in the dark auditorium, a thousand eyes set their sights on us. Ready . . . aim . . .

Without warning, Zoey stops. I bump into her from behind, nearly knocking her over. The audience explodes with laughter.

I cringe, feeling like I'm going to faint—or fart. "Sorry," I whisper.

"It's okay," she says. "Laughter is good. Now hold my skirt tight—I'm going to turn around, okay?"

While I keep my arm wrapped around her waist, Zoey

spins around. Her face is tight and anxious, but she's smiling, trying to stay brave.

"That was good. Now remember: Stand tall. Head high. Calm. Confident."

I lift my chin, raising my head up. Big mistake. The audience floods into view. I whimper. "I think I'm going to die."

"No, you're not. Breathe." She turns my chin away from the audience, toward her. "Don't look out there. Keep your eyes on me. Focus on what's in front of you."

"I can't do this."

"Yes, you can," Zoey says, her eyes wide and shiny. "You've got to. I need you to."

Our song's first chord rises from the speakers toward a crescendo start, and a feeling lifts up inside me—like on the first morning of English class when Scruggs heckled Zoey. I need to be strong. I need to help her. Be brave for her.

In a burst of notes, the singer belts out our song's opening lyric. On cue, Zoey starts our merengue, shaking her hips like when we danced at her house.

I hold onto her shoulder and waist, my gaze clinging to her resolute face. As I learned with Peppy, I don't think ahead, I just take it step-by-step. And like Cesar told me, I try to imagine the auditorium cheering for us.

When the song bursts into its first chorus of la-la-las, Zoey signals the props guy. Peppy rolls onto the stage on Cesar's skateboard.

Surprised, the audience gasps. Peppy bounds off the board into the spotlight, and the board rolls into the wings. While Zoey and I keep dancing, he sits, raises his front paw, and waves hello to Zoey.

The crowd bursts into a ginormous unanimous "Aww . . ."

Zoey stealthily tosses Peppy a pouch treat. But for the audience, she acts like she's snubbing him. Meanwhile I keep following her lead, one step at a time.

As we rehearsed, Peppy doesn't give up. He yips and yaps for Zoey's attention. And when that doesn't work, he chomps down on her torn skirt.

"Hang tight," she urges me while I tug back on the skirt with all my might.

The room is roaring with laughter. As we predicted, Peppy is stealing the show. Sweat streams down my temples. "I can't fight him off much longer."

Zoey wags a scolding finger at Peppy—his cue to let go—and his jaws pop open, releasing the skirt. She sneaks him a treat and shoos him aside. As Zoey pantomimes an apology to me, we resume our dance.

Of course Peppy doesn't really give up—he isn't supposed to. He crouches down to his stomach and drags himself back to us. Sitting up on his haunches, he presses his paws together, begging her for a dance.

I no longer need to imagine the audience cheering for

us—they're actually doing it, loud and enthusiastic. And I think, *I can do this. I AM doing this.*

"Grab your skirt," I tell Zoey. "This is where I take over."

I unsheathe my plastic sword. Seeing his cue, Peppy rears up onto his hind legs. He stretches out his front paw, and we start our swordfight. When he jabs at me, I recoil, and the audience cheers. When I thrust my sword, the crowd hisses and hoots.

But then—unexpectedly—the booing turns to laughter. Out of the corner of my eye, I glimpse . . . Emily.

She's scurrying onto the stage in her kitty outfit and face paint. She hurries toward Zoey, carrying a big plastic clip, and the audience howls. Do they think she's part of our act?

As Emily clamps Zoey's skirt, the crowd laughs so loudly they practically drown out the music. And for the first time since starting our dance, I glance out beyond the stage lights. From the darkness, a thousand faces are watching.

In an instant, my courage vanishes. My legs wobble. I stumble to a stop. The sword freezes in my hand. I can't move. I can't breathe. My ears are ringing. My eyes are going blurry. I can't go on. I'm about to go down.

"Jorge?" Zoey's whisper rises above the music. "Are you all right? Please, I need you."

In the front row glow of the stage lights, Norma leans forward. Her eyes shine, bold and encouraging. She mouths the words, *Be brave, Zorro.* Her pointer finger slashes the air—*swish, swash, swoosh!*—and just as she stabs her finger in my direction, Peppy jams his nose in my crotch.

The shock of his muzzle jolts me back to awareness. I can't bail on Zoey. I can't let her down. A surge of energy rushes through me. And I tell my fear, *Stay back!*

Next to Zoey, Emily is taking a bow. As she scampers offstage, leaving Zoey's skirt securely clamped, Zoey gives me a questioning look. I nod that I'm okay.

With a relieved look, Zoey returns to our skit, stretching out her arms between Peppy and me, stopping our sword-fight. Peppy obeys, backing away, lowering his paw. And I thrust my plastic sword, jabbing at him in a mock stab.

Peppy flinches. He falters. He drops dead—flat on his back, paws pointed up, tongue dangling from his mouth.

Zoey presses her hands to her cheeks, horrified. I toss my sword down and grab her, resuming our dance. The audience hisses and boos me. But then . . . Peppy springs back to life!

He shakes off the rigor mortis, barks, and snaps at me. The auditorium erupts in a resounding cheer. Weaponless, I throw my arms in the air and flee backstage.

"The three of you are awesome," Emily greets me when I reach the wings.

"Thanks for your help," I say, catching my breath.

From behind the curtain, we watch Zoey and Peppy go on with all the tricks they rehearsed—the twists and twirls, leaps and rolls, front flips and back flips—until Zoey presses a hand to her chest, exhausted. That's Peppy's cue.

He dashes backstage to fetch the finale's plastic rose from the props guy, and as the song's last refrain blasts over the speakers, he presents the rose to Zoey.

Taking the flower, she bends to kiss him. Peppy drops down and curls his paw over his head, shy and embarrassed—as if that dog could *ever* be shy and embarrassed.

"Aww . . ." the audience cries, louder than ever.

Peppy gets up on his hind legs, letting Zoey kiss him. As the music winds down, she takes his front paws, they resume their dance, and she calls me to join their circle.

I take her hand in one of mine and Peppy's paw in the other. And she whispers, "Look."

Beyond the stage lights, kids and parents are up out of their seats. Dancing to the song's final joyous la-la-las. Clapping to the beat. Waving their arms above their heads. Filming with their phones. The entire front row is our friends and families. At the center, beaming up at me, is Norma.

"Is that your dad?" Zoey whispers.

"Yep. That's her."

"She's pretty," Zoey says.

I nod proudly. I can see it now. She is pretty.

As the music fades, the applause wanes. People take their seats and vote. Cesar and Victoria come out from the wings to interview us. My brother's usually confident smile is tight and worried—as though he's scared I might point out Norma to the whole auditorium.

I shoot him a look like, *Stop worrying. I'm not going to do anything embarrassing.*

"Peppy?" Zoey calls. And, as she promised at rehearsal, she commands him, "Go to Cesar!"

In a flash, Peppy bounds across the stage, leaps up, and flings himself into Cesar's arms. My brother catches the flying dog as easily as a soccer ball. Peppy flicks out his tongue, giving Cesar a bath.

"Aww," several audience members exclaim. The sight is sure to earn Cesar a ton of votes.

"Wasn't that an amazing performance?" Victoria asks the audience. "So, Zorro, are you going to reveal who you really are?"

No longer needing to keep my identity secret, I peel off the eye mask. My front-row fans burst into cheers. "Yay, Jorge! Go, Jorge! Whoop, whoop, whoop, whoop!"

My body hums with pride at everything I've accomplished this evening. I feel like I can do anything. . . . until a shout booms from the rear of the room, "Your dad's a freak!"

I wince. Throughout the audience, heads turn, scanning the room for the heckler. I stare with them. Although it's too dark to see clearly, I know the voice—Scruggs.

No one says anything. Everybody is waiting to see how I'll respond. I clamp my knuckles around my cape, not sure what to do. Should I ignore Scruggs? Yell back? Come up with some jokey wisecrack? Nothing even remotely funny comes to mind.

My gaze—and hopes—turn to Cesar. His perma-smile appears more tense and nervous than before.

"Well, thank you, Jorge and Zoey," Cesar says, pretending he didn't hear Scruggs. Turning to the audience, he adds, "Let's hear another round of applause for—"

Scruggs interrupts, yelling again. "Your dad's a woman!"

Cesar's smile vanishes. He looks ready to answer Scruggs with his fists. While he squints into the dark, Victoria glances at the front row, at my mom . . . and Norma. As a wave of recognition rolls over Victoria, her brow creases with confusion.

Cesar looks backstage for help. From the wings, Coach Craddock takes a step into view.

I hope he'll take more than just one step, that he'll come onstage and call out Scruggs. Instead he plants himself where he is, arms folded—his classic coach pose—and gives Cesar a stern look as if to say, *You know what to do.*

Cesar takes a breath so deep his chest swells, but no words come. For what seems like forever, the only sound in the auditorium is Peppy panting in my brother's arms. I switch between one foot and the other, waiting. The show has come to a standstill.

Finally Cesar swallows so hard you can hear his gulp

over the mic. "Right now feels like the scariest moment of my life. Scarier than emceeing this show. Scarier than any test I've taken. Scarier than any soccer game I've played." He pauses. "The truth is, I've been hiding something. . . . scared that if any of you found out, you wouldn't want to be my friends anymore. Scared that you wouldn't like me."

Peppy stretches up and licks Cesar's face as though he understands. Somebody in the audience giggles, and Cesar relaxes a little.

"When I told Coach Craddock my secret, he said I need to just be honest. But what if telling the truth means risking everything you want—or think you want?"

Cesar stares out at the audience as though he's hoping somebody will shout the answer. Nobody does.

"I guess sometimes you've just got to face the truth whether you want to or not." He lets out a sigh you can hear all across the auditorium. "So, yeah, my dad *is* a woman—he's transgender."

Cesar gazes down at Norma. People in the neighboring rows peer at the big, broad-shouldered woman, their expressions flickering between shock, confusion, curiosity, disapproval, and everything else. Mom clasps Norma's hand.

"Coach always says that everyone on our team is different in some way—and those differences make us a better, stronger team. Well, now you know how I'm different. And I hope you'll still like me. And whether or not I get elected tomorrow, I'll work to make our school a better place for all of us, no matter how we're different." He pauses, fumbling for how to wrap up. "Who knows? Maybe having a dad who's a woman will make me a better man."

If that was meant as a joke, it bombs. Cesar gazes out at the silent audience and gives a quick shrug. It doesn't matter. What matters is that he's said his piece.

In the front row, Noah starts to applaud. Next to him, Chang joins in. Then Darnell. Then the entire front row.

If my life was a feel-good movie, more people would chime in, one after the other. The entire audience would rise in a roof-raising ovation.

But my life isn't a Hollywood movie. Even when Coach Craddock and Ms. Finnegan come onstage clapping, they rouse only a smattering of applause.

"So can we get on with the show?" Cesar asks nobody in particular. Glancing at his cue cards, he calls out the next act. Victoria arranges a smile on her face, still looking a little stunned.

By the end of the show, our act with Peppy has racked up the evening's highest score. We win first place with a nearly perfect 4.93 stars. And in a backstage corner when nobody is looking, for the first time since our breakup, Zoey kisses me.

CHAPTER 42

"Bravo!" Norma cheers when Zoey, Cesar, Peppy, and I come out the stage door. While Mom is hugging Cesar, I introduce Norma to Zoey.

"Wonderful to meet the girl who dares to be different," Norma exclaims, and I try not to blush.

"Thanks. I love your cookies," Zoey says.

"Well, I hope Jorge brings you over to bake with me sometime," Norma says.

"I hope so too," Zoey says while families bustle past us, casting stares at Norma—some disapproving, others merely curious. An elderly lady pats Norma's arm and says, "You were fabulous—and so are your boys."

"Thank you," Norma replies.

After Zoey introduces her folks and says good night, promising to text me later, Norma turns to Cesar. "Are you riding home with us?"

Cesar thinks for a moment. Then his mouth twitches with a smile. "Sure."

At the car, he takes the front seat beside her, and during the drive we all talk about the show. People have already posted photos and videos of the different acts, of Cesar's speech, and of Norma.

"I was proud to be your dad tonight," she tells Cesar and me. "More than you could ever imagine."

Cesar nods, accepting the compliment. His fury at Dad seems a thing of the past—as if a superhero magician mind-wiped away his resentment.

Once home, Norma suggests that she make us some chimichangas, and Mom seems happy to let her cook.

Dinner is like old times: the whole family under the same roof, talking and joking. And when we've emptied our plates, Norma's eyes twinkle with mischief. Reading her mind, we glance at each other, scoot forward in our seats, and rev up.

"On your marks," she says. "Get set . . ." She glances at her slender, silver watch and exclaims, "Go!"

We spring to our feet. Cesar stacks dishes. Mom gathers glasses. I scoop up forks and knives. Peppy skitters out from under our footsteps. Stopwatch cleanup is back!

"Time!" Norma calls out, shutting the dishwasher door. "Eight minutes and eighteen seconds."

"Our best time ever for chimichangas," Mom says. "Now

I'm going to go soak in a nice warm bath and collapse into bed." She pats Norma's shoulder and yawns. "Talk to you tomorrow."

"Good night, amazing Mom," Norma says, giving her a hug. I'll take it. Even though they're not a couple anymore, it feels like we're still just as much a family.

Norma, Cesar, and I hang out for a while, recapping the show. Cesar tells us he apologized to Victoria backstage for not having told her about Dad.

"But she didn't want to talk about it," he mumbles mopily.

"Give her time," Norma says. "We all go through our own coming to terms."

That fails to stop Cesar from looking forlorn.

Norma smiles a sad smile and asks him, "Can I give you a good night hug, mijo?"

"If you want."

Cesar stands, and Norma encircles him in her big, blousy arms. He slowly returns the hug, and I feel the familiar yearning in my chest. An ache for what used to be.

When I walk Norma to the front hall, she pauses at the doorway of her old office. The room remains vacant, like a shrine to the way things were.

"Hmm . . ." Norma rubs her chin. "You're always saying your comic book boxes cramp your room. Why not make this your creative studio?"

"Because . . . it's *your* room."

"Not anymore, mijo."

After Norma pulls out of the driveway, I stare silently at the empty den for a moment before heading upstairs. Mom is sitting at her vanity in her bathrobe, rubbing on some face cream. She sees my reflection in the mirror. "Ready for school tomorrow?"

I tug at my hands. "I guess."

Mom sets her cream down and swings around to face me. "What's going on?"

"Are you sure there's no way you and Dad can make things work? Maybe you could, like, compromise."

"We did compromise, sweetheart. That's what got us through all these years. But people change. Just like your dad is being honest, I need to be honest. If I'm going to have a spouse, it needs to be a man, not a woman. That's how I'm built. To compromise that would be dishonest. I'll always love your dad, and we'll stay friends, but we can't be like before."

I sit down on the bed. "It hurts so much sometimes. I want the pain to go away."

"I know." She walks over and sits beside me. "Hopefully, it will hurt less with time. I don't know if it will ever stop completely. Sometimes we have to learn to live with the pain—without trying to fight it or fix it. Just let that empty spot be there."

"You feel it too?"

"Sure, I do. I bet Cesar does too. I don't know anybody who doesn't have some empty space from losing someone."

I bury my face in her shoulder, breathing in her bath soap's scent, and wish she could make the hurt go away. But maybe she's right.

When we finally hug good night and I shuffle to my room, Peppy is already nestled in my bed. I tell him he did great tonight, but he barely glances up. For once in his life, he looks exhausted.

I plop beside him with my phone and text Zoey: Good night . . . Thanks for an amazing time

Back at you, she says. I really like your dad . . . your whole family

Thanks, I type. I like them too, I just wish—

I stop and think about what Mom said. Can I learn to live with the hurt?

Peppy gazes up at me, his snout between his paws. It reminds me of the time Zoey and I set the cookies in front of him—how he whined, whimpered, and licked his lips until he finally accepted he wasn't going to get his way. He surrendered.

I pick up my phone again, hit backspace, and type: I like my family too . . . just as they are

I hit SEND. Then I switch off the light, lie down, and rest my head on the pillow, surrendering.

CHAPTER 43

The next morning on the bus and at school, everybody is yakking about only one thing: last night's show. Some people say nice things like, "Your dog's hilarious," or, "How'd you get him to learn all those tricks?"

Other people are jerks, saying stuff like, "Your dad should've been in the show." Or, "No wonder you wore a mask."

By lunchtime, I'm ready to scream from all the jerky comments. But my misery evaporates when I get to Zoey's table. She saved me the seat beside her, just like before our breakup.

Along one wall of the lunchroom, ballot boxes are lined up for the student government elections. Our group agrees to vote unanimously for Cesar, but the election results won't be announced until last period. During afternoon classes,

I can hardly concentrate, I'm so worried for Cesar. Before last night, I thought he had the election in the bag. Today I'm not so sure.

Minutes before the final bell, Mr. Richter's voice crackles over the loudspeaker. I sit up, my heels jiggling anxiously. First he announces the representatives elected from each grade . . . then the treasurer . . . then the vice president. . . .

"And now for the president's race," he says at last. "Only eleven votes decided the election, reminding us how important it is for us as citizens—"

"Just tell us who *won!*" I blurt out, no longer able to contain myself.

"I'd like you to join me," Mr. Richter goes on, "in welcoming our new student body president, Shanaya Paswan."

Throughout the school, applause breaks out. I slump in my chair, feeling bad for Cesar. Right away I text him. I'm really sorry . . . but it was close, huh? You OK?

Thanks, bro, he writes back. I'm bummed but OK. After last night I figured I'd lose . . . But guess what? Victoria didn't dump me! We're still going out

That's GREAT, I type back.

After school, Darnell and Chang come to my house to submit our comic before the contest deadline. During the past few days, between rehearsing and stressing about the talent show, I managed to flesh out the script. Chang cranked out the illustrations. Darnell filled out the entry form.

Now we shove aside my comic book boxes, huddle around my computer, and send off our project. Then we celebrate with chips and salsa, cheering, "One for all, and all for salsa!"

When the guys are leaving, we walk past Dad's old office, and I remember something. "Hey, wait. Could you guys help me move some stuff?"

They agree, and together we lug my desk, chair, and comic book boxes down to the vacant room.

"I wish I had a studio," Chang says when we're finished.

"Whoa," I say. "This is *our* studio, for all of us."

"A noble heart, you have," Darnell says, pulling us into a Jedi-worthy group hug.

After they've gone, I lean back in my chair, admiring the place. Peppy lies at my feet, dozing. On the desk stands a framed photo of Dad and me one Halloween long ago. In it, she—still outwardly a *he*—wears a spandex Super-Dad costume stretched and tugged over his big lumpy body while I sit on his shoulders in my Spider-Man PJs.

My thoughts travel back to that time, when Dad would pick me up in his big, strong arms, and toss me in the air—so high I felt I could fly. He was the strongest, biggest, best dad in the world. And when I dropped down, he was always there to catch me.

As I stare at the photo, my chest aches with longing. I try to just let the feeling be there. Not fight it. Not fix it. Just accept that things are different now.

I get up from my chair and hook Peppy's leash to his collar, not exactly sure where we're going. Maybe we'll go to Zoey's. Maybe to Norma's. Or maybe we'll take Zoey with us to Norma's and bake cookies with her.

Outside, the afternoon sun warms my face. A breeze blows through my hair. And I leap up off the sidewalk, like a superhero reaching for the sky.

A Note to Readers

I was lucky. I grew up in a home where my mom and dad encouraged me to explore who I was—including my gender.

One afternoon I might play shoot-'em-up cops-and-robbers with my toy water rifle; the next day I would play house with Barbie and Ken. When I wanted to be Count Dracula, Mom sewed me a cape and used her lipstick to paint a blood red streak dripping from my mouth. And when I wanted to dress up in her skirt, heels, and makeup, she helped me again with the same lipstick and equal zeal. Even now, half a century later, and with Mom long gone, the scent of lipstick calls back giddy memories of me clomping around our house in her pumps. Make-believe was fun, but it was more than that—much more. It taught me to see myself in others, and to recognize them within me.

In my high school English class, the teacher introduced our class to Walt Whitman's *Song of Myself.* When I first read his verse "I am large, I contain multitudes," a surge of excitement pulsed through my veins. *That's what I am,* I thought. *That's WHO I am.* On the outside, I identified as a boy, but on the inside, I felt far bigger—a mix of masculine and feminine.

As I continued to explore my gender into adulthood, time and again I felt torn between a male identity and the recognition that I often felt more like a girl than a guy. Once again I sought solace in Whitman's verses: "Do I contradict myself? Very well then, I contradict myself."

Over the years I've come to understand that by freeing me to play with so many aspects of myself, Mom and Dad bestowed on me one of the greatest gifts a parent can give a child: empathy. The ability to see yourself in another, to put yourself in the other's shoes, no matter what their gender or how different they may appear on the outside, and to see that other person within yourself. It's a perspective I called upon to write this book.

This story springs from my own experience with gender, from the stories of others I've met along the way, and from that inseparable cousin of empathy: imagination. I spent time with twins, dog whisperers, trans people, kids of trans people, gender-fluid people, people who identified as genderqueer, and people who refused to attach themselves to any label. In each encounter, I sought out how we were alike, no matter how different we appeared on the outside. I strived to see myself in them and them in me. The result was these characters, this multitude.

I hope *The Greatest Super-power* will encourage you to recognize the multitude inside yourself, the mix of feminine and masculine, and inspire you to use your own superpowers to be as large and true as you can be. I wish you peace, and joy, and empathy!

– Alex

Me, age 5, with my mom

Acknowledgements

My huge thanks go to my wonderful editor, Alison Deering, and the amazing Capstone team, including Tracy McCabe, Brann Garvey, and Michelle Bisson. Thanks also to so many friends and family who supported my work on the manuscript with their encouragement and feedback, including Pamela Barres, Leah Bassoff, Jef Blocker, Tomie dePaola, Emily Faulkner, Bruin Fisher, Sean Gowers, Bill and Jackie Hitz, E.K. Jinxx, Tony Mendoza, JoAnne Metzler, John Porter, S. Chris Shirley, Amy Soule, and Angie Zapata. And special thanks to my agent, Miriam Altshuler, for so steadfastly believing in me these past twenty years. With gratitude to you all!

About the Author

Alex Sanchez has published nine novels, including the American Library Association "Best Book for Young Adults" *Rainbow Boys* and the Lambda Award-winning *So Hard to Say*. His novel *Bait* won the Tomás Rivera Mexican American Book Award and the Florida Book Award Gold Medal for Young Adult Literature. An immigrant from Mexico, Alex received his master's degree in guidance and counseling and worked for many years as a youth and family counselor. Now, when not writing, he tours the country, talking with teens, librarians, and educators about books, diversity, and acceptance. He lives East Rochester, New York, and at www.AlexSanchez.com.